THE QE2 LADY
&
OTHER STORIES

by

Valerie Hansard

Grosvenor House
Publishing Limited

This book is published by
Grosvenor House Publishing Ltd
Link House
140 The Broadway, Tolworth, Surrey, KT6 7HT.
www.grosvenorhousepublishing.co.uk

A CIP record for this book
is available from the British Library

ISBN 978-1-78623-893-1

Contents

The QE2 Lady   1

Brits Abroad   32

The Fairground   45

The Critic   60

Music Lessons   62

Louise   73

Sandwiches   80

The Chilla Rat   84

The Stag Do   98

Early Morning Tea   100

Wine Tasting   108

The Reluctant Window Cleaner   120

Gloria   128

Joe's Spanish Adventure   144

Scotch Eggs   149

Going To The Dogs   157

The Beach Hut   173

The Doorman   180

Christmas Pudding   184

Bells   197

Butter   220

Judgement Day   224

The QE2 Lady

Harriet stretched, rolled over and glanced at the alarm clock. It was 7.40 am. Another twenty minutes before Deepak would arrive with her breakfast. She lay back on the comfortable duck-down pillows, trying to decide whether she should shower and dress before breakfast, or eat in her dressing gown. She sat up and glanced down at the floor by the stateroom door. Yes. The ship's *Daily Programme* had already been delivered, along with *Britain Today,* the short news précis, which served as a daily newspaper on board. Harriet slid out of bed and put on her dressing gown. The shower could wait. She would start the day by reading the ship's bulletin and then move on to today's news. She picked up the two thin sheets of paper and took them over to the arm-chair by the large picture window, which opened onto the balcony. Settling herself comfortably she glanced out of the window. Yesterday's view of a vast expanse of sea had been replaced by half a dozen huge cranes, rising several hundred feet up into a leaden grey sky. Grey sky. That could only mean they were in England. Harriet looked down at the scurrying figures below on the quayside tying ropes around bollards and trundling a gangplank into place, which was then secured to one of the lower decks of the ship. Of course! How could she have forgotten? The Mediterranean Cruise had just ended and the ship had docked in Southampton. Soon its hybrid collection of passengers would disembark, to be replaced during the afternoon by a completely new set of humanity, bound for New York and beyond. Harriet glanced at the front page of the ship's *Daily Bulletin*. The departure time was 5.00 pm. There would be plenty of time to go ashore if she wished to do a bit of shopping in Southampton.

There was a gentle knock at the door and Deepak entered bearing a loaded breakfast tray.

'Good morning, Lady Spears. And a very nice morning it is too, though it be a little grey.'

'Good morning, Deepak. It's certainly grey – but I suppose that's what one has to expect in England.'

'Certainly, madam, England is usually grey. That's why we live at sea, so we can travel to sunnier places.'

Deepak set the breakfast tray down on the table. 'And if you want anything else, Lady Spears, don't hesitate to call me.'

Lady Spears smiled through her wrinkles at the slim dark little Indian backing away towards the stateroom door.

'Thank you, Deepak. I might do just that.'

Deepak gave a little bow before closing the door.

Harriet inspected the breakfast tray to see if any item she had ordered had been forgotten. She would discover it quite soon – she usually did. She picked up the crisp white linen table napkin in her gnarled ring-encrusted fingers and shook it out. Should she start with prunes or muesli, or mix them together? A little jam pot caught her eye. She picked it up and inspected it closely, squinting slightly as she strained to read the tiny print with her rheumy short-sighted eyes. Making out the words

APRICOT JAM, she heaved an impatient sigh. How *could* the galley always get things so wrong? And it wasn't as though she were a new passenger… She crossed to the telephone and dialled the number.

Welcome back, Lady Spears,' said the security guard smoothly as Harriet proffered her ship's Photo Identity Card. When these were first introduced Harriet objected to being screened along with the hoi polloi.

'Why should I be screened along with all the other passengers?' she complained. 'After all, I *do* live here. I'm a resident, not a tourist.'

She lodged her complaint at the Purser's Office.

The Chief Purser was understanding, but firm. 'It's the time we live in, Lady Spears. It's a terrorists' world. The screening is for everyone's benefit, including your own. It's the same at all the airports nowadays – and I believe even Harrods inspects their shoppers' handbags.'

Even Harrods! Harriet couldn't possibly imagine having her handbag searched in Harrods. It was just as well she now lived at sea. But it was rather humiliating to be treated the same way as everyone else. She would have to find another way of expressing her individuality – she usually did.

She took the lift up to her suite on the Funnel Deck. There was plenty of time to unpack all her shopping before she changed for dinner.

As Harriet undressed after dinner, something on the pillow flashed in the light of the bedside lamp. She stretched out her knobbly hand and picked up a small square of chocolate covered in tinfoil with CUNARD printed on the outer paper wrapping. It was the ship's custom when turning down the beds at night in the top-standard staterooms to leave a square of chocolate for each passenger; perhaps to satiate the appetites of those who were still hungry. But Harriet had requested that she should receive no more chocolate. It wasn't that she disliked chocolate *per se*: it was just that it served as a reminder of the appalling tragedy that had occurred all those years ago...

At first Harriet's parents were against the marriage. For a start, Donald was fourteen years older than Harriet. Then he had been married before. A brief childless marriage, which had ended fairly amicably when both parties decided that they didn't have sufficient interests in common to spend the rest of their lives together, particularly childless lives. Then there was Donald's Jewish family background. Not that they practised the Jewish religion any longer. Of course not. That would have been bad for business. And that was Donald's big plus point. He was good at business: any business, as long as it made money. But with financial reward came a certain amount of resentment. The resentment of the business rivals he had either swallowed up or obliterated. As long as he came off best in the end, Donald wasn't particular about whom he hurt or damaged.

Donald Spears' parents, Johannes and Elfriede Spiero, had emigrated from Russia in 1911 and settled in London's East End. They were poor and under privileged, but Johannes was resourceful and forward-looking and he was confident that his new life in London would have a successful outcome. From the beginning he realised that if he were going to go anywhere or become anyone he would have to change his name, his religion and learn to speak English. Changing his name and his religion was easy. He called himself John Spiro, insisting that everyone else did likewise. As far as religion was concerned, he stopped going to the synagogue on Saturdays and attended the local Anglican Church on Sundays instead. He shaved off his beard and his side ringlets but there wasn't much he could do about his large nose. People will just have to accept my appearance as it is, he thought. Learning English was a bigger hurdle, but in the end he mastered enough to get by; which was more than his wife ever managed.

By the end of the war in 1918 John Spiro was beginning to do very well for himself. He graduated from a stallholder in Brick Lane and opened a garment factory in the Commercial Road. He used virtual slave labour, exploiting any immigrants who applied for jobs by paying them well below the going rate. His garments were sold in the East End street markets and slowly appeared in the shabby East London shops. Soon his profits enabled him to buy a van, which allowed him to explore outlets further afield in places such as Leyton, Leytonstone, Clapton and Walthamstow. His big break came when he sold an assignment of Russian peasant-style skirts to Marks and Spencer. The skirts quickly caught on and became a much sought-after fashion item, after which he never looked back. Even the war didn't dint his fortunes. People had, after all, to dress themselves. During the war John Spiro had toyed with the idea of going into the business of supplying army uniforms. He investigated various outlets but discovered that the restrictions on the style and fabric quality were too great, so he put that idea aside for a rainy day.

In 1918, when he realised an heir was on the way, John Spiro anglicised his surname still further, calling himself John Spears. To help improve his English he started going to the cinema. Cartoons were quite new to him and he was enchanted by Mickey Mouse and all the other cartoon characters. Donald Duck quickly became a favourite. He thought the name Donald was quintessentially English and decided to call his son Donald.

Soon after Donald's birth in September 1918, John Spears moved his family into a substantial mock-Georgian house in Chigwell, Essex, where Donald, an only child, grew up in comfort and comparative luxury. He was a bright boy and extremely competitive in everything he did. From the beginning he was privately educated and ended up being head boy of his public school. There was talk of his going to Oxford or Cambridge; but bright though he was, Donald couldn't actually imagine himself knuckling down to another three or four years of further study. The matter was settled during his last term by the sudden death of his father. Although both Donald and his mother were totally shocked by their unexpected loss, John Spears' death, at the age of only 56, was no surprise to the medical profession. Since childhood he had suffered a heart condition, which no one had picked up on at the time. Spears left his wife a substantial income for her lifetime, to keep her in the manner to which she was now accustomed. Everything else he left in trust to his son Donald, until he reached the age of twenty-one.

Donald now had to decide how to spend the next three years before he inherited a great deal of money. As he had no need to worry about his mother, financially at least, he began to plan his own life. Should he travel abroad? During the early thirties travel to Europe was becoming very popular among those with private means, so he decided to take a six month tour. He travelled to France, Germany, Switzerland, Italy and Spain. The art and architecture totally amazed him and he became convinced that one day, funds permitting, he would become an art collector. He returned to England financially poorer, but spiritually enriched.

There were still two and a half years to fill in before he inherited his father's wealth, which consisted at the time of several chains of clothing stores and a great deal of money invested in shares and bonds. Sensibly realising that a thorough knowledge of finance would be very beneficial to his future, Donald enrolled in a business management course in the City. With his usual diligent application, he passed the course with flying colours and took a further, more advanced course. Both courses were to form essential bedrock for his understanding of all his future financial dealings.

Donald's twenty-first birthday in September 1939 occurred just a few days after the outbreak of World War II, a fact which held no significance for him at the time. Proud and delighted to find himself with such great wealth at his disposal, he began spending some of it and reinvesting the remainder for his increased benefit. He bought an Edwardian house in Wanstead and started restoring and furnishing it, scouring antique shops and art galleries and acquiring the best that money could buy. But his short-lived spending spree lasted barely a year. Unfortunately for Donald his country was now at war with Germany and, even more unfortunately, he was eligible for call up. In March 1940 he joined the army as a private soldier.

Donald was not cut out to be a soldier and he didn't have a very good war. He lacked the moral authority to be a leader and he was too stubborn and physically too timid to be a natural follower. He saw fighting in France and later he was sent to Italy where he suffered severe fractures to both legs and lost part of his left lung. In 1942 he was invalided out of the army and returned to civilian life. He didn't have much to return to. His mother had died and the large family house in Chigwell had been requisitioned by the government for 'war work'. His house in Wanstead had been badly damaged by German bombs. His shops, all of which had been located in London's East End, had been flattened and his shares had taken a severe tumble.

At the age of 24 Donald Spears was now a semi-invalid, with no home, no parents and no job. He would need all his ingenuity and a great deal of hard work to improve his dismal situation. And he had no idea that the cruel, vicious war would continue for another three years.

VE Day 1945 was a day of huge relief and tumultuous celebration. Donald joined the masses thronging The Mall as they cheered the King and Queen on the balcony of Buckingham Palace. Everyone now expected that life would return to normal straight away. They expected that all the goods they had been deprived of in the last six years would immediately appear in the shops. But of course that didn't happen. There was enough basic food to feed everyone but there were no luxuries. Slowly, people with a bit of push and brass neck managed to track down hidden caches of clothes, furniture, electrical goods and jewellery, which the more affluent members of society had put aside for a rainy day. By the summer of 1945 the rainy day had arrived and the owners of these Aladdin's caves offered their goods for sale to anyone who would buy them at exorbitant prices.

And so the Black Market was born.

Donald Spears seized his chance straight away. His first opportunity came quite by accident as he was visiting the site of one of his former shops in London's East End. It was a depressing trip. Most of the buildings in his old haunts on the Commercial Road had been flattened. Weeds were growing among the rubble on the bombed sites, old newspapers blew around forlornly and rats scurried round among the fetid remains of food long discarded. There was almost no one about. Donald was just thinking of leaving and perhaps visiting his old home in Chigwell when a voice hailed him:

'Don, you auld sod! Whatcha doin' 'ere?'

'Mike, old boy! What good luck!'

They walked down the desolate street together, looking for somewhere to sit and have a drink. Finally, right at the end of Commercial Road they found a workman's caff, open but deserted. Over a cup of bitter stale tea they discussed their war experiences, sympathising with each other's plight. Mike had once worked for Donald's father in one of his shops, now totally obliterated. Mike's home had been flattened. His wife and child, at home at the time, had no chance of surviving. He was bitter and deeply unhappy. He had no home and no money. He had no one to turn to and nowhere to go, so he had taken to stealing anything he could find and selling it off to anyone who would buy.

'There's money in it, mate. Mark my words. The stuff's easy to come by. It's just a question of finding the buyer with enough of the ready... if you get me.'

Donald certainly got him. They hatched a plan. Mike would source the goods and Donald would find the purchasers. They shook hands and drank a toast over the remains of the stale cold tea.

'We're business partners!' said Donald.

''Ere, 'ere!' echoed Mike.

At first the partnership flourished. Mike gave Donald whatever he was able to acquire and Donald paid him well for his trouble, selling the goods on for double or treble. As Mike became more prolific, Donald became more demanding. He no longer accepted items of furniture, worn out carpets or broken electrical goods. All he was interested in now was jewellery - and the more expensive the better.

After about eighteen months Donald had made enough money to buy a shop on the Whitechapel Road. He paid a builder to renovate it and six weeks later he opened his first jewellery shop. He bought a large amount of the jewellery legitimately. The rest he acquired from more dubious sources. Donald had arrived at that point in his life when he realised that it certainly didn't pay to be completely honest - and it didn't pay to be too soft on his fellow human beings either.

Shortly after the jewellery shop opened, Donald dropped Mike. He felt that he knew too much about his nefarious activities. He found other outlets for sourcing his illegitimate stock, changing his contacts as frequently as possible. What he was totally unaware of was the resentment, even hatred, which Mike now felt towards him. Donald was now in the throes of becoming a very successful businessman, but as some of his 'trade' was still not 'kosher', he made as many enemies as he made friends.

In 1948, aged 30, he met and married Margaret, a pretty girl ten years his junior. Coming from a similar working class background, Margaret had lost both her parents and her brother and sister in the brutal East End bombing. With such a shared tragic past she and Donald bonded quickly. But sadly, the marriage was a failure. Margaret was lazy and sluttish in her habits. She would rise late, spend most of the day reading 'girlie' magazines and feel a headache coming on whenever she was expected to do any shopping, cooking or housework. Although they both expressed a desire to have children, none came their way and after eight years, as they grew further and further apart, Margaret agreed to a divorce, provided she received substantial alimony. Donald capitulated, and made a handsome sum over to her.

Donald was now thirty-eight and owned eleven jewellery shops. Following in his father's footsteps, he purchased more jewellery outlets in similar areas where his father had bought his clothing shops before the war in Chingford, Chigwell, Walthamstow and Woodford. By now all his purchasing sources were legitimate. He was amassing a sizeable fortune on the stock market and he had recently bought a substantial Edwardian house in an up-and-coming genteel area of South Woodford.

Now the only accessory that Donald Spears lacked was a wife.

With money in the bank, stocks and shares, and property, Donald was able to employ well-qualified people to run his business empire. Now, with a little more time on his hands, he began to build up his image. He started with his appearance. Contrary to his previous habits, he eschewed East End market stalls and no longer shopped at Marks and Spencer, going instead to Harrods and Liberty's. Finally he went to Saville Row to have bespoke suits made. Soon he had built up a wardrobe of impeccably stylish clothes and accessories.

Next, Donald turned his attention to leisure activities. So far in his life the only time he had had much time for leisure was between the ages of eighteen and twenty-one, the three years between his father's death and his inheritance. During that time he had spent six months travelling in Europe, a trip that had made a huge impression on him. But it was the visit to Italy that he had enjoyed the most. The rich variety of the art treasures had quite bowled him over. He had also spent nearly a year of the war in Italy, a sad and distressing time, but the war was over, the Italian economy was recovering and he was sure that the art treasures were still there and accessible to the public. Donald discussed his planned trip with a business colleague over dinner at the Savoy.

'I'm very drawn to Italy,' he explained. 'But I don't know where to start. I don't know whether to visit Rome, Naples or Florence first.'

'Take a cruise!' cried his friend enthusiastically. 'That'll solve the problem of where to begin. You'll enjoy the luxury of life on board ship and you'll meet other wealthy passengers with similar tastes such as yours. You remember Edward White?'

'Of course.'

'He took a Mediterranean cruise last year. Had a wonderful time. Even met his wife to be on board!'

'Sounds good,' said Donald. 'I'll give it a try.'

As money was no object, Donald booked himself a suite complete with butler on the top deck of the QE2, one of the most luxurious liners afloat at the time. The ship's décor was awash with marble and gold leaf and the cabin furniture was all of solid mahogany. Donald asked the butler how it was possible that the ship could keep afloat with so much heavy furniture on board.

'That's only up 'ere, sir,' replied the steward in his thick burring Devon accent. 'Them cabins on the lower decks; they be small with all them plastic-like fittings. They don't have much comfort or luxury. I wouldn't try a berth down there if I was you, sir…'

Donald had no intention of trying life without luxury.

'And them cabins on the lower decks that some of the crew have to put up with! Quite shocking, some of them. And now if that's all, sir; I'll be getting along to serve Colonel Brownlow his breakfast…'

The month long cruise was nearly at the halfway point when Donald met Colonel and Mrs Brownlow. Donald had formed the habit of going to the Chart Room Bar on the Quarter Deck at 7.30 every evening for a pre-dinner glass of Chablis. He sat at one of the tables for four, selecting a chair from where he could watch the well-dressed couples passing through to dine in the Caronia Restaurant and could also enjoy the endless seascape floating by. Even at 7.30 in the evening the Mediterranean still held its colour of deep azure blue, turning blood red as the sun, now a bowl of fire, sank slowly down into its fathomless depths. Only tonight, mused Donald, the sea is not the Mediterranean but the Adriatic. He felt a flutter of excited anticipation. Tomorrow the ship would berth in Trieste and he would spend the day in Venice.

Donald stood in front of the stateroom mirror struggling with his bow tie. Tonight was a formal dress night. The ship's dress code was very strictly adhered to. On days at sea, dinner jacket was the order of the day. While in port gentlemen were requested to wear jacket and tie. Donald had even heard passengers being reprimanded for being incorrectly attired. Imagine that happening in London! Even at the Savoy. Donald put on his white evening dress jacket and arranged a fresh handkerchief in the breast pocket. He was grateful to his friend Edward for suggesting that he pack a white dinner jacket in addition to his black one.

Donald arrived at the Chart Room Bar at precisely 7.28 and walked over to his usual table. When he discovered that the table was already occupied he felt a sense of shock, almost outrage. Of course Donald realised that he had no right to feel aggrieved. Tables in the bars were not reserved, unlike his table in the prestigious Queen's Grill, which was his alone for the entire cruise. The couple already seated at the table had obviously sensed Donald's discomfort. The lady looked up at him and smiled.

'Good evening. Were you expecting to meet someone else at this table?'

'N-no. N-not at all. Of course not.' Donald gave a little laugh. 'These tables are free for all, aren't they?'

'Perhaps you'd care to join us for a drink?' The gentleman's tone was so friendly that Donald positively warmed to him.

'What will you have?' continued the gentleman, as Donald took a seat. He was just about to reply when a tall slim young lady sat down opposite him.

'You look really lovely tonight, darling,' said the older lady.

Donald looked up and tried not to stare. The young lady opposite was indeed lovely. Not pretty exactly, but fresh and extremely well groomed. The pale blue off-the-shoulder evening gown set off her light tan to perfection, emphasising her beautifully shaped shoulders and elegant long neck. Her face was a perfect oval, with an upturned nose and deep blue eyes, topped by a flaming mass of auburn hair. Donald felt a frisson of sexual arousal.

Donald was thoroughly enjoying his day in Venice. He had decided to make the visit on his own rather than follow a tour guide waving a number or twirling a plastic umbrella. Often the guides spoke such poor English as to be almost unintelligible. He'd taken some excursions on the cruise; this time he felt like spending the day on his own. He had already been to Venice on his six-month tour of Europe before the war and had been quite struck by its unique beauty. But was the beauty only skin deep? Was there not a touch of evil lurking somewhere, or was the evil only in his imagination? Donald left St Mark's Square, the Rialto Bridge and the throngs of heaving tourists to walk along the side streets. Some of these stopped abruptly, leading nowhere at all except into the murky depths of a canal. It would be very easy to become totally lost. Donald took the tourist map out of his pocket. Most tourist maps were quite hopeless, marking only the main streets and this one was no exception. As he tried to work out which narrow alleyway he should take back to one of the main thoroughfares, he glanced up at the completely deserted bridge in front. Suddenly, a tall slim lady walked across, followed by an older couple in their sixties. The young lady had flaming auburn hair. It was the lady whose table he had shared in the Chart Room Bar the previous evening.

Donald was determined to see more of the lady with the auburn hair.

It was easier than Donald had thought. Perhaps the young lady also wished to see more of him too. For the next few days, precisely at 7.30 pm, Donald and the couple with the auburn-haired daughter met at the same table in the Chart Room Bar. Every evening they ordered the same pre-dinner drinks and took turns in adding the amount to their ship's account. On the fourth evening, by which time they were all on first name terms, Colonel Brownlow suggested that Donald join their table in the Queen's Grill for the remainder of the cruise.

'It seems a shame to have an empty fourth place at our table,' he said, in his usual jocular manner.

'Basil prefers symmetry,' remarked his wife. 'We should have had two children. And I'm sure Harriet will enjoy your company, won't you darling?'

Harriet remained silent. Donald wondered what she was thinking.

'He seems such a nice young man, doesn't he, Basil?' remarked Edith Brownlow, as she helped her husband tie his bow tie for yet another evening dress dinner. 'I suppose we shall see more of him when we return to London. Harriet seems to like him quite a lot.'

'I'm sure Harriet likes him. But we know nothing at all about his background. He's very evasive. Whenever I ask a personal question he avoids it. I don't even know whether he belongs to a Golf Club!'

'I realise how important the right Golf Club is. But he must be from a good background. He speaks so well. You can always tell a person's background from the way they speak. He's definitely the product of a good public school. No one from a state school would speak as he does.'

'He certainly speaks well enough,' agreed Basil. 'But speech is not all. There are many other factors to consider when...'

'When what, dear?'

'Oh, I was just looking a little way ahead. We must above all ensure that Harriet has the best that life can offer.'

Edith gave her husband a long look.

'Time for the Chart Room drink. We stop off at Palermo tomorrow. I must confess that I'm beginning to look forward to a bit of dry land.'

'Me too!' Basil stroked his chin thoughtfully as he held the cabin door open for his wife.

'Spears. Where have I heard the name Spears before?'

When, to his utter delight, Harriet accepted Donald's proposal of marriage they went round to the Brownlow's London home in Eaton Square, armed with a bottle of champagne.

'I'm very proud and happy to announce, sir, that your lovely daughter, Harriet, had agreed to marry me.'

Edith got up from the sofa at once and embraced them both. 'I can't say how delighted I am. And I know you will both be very happy.'

A shadow of a frown passed across Basil's face. 'I think we had better have a chat in my study.'

Donald found the interview in Basil's study quite daunting. It wasn't so much a chat as an interrogation along the lines of the Spanish Inquisition. Of course Donald understood perfectly that Colonel Brownlow was about to give his only daughter's hand in marriage to someone about whose background he knew very little.

'Spears,' Basil began, 'that's an interesting old English name...'

For a second Donald wondered whether he could fake his past, but decided not to. Things were bound to come out sooner or later. It wouldn't be fair to Harriet. He was genuinely in love with Harriet and desperately wanted to possess her smooth, slim, silky body. But there was quite a bit of explaining to do. He hesitated, wondering where he should start. In the end, it all came out, even his poor war record and his injuries. As a professional soldier who had fought throughout the First World War, Basil was quite touched by Donald's war experiences. He was particularly impressed by the way in which his future son-in-law had pulled himself out of poverty to become a multimillionaire.

'Of course, it's in poor taste to discuss money, but having money is *so* important, dear boy. I'm so glad we see eye to eye on that score.'

What Donald omitted to explain was the ruthless way in which he had started to make his money, sparing nobody's feelings, leaving no colleagues' bank accounts safe from his predatory machinations.

The omission of the Golf Club membership was quite easily settled. 'I'll propose you for the ... Club,' said Basil, mentioning one of the most exclusive Surrey Golf Clubs.

In an hour it was all settled. Harriet was relieved and very happy and Edith looked forward to arranging a large prestigious wedding.

Almost exactly a year later, in July 1957, Harriet Brownlow walked down the aisle on her father's arm and gave herself in marriage, for better, for worse, for richer, for poorer, to Donald John Spears. Donald was thirty-nine, Harriet was twenty-five.

The next twenty years passed happily enough. Like most couples Harriet and Donald had their little ups and downs but they rarely had a serious row. Early on in their marriage Harriet bore Donald two sons.

Married to a man with the Midas touch, Harriet realised that she would never need to work. So she kept up her piano playing, at which she had always excelled, giving public concerts in church halls for charity. She learnt to speak excellent French, then good Italian and became involved in helping foreign nationals settle into London life. With a limitless personal allowance, she bought designer clothes and more jewellery than she could ever wear, much of it from her husband's ever-increasing chain of shops. She and Donald entertained frequently on the most lavish scale and took as many holidays abroad as Donald's business commitments allowed. And of course, it goes without saying that their two sons were educated at one of England's top public schools.

Harriet was happy and content with everything in her life except one for thing: Donald never discussed his work, or any related aspect with her. Comparing notes with other women friends, she discovered this was quite unusual. From time to time she would try to draw Donald out and persuade him to talk about his day's events, but to no avail. Another thing Harriet noticed was the frequency with which her husband's business associates changed.

Discussing a proposed dinner party, Harriet would suggest a couple that she thought would add to the success of the evening.

'Oh, not him,' Donald would laugh. 'I don't see him any more now...'

Or Harriet would suggest an evening out with one of Donald's managers, or accountants.'

'No, I gave him the sack. He was caught with his hand in the till.'

Or of the accountant: 'he was useless – he couldn't count.'

For their twenty-fifth wedding anniversary Donald booked a cruise on the QE2, where they had first met twenty-six years ago. About two months before their departure Donald received a letter from the Lord Chamberlain at Buckingham Palace.

'On behalf of Her Majesty, Queen Elizabeth II, I beg to inform Mr Donald Spears that he has been recommended for a Knighthood...'

'Arise, Sir Donald!' Donald Spears knelt before Her Majesty The Queen as she placed her sword lightly on each shoulder, bestowing on him a knighthood for his services to industry. Harriet stood watching quietly on the sideline, her heart thumping, clenching and unclenching her hands in excitement. And now I'm Lady Spears, she thought, married to a knight of the realm. How fitting, after twenty-five years of marriage.

After the impressive ceremony Colonel and Mrs Brownlow, now in their eighties, whisked them off to Claridges for a celebratory lunch.

Rather as they had expected, the cruise was a huge success. As their sons were now grown up and independent, Donald and Harriet decided that they would cruise at least twice a year. Now in his sixty-fifth year, Donald, although not contemplating retirement just yet, was allowing his managers and advisers a fuller rein. That is, unless he had just sacked them or caused them personal inconvenience or harm. And if the latter were the case, what better place to be than at sea on a cruise ship, where no one could reach him. So over the next fourteen years Sir Donald and Lady Spears cruised the world.

Gradually Donald Spears discovered that his murky past was beginning to catch up with him. Sometimes in a pub, a restaurant, in a shop or even on the corner of the street, he would catch a glimpse of someone he had wronged. There were several business colleagues whom he had cheated out of money; shop managers he had sacked for no apparent reason, accountants he had dispensed with because he had decided they were devious or low in skills. He began to dream about these people and feared he would be blackmailed or even gunned down.

By the early nineteen nineties computers were becoming more widely available and more and more businesses were installing them. Although now in his seventies, Donald was still very alert. He took a computer course and had several computers installed in his office and some of his jewellery shops. And he used the Internet to try and find out more about the people who troubled his dreams.

There was one man whom he feared the most; Derek Slater, a man Donald had always disliked and distrusted. Donald had interviewed Slater for the post of manager in his Walthamstow jewellery store and had engaged him on the strength of his impeccable CV. Slater had worked for Donald for three years before being sacked for dishonest bookkeeping, which Slater vigorously denied. For several years after that Slater wrote threatening letters, which Donald threw in the bin.

Then one morning in 1994 Donald received a letter from Slater, saying that because Donald had sacked him some years ago for no reason, he was now in financial difficulties. Slater demanded regular monthly payments, stating that if he didn't receive them he would go to the police and reveal Donald's murky past. Donald hesitated and then threw that letter in the bin as well. After this, regular monthly threats arrived in the post and things got to the point when Donald realised that it would be prudent to absent himself from England's green and pleasant land.

Donald suggested to Harriet that they should cruise to South America, one of the few continents they hadn't yet visited. Harriet was entranced by the idea. Now past 60 (although she never admitted it to anyone), and despite the fact that her stunning auburn hair had faded, Harriet had kept her figure and her good looks. South America was an enormous continent with such varying climates that she would need a vast new wardrobe; and as they were to cruise from the outset of the trip, she would be able to take as much luggage as she wanted.

As expected, they both loved being back on board ship. They had selected the QE2 again, still one of the most luxurious liners afloat at the time. With money no object, Donald had selected the best suite, which went hand in hand with the finest restaurant. Crossing the Atlantic into the South Seas took over a week, but with so much excellent entertainment on offer, the days seemed to whiz by in an explosion of self-indulgent luxury.

It was around this time that Donald started having nightmares and talking in his sleep. This disturbed Harriet and she was in two minds as to whether she should ask him what was troubling him so much. Then one day Donald thought he saw Derek Slater lying on a sun-lounger on Number One Deck. Although Donald and Harriet had their own balcony, there were times either when the sun didn't reach it or when it was too hot, so they would seek out a sun-bed or a deck chair on one of the main decks, where unfortunately the facilities had to be shared with the hoi-polloi.

The glimpse of the person he thought was Derek Slater had given Donald a big fright. How could it be possible, he said to himself, that Slater had known he was on the QE2? And if he was on board, what was Slater's motif? Donald went down to the Purser's Office and asked to see the passenger list.

'Thought I'd seen an old friend,' he mumbled.

'Certainly, sir,' replied the girl behind the counter. 'I'll get it for you right away. But I'm afraid you can't take it to your stateroom – you must consult it here.'

It didn't take Donald long to get through the list of Ss. There he was: Slater, Derek, United Kingdom passport. Donald felt a hollow ache in the pit of his stomach as he handed back the list.

Should he tell Harriet? That was the next burning question. For the moment he decided to say nothing. In two days the ship was due to berth in Rio de Janeiro. Why spoil Harriet's pleasure? After all, he had no proof that Slater knew that he, Sir Donald Spears, was also on board. He mustn't blow the situation up out of all proportion.

He returned to his stateroom suite to dress for dinner.

As the QE2 berthed in Rio de Janeiro, everyone was in a state of high excitement. The ship was spending three days in port to allow the passengers plenty of time to explore that fascinating city, considered to be one of the most exotic on the whole South American continent.

On the first day Donald and Harriet explored Rio on their own; the second day they took an exhaustive guided tour; and on the third day they again spent the day on their own, revisiting the places they had particularly enjoyed. They were sitting in a pavement café after a good lunch, people-watching, - always a fascinating past-time, particularly in a new city - when Donald noticed a man standing on the edge of the pavement, staring intently in their direction. He was about to make some remark about its being impolite to stare, when he suddenly realised that the man in question was none other than Derek Slater. Donald froze, turned away and called for the bill.

As Harriet hadn't seemed to notice anything untoward, Donald said nothing.

Later, back in their stateroom as they were changing for dinner, Harriet remarked on the substantial heap of small chocolate squares, each covered in tinfoil with a paper wrapper marked CUNARD, that were piling up on the bedside tables.

'We hardly ever eat them. Should we ask the steward to stop leaving them?'

Donald laughed. 'I think they're just part of the system – like the canapés. It might rock the boat if we asked them to stop. And anyway, I like a little nibble of chocolate now and again.'

'But you can't stand dark chocolate,' objected Harriet.

'They're not all dark. Look! This one says ORANGE MEDLEY'. Donald broke open the wrapping and bit off a small piece of chocolate. 'Delicious! No, let's not say anything. One evening the dessert might be poor …'

Harriet laughed. 'All right – chocoholic!'

With the excitement and enchantments of Rio still ringing in their eyes and ears, the QE2 passengers settled down to another day afloat. As usual on the days when they were at sea, evening dress was *de rigueur*, so Harriet booked a hair appointment. Walking along the long corridor on No One Deck on the way to the hairdresser, she heard footsteps coming along behind her. Harriet intensely disliked the long corridors on the five main decks. Although well lit both day and night, they were endless, soulless and faceless. She was more than relieved that their luxury penthouse suite was on the Funnel Deck, accessible by an obscure lift known only to the few passengers sufficiently privileged to afford such superior accommodation. There was no one else around in the long corridor – except for Harriet and the footsteps, which were coming closer. Now Harriet was too frightened to turn round. Suddenly she felt a hand on her arm. She looked down. It was a male hand. She screamed.

'Don't be frighty!' said a rough voice. 'I won't hurt you, Mrs Spears.'

'Lady Spears, please!' Harriet's tone was haughty.

'I said Mrs Spears. Your 'usband don't deserve 'is knighthood and 'e know it. 'E's trampled on enough blokes to get on – now it's 'is turn to be trampled on. You'd better warn 'im, Mrs Spears. I know where your little eyrie is up beside the funnel. Just warn 'im that if 'e don't start paying Derek Slater wot 'e's arsked, it'll be the worse for 'im.'

Harriet was too frightened and upset to go through with her hair appointment. She returned to the state-room to have a lie down. As they were changing for dinner Harriet recounted her unfortunate experience to Donald.

'Derek Slater.' Donald sat down heavily on the bed. 'Yes, it would be him, wouldn't it? He always *was* a load of trouble. Don't worry, darling,' Donald took Harriet's hand and stroked it. 'I'll think of something – there's plenty of time.'

A few days later, as they were cruising down the coast of Argentina, Donald woke in the night feeling a bit peckish. A good job we didn't give all that chocolate away, he thought to himself. He picked up several squares and took them into the bathroom so he would be able to read the wrappers in a good light. He sat on the lavatory seat, unpacked two squares marked ORANGE MEDLEY and ate them. An hour later he awoke with the most appalling stomach pains. He lay in bed, screaming in agony. In another hour he was dead.

Sir Donald Spears' death sent shock waves round the ship. Although certainly not a young man, he had apparently been in the peak of good health. His wife, Lady Spears, was inconsolable.

The ship's attitude to any kind of stomach upset was extremely rigorous. Any passenger suffering from even one mild attack of diarrhoea was confined to his or her cabin and put on the most stringent diet. No steward was allowed to enter the cabin during a passenger's illness, so the food was left outside the door, to be served by the spouse or partner. After making a full recovery the patient had to undergo an examination by the ship's doctor before he or she was allowed to eat in the restaurant or mingle with the other passengers. On each occasion before boarding the ship, all passengers were requested to sterilise their hands with a sanitising gel and the same procedure was repeated on entry to all the restaurants. These stringent measures were enforced to keep gastric epidemics to a minimum. But no one was prepared for a death. All the food that had been served in the Queen's Grill was thoroughly analysed but no traces of anything to cause alarm, such as salmonella or e-coli were found. The cause of Sir Donald's death remained a complete mystery.

Then some bright spark came up with an idea. Sir Donald had been taken ill in the early morning. By that time his dinner would have been sufficiently digested not to cause a problem. Could it have been one of the squares of chocolate? The stateroom wastepaper basket was inspected, then the bathroom bin. Yes, there in the bin was the paper and the foil wrappers from two small squares of chocolate. All the squares of chocolate in the Spears' stateroom were then sent to be analysed and several of them were found to contain traces of arsenic. Arsenic! How in heaven's name could arsenic have been found in chocolate squares on the QE2, where the hygiene was so strictly monitored? All the remaining squares of chocolate on board were seized and sent for analysis but not a trace of arsenic was found. It appeared that the chocolate delivered to the Spears' cabin had been deliberately tampered with. But by whom? And why?

On the evening of Sir Donald Spears' death, while all the passengers were dining, Derek Slater had made his way up furtively to the Funnel Deck and hovered in the corridor outside stateroom Number 8013. He had checked with the Purser's Office that this was indeed the Spears' cabin. Half an hour later the Filipino steward arrived as usual to tidy up, remake and turn down the bed and place a small square of chocolate on each pillow. In a matter of moments, with the help of a large bribe, the steward was persuaded that Derek's chocolate 'would be just the ticket for my friend.'

The following day the steward was rigorously cross-examined by the Purser and several other senior officers. Had he noticed anything? At first he denied everything. But eventually the story evolved. He admitted having received a handsome bribe from one of the passengers if he agreed to deliver his squares of chocolate to a certain cabin.

'Special for my friend,' the passenger had said.

The steward was asked if he would be able to pick out the passenger in an identity parade.

'No, sir. No possible. All white people same, sir.'

Before the QE2 docked in Buenos Aires, a church service was held for Sir Donald Spears. Afterwards, there was a special plane ready at the airport with a coffin on board to take Sir Donald's body back to London, accompanied by Lady Spears.

And no one, not even the security guards, noticed that Derek Slater had slipped ashore without leave, never to be seen again.

Harriet found life extremely difficult without Donald. She hadn't realised how much she had relied on him and how much he had become part of her very being. For the first six months after his sudden and tragic death she hardly left the house. Her sons took it in turns to do her household shopping on the Internet and came to visit her twice a week. The cleaner and the gardener arrived and left as they had always done, as regular as clockwork. Meanwhile Harriet sat in Donald's old Victorian rocking chair just gazing into space.

After six months of lonely vigil, her sons suggested she take a cruise on the QE2 to lay the ghost. Harriet booked for a Mediterranean cruise, which left in six months. The cruise coincided with the anniversary of Donald's death, which made Harriet nervous, but in fact the whole venture was far more successful than she could ever have imagined. Harriet took up the old threads of past cruising experiences with Donald and she returned to London quite refreshed and rejuvenated. Another six months of depression ensued and again her sons suggested a cruise. This time she cruised to New York, down the US coast to Florida, calling at several ports on the way. The cruise continued through the Gulf of Mexico, the Panama Canal and up the Pacific coast, arriving finally in Alaska.

By the time she returned home, Harriet had come to the conclusion that life on board ship suited her perfectly. She loved the orderly routine, the days at sea when evening dress was *de rigueur*. She also enjoyed the days ashore when she could choose to go on an organised excursion or explore new pastures on her own. She had no need to shop for food or prepare meals. All her laundry was taken care of and she no longer needed a cleaner, a gardener or a window cleaner. In the autumn of 1998 she sold her London home complete with furniture and booked a pent house luxury suite in perpetuity on the QE2. She no longer misses her friends or even her sons. She loves the endless flat seascapes and wouldn't swap this view any day for trees, grass, flowers or mountains.

Harriet is known to many of the QE2 passengers, more by repute than acquaintance. She can be spotted in the public rooms or on deck wearing her trademark sunhat with the brim turned upwards. When she attends some of the concerts she is often mentioned. 'And here is a special request for the lady who lives on board ship.' She is now becoming more and more demanding, insisting that everything be done 'her way.' She arranges bridge foursomes, but complains bitterly if the other three players are not of a high standard. In the prestigious Queen's Grill, if her food isn't piping hot and cooked exactly to her liking, she will send it back.

She is most particular about the arrangement of the furniture in her stateroom and about how her bed is made. And above all, under no circumstances, will she tolerate squares of chocolate being left on her pillow at 'evening turn down.'

When the ship has occasion to go into dry dock, she goes on holiday to Bournemouth or Bognor Regis.

Sadly, in 2008 the QE2 was decommissioned. At 41 years old she was considered too old to continue sailing the high seas. Her familiar red funnel was cut off, her decks were stripped away and hundreds of cabins were demolished before she retired to Dubai to become a floating hotel. The many thousands of passengers who had sailed on her greatly mourned her demise, none more so than Lady Spears, often referred to on board as 'The QE2 Lady.' At 76 years old, Harriet had lost none of her resourcefulness. Realising that a return to living on dry land was out of the question, she booked a luxury penthouse stateroom on the latest liner to sail the high seas, where she lived to the great age of 94.

Brits Abroad

'Have another one, will you, Rene?'

'Ta, don't mind if I do.'

'What was it, ducks?'

'Tequila and lemon, thanks, Reg.'

'Another pint Stan? You're not driving, any rate.'

'You won't be driving neither, Reg, by the looks of you. You'll have to spend the night here. Yeah, I'll have another pint, thanks. May as well celebrate. We'll be well out of this joint this time next week, won't we Rene, love?'

'You lucky, goddam bastard.'

Reg got up unsteadily and went over to the bar. 'Two more pints of bitter, please, Mike, and a tequila and lemon.'

'I hope you're not mixing the tequila with the bitter, Reg? You look pretty tanked up already.'

'I'm OK, Mike. I'll manage. Got to drown me sorrows. I'm losing one of me best mates next week.'

'How's that, Reg? Who is it, any road?'

'It's Stan. Him and Rene is emigratin'.'

'Emigrating? To Australia?'

'No. To Fartie-something.'

'Fartie-something? Where the hell is that? I've never heard of a place called Fartie-something.'

'It's one of them Canaries.'

'Canaries? I thought a canary was a bird.'

'It is, you stupid plonker. It's also a string of islands somewhere past Africa.'

'That's a long way off.' said Mike ruminatively. 'No wonder you're upset. Here, have a pint on me.' Mike gave Reg back some of his change. 'I'll bet it's hot out in this Fartie place if it's past Africa.'

'You bet it is. I hear Rene's taking almost nothing except bikinis with her.'

'Don't they have no winter?'

'Naagh. Not past Africa. It's always hot out there. Thanks Mike. You're a real pal.'

Reg lurched unsteadily back to his seat, slurping the beer on the floor, almost losing the tequila and lemon down a woman's back as he negotiated a narrow gap. The Crown and Anchor was filling up. It was past nine o'clock on a murky November evening. A woman screeched with mirth in the far corner. Unrefined guffaws of male laughter accompanied her high-pitched cackles as someone in the party told another lewd joke. A teenager in torn jeans, stained leather jacket, and a Mohican hairstyle, put a coin in the jukebox and raucous music blared out. The living gas fire blazed on relentlessly at full power making the room unbearably hot.

Reg set down his half-finished pint and leant his head back against the brass rail. In two seconds flat he was fast asleep, snoring loudly with his head slightly on one side, his mouth wide open. Stan took one look at him and burst out laughing.

'God, I ain't half going to miss this place, Rene.'

Stan and Irene Parker first went to Fuerteventura on holiday twelve years ago. It sounded the ideal place: hot sun, sea, cheap booze, and plenty of English tourists to talk to. They booked for two weeks at the beginning of May and had the holiday of a lifetime. Shining down relentlessly from a cloudless blue sky, the hot sun was offset by a cool breeze. The hotel was superbly appointed with three swimming pools, five bars, a games room and a nightly disco. Above all, there was an alternative English menu and three-quarters of the hotel guests were English.

Stan and Irene were not great travellers. They had once taken the children on a day trip to Boulogne but it hadn't been a success. Tracy, then aged eight, was sick during most of the journey home on the hovercraft and ten-year-old Dean never stopped complaining about the food. Unable to speak a word of French, or any foreign language, they had felt isolated and confused. Their only other venture onto foreign soil was a long weekend in Rotterdam. They had been mistakenly persuaded that Holland was just like England and Dutch was very easy to understand. Although they enjoyed the weekend more than their visit to France, for next the few years they took their holidays in England.

Fuerteventura was a complete change and after their first visit they returned every year. By the sixth year they had quite fallen in love with the place. They adored the bustling bars and taverns in the little towns, the endless beaches with fine white sand. They rented a car and armed with a picnic lunch, they explored the barren rocky interior with its lunar-like landscape. They spent one holiday at the southern-most tip and enjoyed gazing out to sea, feeling blissfully free in escaping all the mundane problems of daily life at home in Loughton, Essex.

As the years went by they managed to make more frequent visits to their Utopian island 'just past Africa'. By the tenth year they were making at least two annual visits and had decided when the time was right, they would go and live there permanently.

Stan and Irene had both grown up in Dagenham, Essex. Irene's father had worked on the Ford Motor assembly line; Stan was the son of a lorry driver. Neither had much ambition in life. In the 1960s it was not considered appropriate for working-class people to have any idea of bettering their station in life, so they continued to live and behave just as their parents had done. In the natural course of events Stan became a lorry driver, and as soon as she left school Irene took a job stocking the shelves in the local super-market. They had met at school and, never having dated anyone else, they were married when Stan was twenty and Irene nineteen.

Just as his father had done, Stan formed the habit of passing demolition sites to see what pickings there were, preferably for free, which rapidly became a lucrative little side-line. One day his eyes lit on a handsome old fireplace, in need of some repair.

'Take it, guv,' one of the workmen had said. 'It looks in pretty bad shape to me. I shouldn't think it's worth much.'

As he heaved it onto his lorry, Stan wasn't so sure. In fact it turned out to be Adam and the proceeds of the sale helped him to set up his own demolition business. From then on things only improved materially. They moved to a large house in a desirable area of Loughton and Stan bought a hairdressing salon for Irene.

They had now reached the highest attainments in living standards and possessed everything they needed that money could buy. So their plan to live permanently in Fuerteventura was not a quest for a better life. It was more a desire for a complete change: the chance to live in a completely different environment and who knows...? Perhaps even become two completely different people.

It was a decision not undertaken lightly. Stan sold his business, the hairdressing salon and their desirable, if rather ostentatious house for over one million pounds. So it was with feelings of uncertainty, trepidation and considerable excitement, that Stan and Irene shut the front door of their house for the last time.

Most of the furniture and fittings had been sold with the house and all their crockery and linen had been shipped out ten days ago. All that remained was for them to pack up the rest of their personal items and bid a final farewell to their local friends in the Crown and Anchor.

As so often happens on a November morning in England, the day of their departure was shrouded in heavy fog. Stan and Irene were forced to spend seven hours at Gatwick Airport before their aircraft finally took off. By the time they arrived at the airport in Fuerteventura it was nine o'clock in the evening and they were fraught and exhausted.

On the two previous visits in the search for their dream home they had been met at the airport either by the estate agent or his deputy, Miguel. But this time there was no one to meet them. They waited in the airport arrival lounge for over an hour before Stan called a taxicab, hesitantly giving the address in his extremely poor Spanish.

'Si, señor,' said the driver, obligingly helping with their copious luggage.

It was a two-hour drive to their apartment and well after midnight when they arrived. As they drove along a rough winding unsurfaced road, Stan and Irene felt their excitement mounting. As the taxi turned the corner the moon came out, bathing the whole scene in opaque silvery light. From the apartment complex they expected a welcoming twinkle of lights, but all was shrouded in darkness. Irene sat quite still, her heart thumping. As the moon came out again, Stan got slowly out of the cab and, looking up at their apartment, he saw the walls of unplastered breezeblock were up, but there was no roof. Glimmering in the moonlight was a giant crane.

'It's not finished, Rene,' said Stan hoarsely. 'We've come all this way and it's not bloody finished.'

Irene burst into tears.

They found a hotel for the night and the following morning Stan went straight to the office of the solicitor through whom they had bought the apartment. But the premises were unrecognisable. A different besuited gentleman sat in the office and Señor Lopez's name was no longer on the door.

'Oh no, he left the island it is a month now.'

'Did he leave a forwarding address?' asked Stan, his heart sinking.

'What is dat ... forwarding? I no understand. He is gone away.'

'How can I get hold of him?'

'No understand. Señor Lopez, he is no more.'

Stan gave up and went along to the estate agent expecting to find José or Miguel. He rang the doorbell and an old woman dressed in black opened the door.

'*Buenos dias,*' began Stan hesitantly.

'*Buenos dias,*' replied the woman shortly.

'I wonder if I might speak to José Lopez or Miguel Garcia...'

'All is gone. Gone away.'

Stan tried a few other approaches but the woman's English was just as hopeless as his Spanish so he gave up and went back to Irene at the hotel.

It was several weeks before they discovered that their solicitor had been embezzling clients' money, including their own, and had gone off to live in South America on the proceeds. The estate agent had gone bankrupt, partly due to the solicitor's misdemeanours and partly due to the erratic working methods of the local builder. In short, they had been sold a pup and had lost over £100,000 in the process. But Stan was a man of resilient nature and considerable financial resources. He suggested they enjoy a holiday in the pleasant hotel they had found and look around for another apartment. As they were now on the spot, it should be easier to purchase something suitable that was actually finished, rather than arranging it all from England.

They divided their time between sunbathing at the hotel pool and scouring the island in their hired car for a suitable property. In less than two weeks they found the ideal place: a spacious ground floor apartment with a small garden, in a complex which included shops, a restaurant, bar and two swimming pools. In great excitement they paid the deposit. Stan telephoned for the money to be sent from England and within three weeks they had completed the purchase and moved in. Their dream of ten years ago had finally come true. Stan and Irene were in seventh heaven. At last they owned their own home on their paradise island.

The weeks passed happily until Christmas. There were so many new things to do and see and so much to learn about their new home. They became more adventurous about eating, buying their produce in the local market and cooking with an entirely different set of herbs and spices. They tried to learn Spanish with CDs and a 'Teach Yourself Spanish' book, and spoke only Spanish at breakfast. But it was hard work searching for the right words and they found the pronunciation difficult. They made friendly overtures to the other residents of their apartment complex without much success. It seemed that at least half the residents were German who had no wish to make English friends and the English residents appeared standoffish and superior. One morning Irene overheard an Englishman saying to his wife: 'Oh, not the new couple at No.8. We couldn't invite them with the Willises. They're just too common, darling.'

Irene was upset and extremely offended.

One day the handle fell off the living-room door. As he replaced it, Stan noticed the door was full of a dry powdery substance that had a peculiar musty smell. The handle fell off again the following day. A few days later Irene noticed cracks in the bedroom wall behind the bed. It was an outside wall so Stan phoned the builder.

With his limited comprehension of Spanish, all he could understand was: 'after Christmas.'

Then the plumbing troubles started. The lavatory wouldn't flush properly, the shower pressure was reduced to a trickle, the bidet became blocked and a tap came off the hand-basin. Stan called the plumber.

'After Christmas,' came the reply.

But the compensation for these practical problems was that there was Christmas to look forward to in a new environment. The shops in the local town were festooned with decorations and the market had a festive air. They bought presents to send home to their family and friends and mailed Spanish Christmas cards. With the purchase of a tree and garish decorations they turned the apartment into a Christmas grotto and deciding to break down any social or linguistic barriers, they bought expensive, rather ostentatious cards inviting the other residents to a party on Christmas Eve. At first the replies arrived in a slow steady trickle, then after a few days, in an avalanche of refusals.

'Mr. and Mrs. Brown regret, but they will be returning to London for Christmas.'

'Herr and Frau Schmitt thank so very much but they for Christmas in Berlin will be.'

'Ron and Madge Middleton are so sorry but they will be spending Christmas with their daughter in Switzerland.'

There was not a single acceptance among the replies.

A week before Christmas the weather turned extremely cold. A chill wind blew and it rained endlessly for five days. On Christmas Eve there was a power-cut and they had no light, heat, cooking facilities or TV for nearly twelve hours. Christmas Day dawned bleak and cheerless. The apartment complex was totally silent. There was no one there except themselves. At three o'clock they sat down to Christmas dinner and got extremely drunk. It was the first depressing Christmas either of them had ever spent. New Year's Eve passed in the same lonely isolation and Stan and Irene were relieved when the apartments began to fill up again towards the middle of January.

The builder called and agreed that the cracks in the bedroom wall needed attention. 'Of course, *Señor*.' He would see to it as soon as he had carried out repairs on an apartment block that was just about to fall down. 'An emergency, you understand, *Señor*.'

The plumber came round and reduced the water pressure still further. The blockage was transferred from the bidet to the hand-basin and the tap that had been replaced was so tight it was impossible to turn on.

The weather worsened. It rained for at least half the day and the wind became stronger and colder. Swimming was impossible, walks became a torment. There was nothing to do except stay indoors. Irene busied herself with early spring-cleaning. She scrubbed and polished the whole place from top to bottom. She made new curtains, bedspreads and recovered the cushions. She turned out all the cupboards, rearranged the contents and moved the furniture around.

Stan took out his tools, replastered and re-papered the bedroom walls and turned his ingenuity to the plumbing. While he tried to solve the mysteries of the Spanish plumbing system, they were without water for four days. In the end he was fairly successful, although he had to admit defeat over the hot tap on the basin. After three weeks spring-cleaning and repairing their apartment they were both completely exhausted.

Happily, at the end of the first week in February, the sun came out. Along with all the other residents, Stan and Irene rushed out of doors and lay by the pool all day for three days. In their excitement and relief at the fortuitous change in the weather they had completely forgotten to take any precautions against sunburn or sunstroke. They both turned a deep, angry red; they peeled and blistered. Irene was so ill that they were forced to call the doctor, who ordered her to lie in bed in a darkened room for a week.

By the beginning of March they both felt sufficiently recovered to try sunbathing again. Armed with sun-hats, sun-lotions and an alarm clock they returned to their sun beds by the pool, carefully counting the minutes as they turned their bodies over in the sun, like two joints roasting on a spit. They swam, they went for walks in the cool of the evening; they shopped in the market, cooked delicious meals or ate out in the evenings. For a month they fully enjoyed their paradise island.

It was Irene who first voiced their thoughts. 'All the days is the same.'

'Yes. Exactly the same.'

'The days is going to be the same until next Christmas, and next Christmas will be just like last Christmas.'

'Yes. And last Christmas weren't much fun, were it?'

The days passed, each one like the last. The sun shone down endlessly, becoming dangerously hot as April moved into May. By June it was straight over-head, covering the island in an intense, shimmering white heat. The temperature rose to 35 degrees Centigrade and by ten o'clock in the morning it was too hot to do anything except lie in the shade. The neighbours remained equally aloof as before. Many gave drinks parties and barbecue suppers but no one invited Stan and Irene. They were beginning to tire of the limited local produce in the markets. Meals in restaurants all began to taste the same. They became bored with swimming; there was nowhere new to walk; they were already tanned so there was no point in sunbathing. Their Spanish seemed to get worse, and above all they longed for English television and English pubs.

In short, they were homesick.

They visited the hotels in the hope of meeting other English people. They struck up friendships, sadly too short-lived, with people who were more of their ilk than the residents in the apartment complex.

'It's been wonderful meeting you.'

'We'll give your love to Essex.'

'You lucky sods living in a place like this.'

'We'll write, of course.'

But no one ever wrote.

As the hot summer wore on, Stan and Irene's loneliness increased and they began to long more and more for England. The weather never changed and their routine never altered. Their newfound friends came and went but no one kept in touch. The English papers were always at least two days late and the TV programmes worsened. They stuck it out until November. One night, after a great deal of cheap Spanish brandy, they struck up a friendship with a particularly nice couple from Romford and revealed their miserable secret.

'Sell up and come home,' advised Tony. 'You've tried it for a year. Don't make martyrs of yourselves. Some one'll buy your place. Tell you what: come and have a bunk down with us for Christmas and stay on till you find what you want back home.'

It was an offer too good to refuse. The thought of another lonely silent Christmas and the monotony of the year to follow persuaded Stan and Irene to put their apartment up for sale and accept Tony and May's generous invitation.

In two weeks they were back in England.

With three days to go before Christmas, the Crown and Anchor was crowded. Stan battled his way back with drinks from the bar to the corner where Irene and Reg were sitting. The atmosphere in the pub was warm and friendly. Outside it was cold and foggy and had just started to snow. The door opened and a couple came in, well muffled up in coats, scarves, hats and gloves. They saw Reg in the corner, waved and came over to join them. Reg turned to Stan.

'This is the couple I was telling you about. Don and Mavis.'

The couple pulled up chairs and took off their outdoor clothes. Mavis was talking in a bubbly, excited manner.

'You see, Reg, we've just bought an apartment in Fuerteventura. We haven't even seen it yet. Isn't that crazy?'

'Yes,' continued Don, 'we bought it off of this English couple who apparently got tired of the life out there. Imagine getting tired of all that sun and sea! There are some queer folk around, I'll say.'

Stan turned to him and asked curiously:

'Can you remember the name of the bloke you bought it from?'

Don stroked his chin reflectively.

'Yes,' he said slowly, 'his name was Parker, Stan Parker.'

The Fairground

'Ere, listen to this, Brigid.' George picked up the paper and peered at it more closely. 'Cocaine smuggling rife. Two out of three people attempting to smuggle cocaine into Britain are successful. Ingenuity knows no bounds. A Thai diplomat was caught at Heathrow Airport yesterday with 10 kilos of pure cocaine secreted in Asian dolls.' Just imagine! I wonder how much 10 kilos would be worth?'

'Quite a lot I should think,' replied his wife. 'But think of the poor lives that stuff'll destroy. They deserve the rope, them smugglers, they really do.'

'But think of the money.' George wiped his mouth on the back of his hand.

'George! That's a terrible thing to say!' Brigid sounded really angry. 'There are many ways of making money without destroying peoples' lives into the bargain.'

'There's certainly other ways - and I've picked a mug's game, that's for sure! Standing all day and night at a rifle range watching people trying to shoot at harmless little teddy bears!'

'Oh, go on wi' you.' Brigid gave him an affectionate push. 'At least you're your own boss an' all.'

'I suppose so,' said George grumpily. He stood up. 'I'd better get going, then. Dinner at eight?'

'Yeah, at eight. I've something special for you tonight.'

It was a hot, still afternoon as George threaded his way slowly through the haphazardly parked vans and caravans towards the main fairground. The harsh jangle of music could be heard in the distance and all was bustle, activity and noise. It was August Bank Holiday Sunday and a large crowd was expected.

'Sit tight everybody and hold ... on!'

Clang, clang, whoosh; clang, clang, whoosh! The 'soul machine' soared into orbit. Teenagers laughed and the younger children screamed in anticipation of the terrors to come. Lighting a cigarette, the youth in charge leaned back against the small pay-booth. Five minutes rest, he thought. It was mid-afternoon and already the crowds were thickening. The 'soul machine' was nearly full up. Almost thirty quid, mused the youth. Should be a good weekend.

Across the pathway his mate was in charge of the dodgems. Amid much shouting, screaming and laughter the cars bumped and crashed into each other. Fathers accompanied small children as the youngsters argued about who was to take the wheel. Mothers and grand-parents watched nervously, mollifying the youngest children with fluffy sticky candyfloss or dentally destructive sticks of lurid pink rock. An appetising smell of frying onions wafted across the park as the queue built up by the hot-dog stall. The metallic-looking hydrogen balloons were selling well and the skittle-alley, video-bingo and punch balls were also riding high in popularity. George threaded his way carefully past the hydrogen balloons and skirted the punch balls to his rifle range. It had become a way of life. He couldn't remember any other. Day in, day out, come sunshine or showers, come hell or high water, he loaded rifles and collected the money. Or he hoped to collect money. The bad days were those when it was cold and wet and he felt the English damp gnaw at his bones. The only respites were meal times, when his mate, Ed or Ed's wife, June, stepped in for him, and the days when he drove the caravan on to the next venue. He enjoyed the driving. It was cosy sitting in the cab of the van with just him and Brigid and young Tom squeezed in between them.

Tom. He must try and do something better for Tom. Tom deserved a better deal than the others. Tom was ten years old and the apple of his eye.

George ducked under the counter of his rifle range. 'Hi, Ed,' he greeted his mate with an affectionate slap on the back. 'How's tricks?'

'Could be worse, could be worse. Could be better o' course.' Ed's gloomy outlook and saturnine manner belied the kindness and loyalty beneath. 'Notes in the box. Small change in here.' He took off the money belt and passed it over to George.

'Best go and help Junie at the hula-hoops now. See you later.'

'You're a pal. Thanks a million.' replied George. 'I'll be along to relieve you prompt at seven.'

''Bye, then.' Ed ducked out under the counter and was gone.

The contenders queued up at the rifle range in a rather disorderly fashion.

'A quid for three goes! Only a quid,' called George without a great deal of enthusiasm. 'Win a cuddly toy or a bottle of Scotch. Only a quid.'

His game was difficult. He knew he didn't stand to lose much. It was much more difficult than Ed and

June's hula-hoops next door. Most people managed to place one hoop around the object of their desire, which gave them the incentive to continue. Recently Ed had made the game more difficult by requiring the contestant to secure the prize with all three hoops. Most managed at least one or two, but very few were skilful enough to throw the third one on top. Following Ed's lead, George had also changed the format of his game. Formerly the contestant had paid £1 for three shots and had to place the bullet in the centre of each of the three hearts. The bullet had to strike inside the heart - it didn't count if it landed on the red outside edge. If he centred all three hearts the contestant won a fiver. On discovering that cheap toys from Hong Kong could be bought for a few pence, George duly acquired a consignment of hearts that had fallen off the back of a lorry. Hanging the target heart over each prize, he made it look more attractive by displaying a dummy bottle of whisky and a couple of the more expensive cuddly toys. Pandas and koala bears were the most popular.

'No leaning on the counter, guv,' he called sternly to a middle-aged man. The man stepped back and aimed at the dummy bottle of whisky. Crack! One in the red. Crack! One in the centre. Again: crack! Last one in the red.

'I won it! I won the bottle o'whisky. Gimme the real bottle.'

'No way,' said George firmly. 'You got to get all three o'them shots right through the centre of that there heart.

'OK. Gimme another go, then.'

George loaded another rifle and took the man's £1 coin. Crack! Right in the centre. Crack! Just on the edge. Crack! A third time: right in the centre.

'You're improving, guv. 'Have another go.'

'Pah!' said the man in exasperation and slamming the rifle down on the counter, he strode off in high dudgeon.

At the hula-hoops next door there was a slight commotion. A small crowd had gathered to watch a successful contestant in full swing.

'Ooh!' went the crowd. And 'Ooh!' again. 'One ... two, ooh! ... three...! He's got another one.' 'What a skill!' 'What an eye!' 'What a shot!'

George peered cautiously round the side of his booth to make sure everything was in order. If Ed had popped out for any reason he had to make sure that Junie was OK. Any slight anxiety was allayed as he caught sight of Ed lifting three hula-hoops off a koala bear and handing it over to the successful contestant. At that moment someone called to him.

"Ere, mate, can I have a rifle, please?'

As the man who had won the koala bear turned round to leave the hula-hoop stall, George caught a glimpse of a halo of fuzzy, almost-white hair and pink eyes glowing in a very fair-skinned face. He was carrying a bulging carrier bag, and looking nervously behind him as he made off in the direction of the dodgems. Settling down to a hot, noisy, exhausting and fairly lucrative afternoon, George thought no more about him. He had barely taken the money and handed over the loaded rifle before he had taken it back again, loaded it and handed it on to the next contestant. Fortunately there weren't many winners. Several people put two bullets through the centre of the heart but very few managed three.

The dummy bottle of Scotch became more and more pitted with miss-hits while the real thing lay unclaimed under the counter. The luxury panda and koala bear remained unharmed. Rather than put in cheap and unattractive-looking substitutes George had merely mounted the heart onto a large surround which left all of the animal covered except the nose, peering cheekily over the top of the disc, appealing to someone to win him and take him home to a loving young master or mistress.

By five o'clock the crowds were so thick they were jostling shoulder to shoulder and the queues for the stalls were indistinguishable from the general mêlée. Looking up occasionally, George marvelled at the number of people and the continuous roar of sound. No longer could individual voices or cries be heard - all was swallowed up in a tumultuous Babel.

The police presence was heavy. Just as well, thought George, though he didn't care too much for the Old Bill. I suppose they're here for our protection. Pick pocketing must be rife in a crowd like this. Even so, the police made him feel uncomfortable.

For the next hour the pace was so hectic that George didn't even have time to realise how hungry he was. At two minutes to seven his pal from the dodgems came to relieve him and he ducked under the hula-hoop counter, strapping Ed's money belt to his waist as June locked hers into a drawer under the counter. Within a minute they had both left and George was in charge of the hula-hoops.

Not so much aggro here as at the rifle range, he thought. At least I don't have to load rifles. But the contestants on this stall seemed to have a greater skill, or at least a higher success rate, than those with the rifles. George found himself extremely busy, extracting hoops from the toys, handing out the prizes, and then replacing them.

Whoosh! Whoosh! Whoosh! Three in a row. There goes another koala bear. George lifted off the three hoops, picked up the little bear and handed it over the counter. As a hand stretched out to receive the prize, George looked up and found himself staring into a pair of pink eyes a few inches across the counter. Pink eyes under white lashes, set in an almost dead-white face framed by fuzzy almost-white hair. The man gave George a long, hard look, stuffed the koala bear into a carrier bag already bulging with similar toys, and sloped off. Bloke seems to have a taste for koalas, thought George and then thought nothing more about it.

Promptly at two minutes to eight Ed and June arrived back at the hula-hoop stall.

'There you are,' said Ed as he quickly whipped the money-belt from round George's waist and tied it round his own. 'Thanks a million. You're a pal. Watch your step out there,' he continued, nodding towards the dense crowds. 'The place is full of the Old Bill. I dunno what they think they're going to find here.'

'Just watching for pickpockets, I should think. Place must be rife with them.'

'Nah, not that lot. There's a whole station-load out there. They're looking for some'at, I reckon.'

George laughed. 'What a vivid imagination you've got. See you just before nine o'clock. 'Bye. Thanks mate.'

George struggled through the jostling crowds. Feeling a hand roaming down the side of his trousers, he looked down and grabbed a slim wrist. It belonged to a boy of about ten.

'Just you be careful where you put your hands, laddie, or I'll hand you over to them coppers.'

'I didn't mean nuffink, guv, honest I didn't,' whimpered the boy, 'It's not so easy being small in a crowd like this, I gotta hold on to somefink, see.'

Letting go of the frail wrist, George gave the boy a pat on the shoulder. His vulnerability reminded him of Tom.

'OK, lad. Be off with you - and keep out of trouble.'

'Yes, sir. Thanks, sir. I will, sir.'

The small boy darted off into the crowd, skilfully threading his way through the morass of legs and thighs, vowing to pick his pockets with greater care.

George watched him go, suddenly overwhelmed by an almost paralysing tiredness. His head ached, his back felt stiff, his hands were sore and his knees felt like jelly. Must be getting old before me time, he thought. It's a helluva tiring existence. Wish I could think of some'at better to do. Then a thought struck him and he stopped dead in his tracks. What about them drugs then? I'd only need one little lot to make a bit o' dough, then I could retire. Buy a nice house - send Tom to a posh school so he could learn to speak proper and 'ave a better start in life. How do you get in the know about these things? he mused. Certainly no one at the fairground could be involved. Otherwise they'd quit the life. It's a mug's game working the amusements - a hard slog and almost nothing at the end of it.

But what about Brigid? He had to consider Brigid. She might even threaten to leave him if she knew he was pushing drugs. Destroying people's lives, she would say. He sighed. There were always two sides to a coin. He didn't want to be responsible for destroying people's lives. And he certainly didn't want to jeopardise his marriage to Brigid. Then there was Tom to consider.

Ironically it was for Tom's sake that he had considered the idea in the first place. Just so that Tom could have a better deal in life. But what if he were caught and imprisoned? Then Tom would be dragged down with him, not to mention Brigid too. No, it wasn't worth any further thought. Nevertheless, a nagging temptation remained. Two out of three people successfully smuggled dope into Britain. Surely he would be among the privileged two? After all, he deserved a break. Life owed him something.

He walked on slowly as increasing hunger pangs dulled his thoughts. As he approached the group of caravans and trailers at the edge of the fairground, the crowds thinned and petered out altogether. The area was cordoned off and guarded by two large and menacing-looking Dobermans, straining at their leashes. Giving them a wide berth, George picked his way between the irregularly parked vehicles until he reached his own caravan, parked right at the end of the lot.

'Hi, luv!' he called out as he placed his foot carefully on the metal step outside the caravan and stood in the doorway. Brigid was bustling about at the stove just a few inches from where he stood. That's the trouble with living in a caravan, he reflected. It's so cramped that only one person can stand up in it at any one time.

Brigid looked up and smiled at him. 'You can come in in a minute. I'll just get the food served first.'

She heaped two plates with a steaming dark rich stew and piled on several large floury potatoes apiece. She carried them two steps to the table at the front of the caravan and set them down carefully.

'There you are, luv. Your favourite. Me good old Irish stew.'

'Lovely jubbley,' George came in and sat down on one of the two upholstered benches at either side of the table and tucked into his food with gusto. There was a long silence as they both enjoyed their dinner. At last George spoke.

'Where's Tom? I thought he had to be back by seven?'

'That's so. I haven't set eyes on him since his midday dinner,' Brigid sounded anxious.

'You shouldn't let him go off like that for the whole afternoon. You must get him to come back every two or three hours so you can see he's all right.'

'And how can I make him do that? The lad is ten years old. How can I control a ten-year-old boy in a fairground? Sure, a fairground is no place to bring up a child proper.'

'You was the one what said it, not me. I'd quit this game tomorrow if I could think of some'at else to do. But I ain't got no skills and I'm too old to learn anything new. I've no choice but to stick it out in the fairground. They wouldn't even take me in a circus.'

'I'm sorry, luv.' Brigid took his hand across the table. 'Don't worry. We'll manage. Tom'll turn out all right. He's a bright lad. The other two didn't do so bad neither.'

George gave a non-committal grunt. 'No. I suppose not.'

Suddenly there was a sound of footsteps running along the path outside and the two Dobermans began barking wildly. The caravan lurched as a boy of about ten bounded in panting, flushed with excitement.

'Hello Mum! Hello Dad! Sorry I'm late. I've been having a wicked time.'

'Steady on there, Tom. You'll knock the 'van over if you keep jumping about like that. Sit down quietly now and tell us all about it.'

George was too relieved to be angry.

'I'll get you some dinner, luv,' said Brigid getting up. 'It's your Da's favourite Irish Stew.'

Tom attacked his plate voraciously and spoke in short bursts between mouthfuls.

'Guess what? This afternoon me and Joey took a bus to Balham and had a go on them fruit machines in the amusement arcade. I won three quid and Joey won four. It was great. So we went into this big toyshop across the road. It's an enormous toyshop - the biggest I've ever seen after Hamleys in London. We was wanting to spend our money on something proper, see, before we was tempted to lose it all again on the fruit machines. Joey was thinking he'd buy one of them computer games but he didn't have enough money. We spent so long looking around that I think the shopkeeper was getting suspicious. And there was no one else in the shop. Then a bloke came in. He was looking for koala bears. The shopkeeper said how many did he want? The bloke said it didn't matter; he wanted all of them. Said he was collecting koala bears to send them to Australia. Isn't that stupid? That's where the koala bears come from, don't they? There'd be no point in sending them back there, would there? So any rate, this man, he bought three koala bears and paid for them in cash and he was just going out of the shop with these three koala bears, like, and he kind of bumped into Joey and me because we was going out of the shop at the same time. We'd decided by then we didn't have enough dough to buy what we wanted so we might just as well go and blow it all on the fruit machines, anyhow ...'

Tom paused for breath. George and Brigid remained silent. Tom finished his plateful of food, wiped his mouth on the back of his hand and pushed the plate away.

'... And as all three of us was leaving the shop together, see, this bloke, that had bought the three koala bears, he started chatting up me and Joey. Oh, he was ever so friendly like, ever so gentlemanly. He explained how he was a collector. Sometimes he collected stamps; sometimes he collected matchboxes. Not for himself, he said. It was for his pals; he always liked to help his pals. So any rate, this time it was koala bears for his mates. He asked Joey and me if there was any more big toyshops around, 'cos he didn't know this part of London very well. I said yes, there was a big toyshop in Clapham. Did he know Clapham? And he said he didn't so Joey and me explained about the buses and all and he was most grateful and he said could he buy us an ice cream and we said yes, that would be lovely. So we all went to the ice cream shop along the street and he bought Joey and me a big double cornet each. Joey had pineapple and chocolate and I had peppermint and toffee and it was really delicious ice cream...'

'You shouldn't accept food from strangers,' interrupted Brigid tartly.

'We didn't accept it from the stranger. He just paid for it. Any rate, the man in the ice cream shop was a stranger too.'

'He's got a point,' remarked George with a twinkle in his eye. 'Go on, Tom.'

'Well, we was walking along the street eating this lovely ice cream...'

'I hope you said 'thank you," said Brigid loftily.

'Of course we did.'

'And was this stranger having an ice cream too?'

'No. He had too many things to carry, like all his koala bears. So we was walking along, chatting in a friendly way and I said to this man, I said, did he know there was a big funfair on Clapham Common this weekend? And he said, no, he didn't, and I said it might be worth his while going along because he could have a chance of winning a koala bear or two if he was a good shot with a rifle or nifty with the hula-hoops. So we told him about the buses and he was most grateful and he went off and we finished our ice cream and went back to the fruit machines.'

Tom paused in his narrative and looked up. 'You know, it wasn't just collecting koala bears that made this bloke seem odd. He had pink eyes and white fuzzy hair - and he wasn't old.'

George felt a chill of fear pass through him.

Back at the rifle range it was nearing eleven thirty pm and George knew the compulsory closing-down time of midnight would be adhered to. The Old Bill would see to that. He'd never known such a large crowd - either of police or the public. And he'd never known it so hot. It must be the global warming everyone was talking about: the greenhouse effect. Well, he felt as if he was in a greenhouse with the sun beating down in the middle of the day. It would be preferable to being in a crowded rifle range with a pale sickle moon peeping in as it was at the moment.

'Here's a quid, guv.'

Automatically he handed over the loaded rifle. Crack! Crack! Crack! No good. All three shots fell at the edge of the target. The disappointed youth put the rifle down on the counter and struggled to get out of the booth.

The music blared out: 'I love ya ba-ba-by. I love ya ba-ba-by. I love ya. I love ya so, I do.' The song wailed on, momentarily drowned by the noise of whining, clanking machinery and the cries of the stallholders. 'Roll up! Roll up!' 'Have a ride on the dodgems.' 'Have a go on the soul-machine.' 'Try your luck with the hula-hoops.'

George joined in the cacophony. 'Roll up to the rifle range! Three shots for a quid. Only a quid. Three shots. You might win a koala bear... or even a bottle of Scotch. Roll up, roll up to the rifle-range.'

He handed over a rifle. The man shouldered it and took careful aim. Crack! The first one was dead in the centre. Crack! Followed by a second success. There was a pause. The contestant put the rifle down on the counter for a moment to rest his arm. Anticipating a possible victory, his two fellow competitors, although aiming for different prizes, did him the courtesy of stopping for a moment. Looking up as the man raised his arm for a third shot, George noticed two police officers standing behind him. The man paused for just a second and then took careful aim. George realised he was going for the koala bear and noticed with a stab of fear that it was the man with the pink eyes and the fuzzy, almost-white hair.

The man pulled the trigger. Crack! He had aimed too high. He had shot off the nose of the koala bear and out poured a fine white powder. The man lunged across the counter and tried to grab the bear.

'Gimme that! I shot it so I've won it!'

But George was quicker. 'No you ain't,' he snapped back. 'You're meant to hit the heart of the target in the centre, not aim at the bloody bear.'

Realising he'd lost out, the man panicked. He backed away from the counter and turned to leave the booth but finding his escape route barred by several uniformed police officers he decided there was only one option open to him: he had to create a diversion. He rushed back towards the counter and gave it an almighty push. It landed with a great crash on top of George, scattering plastic dolls, pencils, crayons, sweets, packets of sherbet, bubble liquid, pandas and koalas in chaotic profusion. In the ensuing pandemonium he ran through the torn canvas at the side of the booth. Clutching his bulging carrier bag full of koalas he ran off into the darkness and disappeared among the crowd. George was left holding the injured koala with the fine white powder still seeping out of its nose. As the crowd in front of the booth melted away, two burly police officers stepped forward and stood on either side of George.

'This your koala, guv?' questioned one.

'Yes,' replied George, without hesitation.

'In that case,' said the other officer, 'you'd better accompany us to the station.'

The Critic

'But there's no colour! It's all beige! I do like a bit of colour. Why just beige?'

Margaret stopped abruptly in the doorway, causing her hostess to bump into her and almost drop a pile of dirty plates on the tiled floor. Walking slowly into the soulless, featureless, totally symmetrical kitchen, her acid comments flowed on ruthlessly.

'Even the floor tiles are beige! *And* they're exactly the same beige as the cupboards, the walls, the ceiling and the work-tops.'

She opened a cupboard at random.

'I don't know how you can tell one cupboard from another – or how you can find anything. What's in here? Goodness, me! It's the fridge! And what's in this one? A *microwave!* I didn't realise you'd lowered your standards to the depths of microwave cooking. That'll be awfully bad for Harry's cholesterol. If you feed him exclusively on microwave food he'll end up having a heart attack!'

'I've no intention...'

'You think you haven't! But once a housewife owns a microwave she never uses the oven again. But perhaps you don't have an oven any more? That chicken was awfully dry. Was it a microwave job or a take-away?'

Margaret's green eyes narrowed, her sinewy feline body ready to pounce as she opened another cupboard.

'If I can pin-point your dustbin I'll have proof...'

'Margaret, I wouldn't ever...'

'And why wouldn't you? I would if I had a kitchen like this. I'd be so mesmerised by the sameness that I wouldn't ever cook a proper meal again. Just finding the equipment must take at least half an hour. Why didn't you tell me you were having your kitchen replaced? Mind you, it *was* about time. The last one was pretty awful. None of the cupboards fitted properly; the blinds clashed with the floor; the drawers stuck constantly and even you said you couldn't find anything. So I suppose this is an improvement. But if you'd told me beforehand I would have advised you - and I'd certainly have suggested some colour instead of this utterly monotonous beige...'

'How do you like the new kitchen, Margaret?'

Harry's deep voice from the doorway interrupted Margaret in mid-flow.

Margaret turned to face him, her eyes deepening to a softer green.

'It's beautiful. I just love all that beige.'

She'd always rather fancied Harry.

Music Lessons

Sergei Smith walked slowly across the quad. As he neared the northern end his nervousness increased, his stomach tightened and his mouth felt dry. He looked at his watch. Five minutes to ten.

Is there time for a quick drink from the fountain? he wondered. Deciding in the affirmative he turned left off the main cloister and went through the swing doors towards the cloakroom.

'Smith!'

'Sir?' he answered hesitantly, his heart sinking, his stomach now churning. 'Yes, sir?'

'Where are you off to at this time of the day? It's nearly ten o'clock. Shouldn't you be in the Latin room?'

'Yes, sir. No, sir, That is to say, sir...'

'What are you trying to say, Smith? A boy of your age and in your privileged position should be more coherent in his speech.'

'Yes, sir. I am, sir. I do try, sir.'

'Trying is not sufficient, Smith. Nothing succeeds except success.'

'Yes, sir. I know, sir. I'm trying to be a success.'

Mr. Willets, the deputy head, was well known for his irascibility. Many of the boys said his bark was worse than his bite but Sergei, finding his bark quite sharp enough, made sure he didn't get close enough to get bitten.

'Aren't you going to the Latin room, Smith?' demanded Mr. Willets in stentorian tones.

'No, sir.'

'And why not? Are you not an Omega boy, Smith?'

'Yes, sir.'

'Then you are due to leave us at the end of this term, I believe?'

'Yes, sir.'

'Then you should take your Latin studies more seriously.'

'I do, sir. I really do, and I intend to make up all the work I've missed, sir. The class is doing the Ablative Absolute this morning, sir, and McTaggart is going to lend me his notes...'

'And why should McTaggart lend you his notes, Smith? Surely as an Omega boy you are quite capable of taking your own notes.'

'I am of course, sir. But the fact is, you see, sir,' the words came out in a rush. 'I'm going to a piano lesson.'

'A piano lesson?' thundered Mr. Willets.

'Yes, sir.' Sergei's stomach muscles tightened even further and tears pricked at the back of his eyelids.

'Why a piano lesson, Smith? I thought you were learning the flute?'

'Yes, sir. I was, sir. But I wasn't very successful with the flute.'

'I thought you said a moment ago that you were trying to be a success, Smith?'

'Yes, sir. That's why I've stopped learning the flute: because I wasn't a success. But I'm going to be very successful with the piano.'

He didn't sound very convincing.

'I see, Smith,' replied Mr. Willets slowly. 'So you've stopped learning the flute because you weren't successful and now you are going to make a success of the piano.'

'Yes, sir.'

'I would have thought the study of the Ablative Absolute would be more important than that of the pianoforte, but let's hope you can combine both - successfully.'

'Yes, sir.'

'Don't be late back.'

'No, sir.'

Sergei heaved a great sigh of relief as made his way to the cloakroom and took a long draught of water from the drinking fountain. What damn bad luck running into Weasly Willets. Hope it's not a bad omen, he thought. My God! Look at the time! Nearly five past ten! I'm going to be late! And it's the first lesson too! Sergei hurried back through the swing doors and started to run along the north side of the cloister. A rhythm started to throb in his head. I mustn't be late, I mustn't be late, I mustn't be late.

But he was late - for the first lesson.

As his steps hastened and his anxiety increased, thoughts of past music lessons began to swirl around in his brain. He had always wanted to play a musical instrument. He really wanted to play in a big orchestra and be part of that tremendous wave of sound: to play the shrill notes of the piccolo; or twirl his bow in fortissimo tremulandi in the violin section. The cello would be an acceptable alternative. Cellos often got the big, sweeping tunes and he liked the sound of the fruity pizzicato in the lower register. The trumpet might be fun, as it often added excitement to the brass section. Even the oom-pah, oom-pah of the trombone would be better than nothing.

Sergei had not had an easy childhood. His father was a career diplomat, his mother a concert pianist. Constant travel seriously disrupted his education, making the study of a musical instrument impossible. His frequent requests for music lessons were met with such replies as:

'We'll see, Sergei, darling. Perhaps when we've moved to Paris.'

Or, from his father: 'I don't think we can place any further burdens on your mother, Sergei. After all, the practice supervision would fall on her and she has her own career to think of.'

So it seemed there would be no music lessons for the moment.

When he was nine, Sergei's parents divorced. During this stressful time he was shunted from grandparents, to aunts and uncles or cousins, from country to country and from one school to another. Some of his guardians were patronising and gushing, others were brusque and cold. Having barely settled down in a new home, he found himself whisked off to another country and a new set of bogus aunts and uncles, which resulted in his retreating more and more into himself. Newly formed friendships were frequently broken and in the end partings became so painful that he stopped making friends at all.

When he was ten and a half he was sent to Cholmondley Hall, one of the best-known Preparatory Schools in England. His father, Sir Charles Smith, had decided that the end goal should either be Eton or Winchester, so preparation, although a little overdue, was now of prime importance. With his customary lack of skill in planning his son's upbringing, Sir Charles delivered Sergei at Cholmondley Hall just after half-term in the Lent term. He hadn't the remotest idea how upsetting it could be for a boy to arrive at a new school in the middle of the school year, never mind in the middle of the term, but as he was due to take up a new post as Second Secretary in the British Embassy in Saigon, the timing was convenient for him.

Sergei had never been to boarding school before and had great difficulty in settling down. In the United States he had attended local day schools, and in Europe he went to schools that specialized in teaching the children of itinerant parents. And if no suitable school could be found, Sir Charles engaged a tutor.

Among the biggest problems he had to surmount at Cholmondley Hall were the hustle and the bustle, the rules and regulations, the constant ringing of bells and the tyrannical discipline. For example, the rules adhering to wearing the school uniform were most stringent. The house tie had to be worn with the sports jacket; the school tie with the suit. The same rigid rules applied to the sports' kit. Socks with coloured tops were worn for football; plain white socks for gym. Anyone who turned up wearing the wrong socks was given a detention after school hours with endless lines to write out.

The petty discipline extended to lessons. Each subject had a colour-coded exercise book and if they were mixed up, the miscreant was punished. Accustomed as he was to doing his work on loose sheets of paper, Sergei frequently arrived in class with the wrong book - or no book at all.

But the hardest adjustment he had to make was the lack of privacy. Except in the bathroom, he was never alone, day or night. He shared a dormitory with eleven other boys in a large bare room with no carpet, curtains or wall decorations of any kind and nothing to separate one bed from another except a stark wooden locker. Every activity was mass participation. Hordes of young boys, dressed alike, going through the same daily routine at the summons of the school bell. The first bell rang at 7.00 am; followed by bells for breakfast, prayers, lessons, break, lessons, lunch, games, tea, prep, supper, evening activities, prayers and bed. Even the evening activities were fully supervised.

Deprived of any permanent friendships before arriving at Cholmondley Hall, Sergei finally persuaded himself that he no longer needed people, for he had discovered MUSIC. Sir Charles was a cultured man with eclectic tastes in music, art and literature. He took his son round the art galleries and the great churches of Europe, to concerts and the theatre. Sergei was receptive to beautiful things, especially music. As part compensation for his rootless life and the refusal of constantly requested music lessons, Sir Charles gave his son the best equipment for reproducing music that money could buy and an endless supply of whatever CDs he asked for. By the time he arrived at Cholmondley Hall, Sergei possessed a greater knowledge of classical music than most boys of his age.

As he listened to music on his personal stereo in the bare over-crowded dormitory, Sergei was completely transported. The music cut him off from everything he disliked about his life around him: the bare walls, the constant ringing of bells and the idle chatter of the other boys. Whenever the rules permitted, he would go to the dormitory, select a CD, and listen, enraptured, to the music on his earphones. Sadly, this activity had one rather unfortunate result. Listening to music made him cry. It was quite involuntary. For no apparent reason the tears just poured down his cheeks and there was nothing he could do to stop them. At first the other boys thought he was homesick. A few teased him but most were sympathetic. After all, it was hard on a chap to be sent to a new school in the middle of term. One boy in particular tried to be friendly. He came and sat down on the bed next to Sergei. He had bright red hair and pale blotchy freckles.

'Hello,' he said, 'my name's Bottomley, Martin Bottomley, but I'm always called Bottom. You're new aren't you?'

Sergei turned off the stereo and removed the headphones. Gradually his tears ceased.

'Don't cry,' said Bottom, 'though I bet you miss your mother. I missed mine dreadfully at first.'

'No, I don't miss my mother,' replied Sergei. 'It's the music that makes me cry. It's so beautiful and powerful.'

'Oh,' said Bottom, 'I like music too. I've got loads of Madonna and Boss CDs. I'll lend you some if you like.'

From then on Sergei listened to music alone in the toilets.

Sergei had to wait until the autumn term before he was able to start learning a musical instrument. At Cholmondley Hall there was a long waiting list for all the extra-curricular activities. The boys were keen to start, even if the dropout rate was high. Sergei had decided to learn the violin. The most expressive of all the orchestral instruments, it certainly played the most notes and Sergei liked total involvement. He waited with mounting excitement for the day of his first lesson. A violin had been bought for him through the school hire-purchase system. He already had it in his possession and he would take it out of its case in the privacy of the lavatory and fondle it lovingly. He plucked the strings, but they were slack and out of tune and only gave a dull 'thwang'. Feeling saddened and a little cheated he put it away, counting the days and then the hours until his first lesson.

The great day duly arrived and he presented himself in the music block at the appropriate hour.

'Go to Room No. 9,' the Director of Music told him. 'Your violin teacher will be Mr. Gropius.'

Mr. Gropius was short, bent, grey and wrinkled. One could with kindness call him elderly, but he had a reputation as a fine violin teacher. Sergei was a diligent and gifted pupil and listened carefully to Mr. Gropius' instructions. He practised assiduously every day and made rapid progress.

There was only one problem. As soon as he had played a few notes his tears started to flow, gushing out with a mind of their own. At first he felt no sadness, no emotion, but as the tears increased he became more and more involved. In his head he heard his CDs of the beautiful music he so much wanted to play: the violin concertos by Beethoven, Brahms, Max Bruch and Mendelssohn. Then his whole body became so convulsed with sobs that playing was no longer possible.

Mr. Gropius was quite non-plussed. Although not an over-exigent teacher, certain critical comments were necessary and the more he corrected Sergei, the more the boy cried. After two terms Mr. Gropius was forced to admit to the Director of Music that the boy was unteachable.

The lessons ceased and so did Sergei's right to possess the violin.

The following term he started trumpet lessons. These went well at first and for half a term he didn't cry once in a lesson. Then as his grasp of the instrument increased, so did the critical comments of his teacher, a young man with a ginger moustache called Mr. Yelp.

'You didn't hold on to the tied semi-breves for long enough,' remarked Mr. Yelp.

'Can't you see I'm trying, sir?' And Sergei's tears started to flow.

It was Sergei himself who terminated the lessons this time. He told the Director of Music that blowing the trumpet adversely affected his sinuses.

Bottom was sympathetic.

'It's a shame you have to stop your lessons when you're so good.'

Bottom was a little envious of Sergei's musical ability. He had tried learning the trumpet, but despite three years of lessons he had only managed to produce four notes. Sergei spent a term without taking instrumental lessons and seemed a lot happier. He listened to music alone in the lavatory and managed the whole term without crying in public.

Now twelve years old and much more securely settled into the rigorous routine of Cholmondley Hall, Sergei decided to learn another instrument. He undoubtedly had musical ability and it was what he wanted to do most. His next choice was the flute.

The flute teacher was a man in his early thirties trying to make a career as a soloist. Because of his outside professional engagements the lessons at Cholmondley Hall were a little irregular and sometimes cancelled at short notice. This kept the pupils constantly on their toes; a state of existence which benefited some pupils, though not all.

At first Sergei was one of the beneficiaries and made good progress. Then one day towards the end of term Mr. Blightwell corrected his phrasing, playing the music himself as he wished it to be played. Sergei tried again.

'No, no, not like that - like this,' and Mr. Blightwell played the phrase again, the notes of his golden flute filling the room with a glorious, mellifluous sound.

'I can't play like that! Not on this horrible old tin flute'.

And the tears started to flow. At the end of term Mr. Blightwell terminated the lessons, saying that due to his increasing professional commitments some of his pupils at the school would have to go. A twelve-year-old boy who cried in lessons was an obvious choice for dismissal.

The flute went too.

In his last term at Cholmondley Hall, Sergei felt he should give himself one more chance. After all, he would be thirteen just after the beginning of the autumn term. Thirteen was nearly grown-up; surely too old to cry in a music lesson. So he requested piano lessons.

The piano! It was such an obvious choice. Why hadn't he thought of it before? Why had he wasted time and tears learning an orchestral instrument when he could be the soloist with an orchestra? And the piano was surely the easiest of all the instruments. There was no problem of actually making the notes, as there was on the violin, or the problem of blowing across or down a tube as on the flute or the trumpet. It must have been the blowing that had made him cry. All the pianist had to do was press the notes that were already there.

Sergei reached the end of the quad and turned the corner. The handsome music block was set apart from the main school, isolated because of all the noise it had been built to create. He pushed the door open and walked slowly up the stairs. A cacophony of sound assailed his ears: a soaring violin; a squawking oboe; a spluttering flute; a strident trumpet; a rumble of tympani. All the sounds were so evocative of his past efforts to learn a musical instrument that his stomach muscles hardened further, his mouth dried completely and a wild rhythm thundered in his head.

His teacher was Miss Hacket in Room No. 3. The rhythm grew louder and louder and his head felt as if it was going to burst. Hacket and Bracket, Hacket and Bracket, Hacket and Bracket. As he reached the top of the stairs sweat broke out on his forehead. His hand trembled violently as he placed it on the doorknob.

Hacket and Bracket. Hacket and Bracket.

He turned the door handle and walked into the room. Miss Hacket looked up from the piano and smiled radiantly.

'Hello. You must be Sergei. Do come in.'

She was young and slim, with shoulder-length honey-coloured hair, wide-set laughing brown eyes and a sensitive, sensual mouth. She was quite beautiful and reminded Sergei of his mother.

He burst into tears and fled.

Louise

'Are you still in touch with Louise?' enquired Amanda as she walked with him to his car.

'Louise?'

'Yes,' said Amanda lightly. 'I seem to remember you were very keen on Louise. At one time John and I even thought...but she was married to a Frenchman, wasn't she? I mention it because the other day in St. Léger I heard a lady speaking English to a tourist on one of the barges. She reminded me so much of your Louise that I asked Jeanine at the post office if an English lady had recently moved into the area. 'Yes,' she said. St. Léger's not far from here – and not too much of a detour. You could surprise her.'

'Louise.' His heart skipped a beat. 'I knew a Louise in Paris but I can't imagine her living in deepest Burgundy. I can't just drop by! Not without letting her know I was coming.'

Amanda smiled and gave him a playful push. 'You didn't let me know you were coming.'

He looked at her quizzically. 'N...no. But you're different. We've always kept in touch. And if it isn't her after all?'

'What does it matter? You might strike up a new friendship.'

He waved Amanda goodbye and set off towards St. Léger. Louise. He had adored Louise. It would be wonderful to see her again after all these years. But could he just turn up unannounced? On the other hand, why not? It seemed an opportunity too good to miss, especially as he was almost passing by.

He drove along the canal as a barge came into view. A bikini-clad girl lay stretched out on the deck, sunbathing, and a tanned young man, wearing shorts, was making ready to operate the locks. He sighed, feeling envious and a little sad. Oh, to be young again and have one's whole life ahead.

He found St. Léger without difficulty. It was like so many other French villages, shuttered and deserted in the warm afternoon sunshine. He wondered where all the residents were. Did everyone in the country spend the afternoon in bed?

He found a shop that was open.

'*Oui, bien sûr monsieur,* you must mean *Madame Perché.* The house isn't far from here. You can't miss it. It's a double fronted two-storey stone farmhouse with green shutters, set at right angles to the road. The courtyard is filled with flowers.'

Perché? He couldn't recall Louise being called Perché. But of course her husband was French. According to Louise, that had been part of the problem.

At the end of the lane stood a stone farmhouse with green shutters and a courtyard in full bloom. He felt a sense of mounting excitement. Louise! How would she look after all these years? Would she be pleased to see him? Would she remember him? Would he recognize her? Or was he being too precipitous.

He parked by the wall of the house and walked along the lane to the big wrought-iron gates. He looked up at the house, standing silent and somnolent, the green shutters closed. Maybe Louise was away? Or resting? Perhaps she wasn't alone?

He pulled the bell-rope and a bell jangled harshly through the still summer air, followed by silence even more deafening than the clanging of the bell. Nothing moved, nothing breathed. As he was debating whether or not to ring the bell again the shutters on the ground-floor window on the far side of the house were thrown open and a head half-appeared through the window.

'*Bonjour, monsieur. Vous cherchez quelqu'un ?*' said a woman's voice.

'*Bonjour,*' he replied. '*Je cherche Madame Perché. Elle est là?*'

'*Mais bien sûr. Je suis Madame Perché. J'arrive à l'instant...*'

The head disappeared, the shutters were closed and a few moments later the front door opened and a diminutive figure appeared. She was smaller than he had remembered. But people often grew smaller with age. The grey hair, too. That was quite a shock. But then he had practically no hair. That would be an equal shock for her.

She came across the courtyard towards the gate with a light springy step. Oh, yes! He remembered her walk and her perfect carriage. There was no doubt then, was there? No doubt at all. She wrestled with the heavy bolt of the gate. There was nothing he could do to help her from his side. He found the tension unbearable. Should he take her in his arms right away? No, maybe not. Better wait a bit.

At last the heavy gate swung inwards. He took a step forward and held out his hand.

'*Bonjour.*'

He shook her hand, numb with emotion.

She led the way through another much smaller gate into a beautiful garden full of flowers, now at their best in the bright July sunshine. In a corner a table was laid for two.

'I've been expecting you,' she said. 'Do sit down.'

He held the chair for her and sat down opposite.

She poured two glasses of wine.

'I don't bother making tea any more. I rarely take any refreshment during the afternoon - only if I have visitors. The wine here is so good - and it's cheap. Teetotallers can always have water.'

She laughed a deliciously fresh, tinkling laugh. He was entranced by her. She quite exceeded his expectations and his fond, distant memories.

'I live in Paris now,' he said.

'What *quartier* do you habit? Or is it co-habit?'

She laughed her beautiful tinkling laugh again.

'I don't think that's correct, is it? You must forgive my English. I have so little practice now.'

He laughed with her.

'No, it's not habit. One lives in a place. I live in the 7th arrondissement in the *Rue de Verneuil*, just off the *Rue des St. Pères*.'

'Of course', she said, 'such a nice part of Paris. But I never really enjoyed living in Paris. I've always preferred the country. It's so peaceful here. Look how beautiful it is.' She indicated the view with a sweep of her hand. 'But you loved the countryside too in those days.'

'Yes, I suppose I did.'

He sounded a little doubtful, but of course he must have loved it then, just for her sake.

'I love the bustle of Paris,' he said. 'It never seems to stop or close down. It throbs all night long. These little country villages seem shuttered and deserted most of the time. Where do all the people go? What do they do during the day?'

She laughed again.

'We are very busy here - getting up to things, I suppose.'

Getting up to things... What things? Or was that another example of her slightly idiosyncratic English? It added so enormously to her charm. He was sure that in the past she had spoken perfect English.

'How long is it since we have seen each other?'

'Oh, don't let's count up the years that have passed. Let's just enjoy the present and hopefully look forward to the future.'

To the future? Together? Surely that was more than he could hope for.

'Tell me about your family,' she suggested encouragingly. 'You have two sons - yes?'

'Yes.' How clever of her to remember. In the past they had tried to avoid speaking about each other's children.

'They've both done extremely well. Mark is a solicitor in London. Paul became a dentist and emigrated to Canada.'

'Grandchildren?'

'Seven.' He laughed. 'Mark has three and Paul four. More than I would want, but I suppose there's a lot of space to fill in Canada.'

'Yes. And you are not lonely since ... since ... your wife ... Madeleine ... was it?'

'No, Marguérite. It was all very amicable really. She just fell for Alain ... you know ... Sometimes these Frenchmen ...'

'Yes, yes, I know,' she sounded bitter. '*Un coup de foudre* - was it?'

'Love at first sight?'

'Yes.' He felt something stirring in him deep down. She was so lovely, so charming, so captivating.

'Tell me about your sons,' he prompted.

'Sons? No sons, just two daughters. Don't you remember how Michel always wanted sons? It irked him not having sons.'

'Of course. I remember Michel always wanted sons. I must have been thinking about someone else...'

But he was sure Louise had sons.

'They're both married. Claudette has two sons and lives in Bordeaux. Françoise has a son and two daughters and lives in Villefranche. It's not too far from here so we see each other quite often.'

'That's nice,' he said without thinking. 'And Michel is...?' The question had to be broached at some time or another.

'Dead.'

'I'm so sorry,' he said, trying to sound sympathetic.

'You needn't be,' her laugh had lost its tinkle. 'He was... well... you know how Frenchmen can be...'

'Yes.'

His heart was pounding for joy. Caution. He mustn't rush things.

'Would you like to see the house?'

His heart leapt again. 'Yes, I'd love to. What about...?' He indicated the glasses and plates on the table.

'Don't worry about those. We can do them later.'

The 'we' sounded like music to his ears.

He followed her across the courtyard into the house. As they stood in the hall she explained what a dreadful state the house had been in when she had first bought it.

Watching her, he longed to take her in his arms and murmur endearments. He wanted to kiss her passionately, to caress her and possess her completely.

In the *salon*, a graceful rectangular room that stretched the length of the house, she turned towards him to point out a particular item of interest. On a sudden impulse he took her hand. He held it and stroked it gently. He touched her hair. It smelt fresh like the countryside. Desire rose in him until he felt he would burst.

'Oh, Louise,' he murmured.

She stepped back a little in surprise.

'Oh, Jack!' she said. 'I knew you'd come. Will you stay for a while? But my name is Katherine.'

He took her in his arms. He no longer cared what her name was. He just knew that at last he had found heaven on earth.

In fact his name was Charles.

Sandwiches

'Hello, Mummy! It's Charlotte!'

'Charlotte! Where are you, Charlotte?'

'I'm staying at Argyle House - with Daddy.'

'With your father! Well, I never. I hope you're coming to see me.'

'Yes, Mummy. I thought I'd call round tomorrow. Perhaps we could have lunch out together?'

'What day is it tomorrow?'

'It's Wednesday, 28 May.'

'I'm never free on a Wednesday.'

'Oh, I see. What do you do on a Wednesday?'

'I just keep Wednesdays free so I can have some time to myself.'

'Oh, I'm pleased to hear you have such a busy life… How about Thursday?'

'I think I could manage Thursday. Perhaps you would care to meet me at the Burlington Hotel for a light lunch? The hotel is round the corner from my flat, which I find very convenient. I don't often go into Grafton Street nowadays. I can't manage the bus and taxis in Dublin have become exorbitantly expensive. It's a new hotel – your father will tell you how to get there. Meet me in the lounge at 12.25 pm.'

'Yes, Mummy. 12.25 pm in the lounge of the Burlington Hotel. Till then…'

Charlotte arrived at the Burlington Hotel at 12.15 pm and sat at a table for two waiting for her mother. She hadn't seen her for so long she wondered if she would recognise her. A waitress arrived and asked for her order.

'I'm waiting for a friend,' she mumbled.

Keeping her eye on the door, she watched people coming and going. A little old lady came in leaning heavily on a cane. Charlotte half got up: 'Mummy?' But the little old lady walked on and greeted another little old lady seated at a table just behind her. She looked at her watch. It was twenty minutes to one, but her mother had always been notoriously unpunctual. At ten minutes to one another old lady entered. She walked erect without a stick, her head held high, peering around short-sightedly. She came up to Charlotte's table.

'Charlotte! Is that you darling?'

Charlotte stood up and gave her mother a peck on the cheek.

'How nice to see you, Mummy! You do look well.'

She had barely recognised her own mother.

Mrs Boland settled into a chair and waved her hand imperiously. 'Waitress! Waitress! I'd like to order please!'

The waitress was by her side in an instant. 'Yes, Mrs Boland, and what can I get you?' in a somewhat resigned tone.

'Charlotte, will you have an egg or a prawn sandwich? Both are highly recommendable provided my instructions are carried out to the letter. You'll remember, won't you,' turning to the waitress, 'that the bread must be wafer thin, no butter, just your excellent home-made mayonnaise... I hope the chef has made his mayonnaise today? The last time I lunched here there was no fresh mayonnaise and I had to make do with that dreadful Heinz Salad Cream…'

'The mayonnaise is freshly made today, madam.'

'I'm glad to hear it. Well, Charlotte, would you prefer egg or prawn?'

'Really, Mummy, it doesn't matter. I like both equally…'

'Don't you have definite opinions any more, Charlotte? I see my daughter is unable to make up her mind so I shall be forced to make the decision for her. I think if we start with one of each? Then we can share and augment the order later if necessary… And will you have a glass of wine?'

Charlotte wondered how she would be able to survive the ordeal without a glass of wine. 'Yes, please, Mummy. A glass of wine would be lovely.'

Mrs Boland looked up at the waitress, who glanced pityingly at Charlotte. 'We'll have two large glasses of Chablis, please.'

'And how are you enjoying your visit to Dublin, Charlotte? You must tell me all about your busy London life and your two little boys. How old are they now? Are they still at school?'

'Well, Tom is…'

When the sandwiches arrived Mrs Boland inspected them closely. 'I don't think I mentioned chives did I, young lady?'

'No, madam.'

'I dislike chives intensely. Please take these sandwiches away and make fresh ones – free of chives.'

'Would madam like some parsley? Just to give the sandwiches a little lift?'

'No parsley, thank you.'

'A little basil or sage?'

'Not even basil or sage. Just some mayonnaise.'

'Just as you wish, madam.'

As the waitress cleared the plates, Mrs Boland turned to her daughter.

'Now, Charlotte, as you were saying…'

The Chilla Rat

'Eric! Hurry up! Your dinner's getting cold.'

'Yes, Mum, I'm coming in a minute.'

Eric opened the cage and took out a gerbil, shivering as it sat on his hand. Its eyes were rheumy, the tiny nose dry to the touch. Eric stroked it gently and the shivers became more violent.

'Poor, poor Germaine. I don't think you're very well. I'll see what I can get for you to-morrow.'

Eric rearranged the food and water to make it look more tempting and returned the little creature to its cage.

'Eric! Come on down.' The female voice from downstairs was becoming irate. 'Leave those damned animals alone and come and have your dinner!'

'Yes, Mum, I'm coming,' replied Eric, too softly for his mother to hear through the closed door. He stood with his hand on the door-handle and looked around at the array of cages: twenty seven of them, all containing one or more rodents. There were mice, hamsters, guinea pigs, rabbits and gerbils: some sleeping, some eating, some riding round on a large slatted wheel like a tread-mill, some just sitting. Eric heaved a great sigh. He hated to leave them, even for meals. He made his way slowly downstairs. He wasn't very hungry. He never felt hungry when one of his rodents was ill. Shuffling awkwardly into the kitchen, he sat down opposite his mother, who had already started her dinner.

'I'm sorry I'm late, Mum. Germaine isn't very well.'

'I'm sorry about that', replied his mother. 'Which one is Germaine? One of the guinea pigs?'

'No, she's a gerbil', said Eric. 'The guinea pigs are George, Gertrude, Garbo and Greer.'

'Is Germaine the feminist one, or is it Greer?' enquired his sister tartly.

'Oh, don't tease him, Lucy', pleaded her mother. 'He's bad enough as he is with all those caged animals up there.'

Eric picked up his knife and fork and examined his food carefully.

'What is it, Mum?'

'It's rabbit', said Lucy with glee. 'It's two rabbits, actually. Mum thought one wouldn't be enough for the three of us.'

Eric gave a cry of anguish and pushed back his chair.

'Mum! You know I won't eat rabbit! It's disgusting! Rabbits are my friends.'

'Haven't you missed two of your friends lately?' taunted Lucy. 'When I came home from school yesterday I went into your room and pinched two of your rabbits for the pot. Didn't I, Mum?'

'Oh, Lucy, for God's sake, will you leave Eric alone,' demanded her mother. 'Stop tormenting him.'

She turned to Eric. 'Of course it's not rabbit, love. I'd never give you rabbit.'

'Maybe it's guinea pig after all', said Lucy, with a smirk.

'I can't stand any more of this'. Pushing his plate away, Eric stormed out of the room.

'Now look what you've done, Lucy.' said Mrs Sanderson reproachfully.

As a small boy Eric Sanderson had always been different to other children. He was a silent, taciturn child who found it difficult to show affection. When his mother tried to comfort him he didn't know how to react. He would never 'cuddle in' or put his arms around her neck and he disliked being kissed. He disliked cats and had a great aversion to dogs, especially the larger breeds, to which he always gave a wide berth. His first real show of affection was towards a rabbit, which he first saw when visiting a friend's house for tea. Without asking permission, Eric let the large white rabbit out of its cage and allowed it to roam freely in the garden, sticking closely to its side as if he were its minder. When his mother arrived to take him home she enquired of his hostess how Eric had got on with her son.

'He took no notice of George at all,' the good lady replied. 'He spent the entire afternoon playing with the rabbit. I don't understand it. George is such a friendly little boy.'

Mrs Sanderson didn't comment. Needless to say the invitation to visit George was not repeated. Neither did Mrs Sanderson invite George to tea with Eric.

Eric begged his mother to buy him a rabbit. At first she refused. Enjoying the independence of her two cats, it was against her instincts to own a caged animal. Sadly, they had had to sell the Doberman. Eric became so terrified of it that he wouldn't come downstairs to meals unless the dog was chained up in its kennel outside. Whenever they went out shopping five-year old Eric managed to slip off on his own. The first time this happened his mother was so distraught that she went to the police. Two hours later Eric was eventually tracked down in the pet shop playing with the rabbits, guinea pigs and dormice. After the fifth visit to the pet shop Mrs Sanderson capitulated and bought him a large white rabbit. At first the rabbit lived in its hutch at the bottom of the garden and whenever he was at home Eric let the rabbit out and played with it for hours. When winter set in, he persuaded his mother that the rabbit was cold and should come and live in his bedroom. After some argument Mrs Sanderson gave in, although she worried about the smell and the difficulty of cleaning out the cage in an upstairs room.

'Don't worry, Mum, I'll do it,' Eric reassured her.

By Christmas Eric succeeded in persuading his mother that the rabbit was lonely and needed a companion, and as one rabbit was male and the other one female there were soon many more rabbits. By Easter there were a great many rabbits indeed and by the following Christmas Eric had seven cages of them in his bedroom. As he felt the rabbits were much safer in the house, the cages were never returned to the garden. Despite being the owner of eleven rabbits, Eric yearned for a hamster. He was now eight years old and the recipient of regular weekly pocket money, most of which he spent on the rabbits. However, he managed to put a little aside each week and a visit to the pet shop one day to buy rabbit food resulted in the happy ownership of two hamsters. Soon the hamsters emulated the sexual activity of the rabbits and there were a great number of hamsters as well.

Mrs Sanderson had long ceased to visit Eric's bedroom. Bedtime stories, never very much appreciated by Eric even before he could read, were now a thing of the past. His mother left clean laundry on a chair on the landing outside his room and Eric was responsible for changing the bed linen and cleaning the room himself. With more than twenty-five rodents roaming freely in the room for four or five hours each day, this posed an ever-increasing problem. In the end Eric became unequal to the task and the room became very dirty and smelly. He was aware his room smelt and quite understood why no one wanted to visit it. However, he still possessed a fairly high standard of personal hygiene and always showered or bathed regularly, but it was becoming more and more difficult to eradicate the odour of rodent droppings from his clothes.

Eric had never been popular at school. Even at his nursery school, long before he owned any rodents, his peers avoided him. He was unable to share toys or join in with group activities. His thought process was limited and he spoke slowly and with difficulty. Physically he was well developed: a handsome little boy with fair, curly hair and large blue eyes. But he seldom smiled and almost never laughed. He rarely cried either, even when he fell over, which was quite frequently, for his movements were clumsy and awkward. He couldn't run very fast and he seemed to have no natural aptitude for climbing or jumping. He remained on the periphery: always an outsider.

By the time he reached secondary school Eric was a loner. Some of the bigger boys teased and bullied him; most just left him alone. As he was still good looking, many of the girls showed some interest in striking up a relationship, but as they got to know him better they found him gauche and lacking in any sense of humour.

So one by one they melted away, leaving him to his own devices.

For the first two years he did well at his schoolwork, coming near the top of the class in most subjects. His parents were extremely relieved. Conscious that their son was rather different from other boys of his age, they considered discussing the matter with their doctor but soon abandoned the idea. There didn't seem to be any definite symptoms to go on, nothing concrete to explain their anxiety. Unfortunately Eric's good scholastic performance was short-lived. By the end of the third year he had lost interest in most of his schoolwork, which became perfunctory and slip-shod, his homework often left unfinished. The only subject in which he retained any interest was biology, at which he excelled.

By now his menagerie of rodents had become an obsession. He bought books about them and worked on a treatise: an exhaustive study, which took precedence over everything else except actually caring for the rodents themselves. So far he had written over 40,000 words. He discovered that there are over 1,000 species and well over 6,000 named varieties. The group to which the common house rat belongs, known as Rattus, has over 500 named forms. That still left other varieties such as the squirrel, porcupine, beaver, mole and hare to classify, as well as the more exotic breeds not found in England such as the marmot, chinchilla, musquash and lemming. But most absorbing of all were the breeds he owned himself. He now had sixteen rabbits, eleven gerbils, nine guinea pigs and seven hamsters in cages in his bedroom.

At sixteen Eric did badly in his GCSE exams, even worse than his parents or teachers had feared. He only passed in three subjects: English Language, Maths and Biology, with an A in Biology. His headmaster refused to allow him to proceed into the Sixth Form to study for A-Levels unless he re-sat some of the subjects he had failed. Eric refused to retake any GCSEs. He felt quite confident that he could obtain high grades at A-Level in Anatomy, Biology and Zoology. These were the only subjects that interested him and the only ones he was prepared to work at. He was hoping to become a vet.

For three weeks before the start of the Autumn Term the argument raged between Eric and his headmaster. Eric's parents supported their son. They felt his passion for rodents should be constructively channelled. They realised that a boy as unusual as Eric would only work if his interest were aroused. It was pointless expecting him to study History or Geography.

In the end Eric and his parents lost. At the age of only sixteen, with no other qualifications than three GCSEs, Eric's chances in the labour market were slim. He tried being an errand boy and then served in a shop. But he hated both occupations so much that he only lasted a few days in each job. Feeling depressed, unwanted and increasingly isolated, he decided to treat himself to a day at the Zoo. Predictably, he made straight for the rodents' enclosure. On the door was a notice:

'Assistant wanted. Please apply within.'

He went in and within minutes was appointed fifth assistant to the rodent keeper at the Metropolitan Zoo.

His job at the Zoo changed Eric's life. He now had a purpose, a mission in life and was spending twenty-four hours a day with rodents. He spent his entire working day tending his charges at the Zoo and, because he felt he neglected his own pets at home, he took to eating his meals in his bedroom. Allowing the animals free range of the room during the night, he woke up each morning to find the whole bed covered with droppings.

By now the smell permeating the house was appalling. Eric's parents became distraught and at last decided to seek medical advice. Eric's obsession with rodents and its resulting unpleasantness had begun to place a great strain on their marriage and Mr Sanderson threatened to leave home unless something was done about Eric.

For six months Eric was referred from one doctor to another. Finally he was sent to see Dr. Solomon Blochstein, a specialist in the study of obsession and autism and considered among the most eminent psychiatrists in the British Isles. He diagnosed Eric as having Asperger's Syndrome, a condition characterised by obsessive and narrow interests.

'It's a form of autism and often affects the sufferer's communication and social reaction with other human beings.' said Dr. Blochstein. 'It's a rare and little understood condition. Not only does the intensity vary, but also a wide range of obsessions can be included. For instance, most people wouldn't consider train spotting to be a particularly abnormal activity; but carried to extremes it can become an obsession. The danger lies in activities in which people engage in on their own. The more absorbing the interest becomes, the less need there is for human contact.

'One of my patients was a boy of eight who had a passion for frogs. He had nearly a hundred frogs in tanks in his bedroom. This case shows a parallel with Eric's case; though with the advantage that at least the frogs remained in their tanks. One solution is to transfer the obsession. I suggested to the boy's parents that they try to interest him in some other animal. It took some time, of course, but eventually his passion was transferred to horses and he became a most successful jockey.

'Quite often the obsession concerns food. I remember a boy who would only eat carrots. This continued for several years. He was persuaded to try other foods with great reluctance and eventually developed a similar passion for leeks.

'The condition is virtually incurable,' admitted Dr Blochstein. 'It's a question of finding a less distressing substitute. I can certainly understand your objection to rodents.' He repressed a shudder. 'Nasty smelly dirty things. Maybe you could interest Eric in tropical fish?'

'Or stamp collecting?' suggested Mr Sanderson. 'It would be a relief to get away from animals.'

'That would be a remarkable achievement,' agreed the doctor, 'but most unlikely given the severity of Eric's particular case. Medical history has so far shown that the substitute passion needs to have a fairly close proximity to the original one. From food to food; animal to animal, if you follow me.'

Eric's parents left without much feeling of encouragement and for the next few months they tried to broaden Eric's interests in any way possible. They suggested horse riding, swimming and tennis lessons; but to no avail. They tried to persuade him to get rid of the rodents altogether and give up his job at the Zoo. They suggested sending him to an expensive crammer where he could retake his GCSEs or take any A-Levels he wished. The harder they tried to persuade him the more adamant Eric became.

Finally Mr Sanderson couldn't cope any longer. He left home, leaving a note on the kitchen table saying he was unable to continue sharing a house with so many disgusting animals. Mrs Sanderson was distraught but held no ill feelings against her husband. The house smelt like a Zoo. Eric had become unkempt and filthy and the whole situation had reached crisis proportions.

Meanwhile Eric was becoming more and more absorbed in his job at the Zoo. In addition to the care and maintenance of the animals, the breeding programme was an important part of the work. Particular attention was paid to the breeding of the more rare species that were in danger of extinction. Eric, now nearing twenty, was fascinated by the sexual urges of the rodents. He watched them at their procreativity for hours on end, intrigued by how some breeds mounted each other and how others did it lying down. He wondered what would happen if two different breeds mated and decided to try an experiment.

Although Zoo policy totally forbade any crossbreeding between species unless the highest authorisation was received in writing, Eric decided to risk experimenting on his own. He also decided to contravene another of the Zoo's strict rules forbidding the removal of animals from their cages or compounds. However, Zoo security was very lax. Only new employees were searched or questioned on leaving the grounds in the evening. As he had now worked at the Zoo for nearly four years, the guard at the exit gate just saw Eric out with a nod. It was no trouble to leave one evening with an African mole rat in one pocket and a chinchilla in the other.

Eric spent many hours watching the African mole rat and the chinchilla indulging in the most bizarre sexual capers on what was left of his bedroom carpet. This stimulated his own sexual arousal. Dimly aware that this was a past time also enjoyed by humans, he felt it was something he might be missing out on. But the complication and aggravation of finding a suitable partner put it out of his mind and he suppressed his natural desire in the vicarious pleasure of watching the rodents.

A few weeks later the chinchilla gave birth to a litter of half-African mole rats. There were eight tiny babies, all with their eyes closed. Eric decided to call them chilla rats.

The chilla rats grew very fast. There was one in particular which seemed to outstrip all the others. Eric was careful to keep the chilla rats quite separate from all his other rodents. There was something a little sinister about them, especially the biggest one. He was ominously ugly and growing at an alarming rate.

One evening Eric let the chilla rats, plus their parents, out of their cages to roam freely in the wreckage of his bedroom. All the other rodents were safely locked up. Since the birth of the chilla rats Eric's interest in his other rodents had diminished considerably and their number had decreased. He let some loose on Hampstead Heath, sold some to the pet shop and others died, either through illness or neglect. Eric was now in the throes of the most advanced form of Asperger's Syndrome. His obsession had narrowed down to chilla rats and to one of them in particular.

Leaving the chilla rats to play, Eric went to the bathroom to take one of his increasingly rare showers. As he was drying himself, he heard a terrible commotion in his bedroom. Shrieks, squeaks, wails and scuttling noises were heard coming through the door. Wearing only a bath towel, he rushed into the room to find a scene of complete devastation. The floor, bed and chair were littered with rodents' remains and there was blood everywhere. Sitting up in the middle of the bed smacking his lips with an evil grin on his face was the largest chilla rat.

He had eaten his entire family.

From that day on Eric went into a decline. He left the Zoo and rarely left his bedroom. He no longer washed or changed his clothes and he rarely spoke to his mother or sister. Mrs Sanderson left his meals on a tray outside his bedroom door.

It was nearly Christmas. Mrs Sanderson begged her son to join them downstairs for Christmas dinner. It was a special day, she pleaded, a family day. And perhaps a glass or two of wine would buck him up. Grudgingly Eric agreed. His mother was feeding him three times a day so he did owe her something. He needn't speak to Lucy whom he hated, with her endless prattling conversation and irritating, high-pitched laugh.

By twelve-thirty a delicious aroma of roasting turkey pervaded the house, partly blotting out the pungent, sour smell of rodent droppings. Eric let the sole remaining chilla rat out of its cage to have free run of his bedroom. The creature had now grown enormous and was almost as large as a terrier. It was black, with a long narrow head, its sharp incisors often exposed in a malevolent leer. Its paws were prehensile, the adept fingers ending in long vicious claws. It rubbed itself against Eric's leg, seemingly in a display of affection. Eric stroked its stiff fur with loving pride; glancing at the other cages to make sure the other rodents were securely locked up before he left the room.

He made his way downstairs unsteadily to join his mother and sister for Christmas lunch. He ventured

down to the ground floor so rarely nowadays that nego-
tiating the steps was quite a feat. His mother greeted
him nervously. She had made a great effort for the occasion. The table was beautifully laid with a lace cloth and
decorated with crackers and a bowl of flowers. A
Christmas tree stood in the corner with some gaily-
wrapped presents lying underneath.

'How nice,' said Mrs Sanderson, attempting to give
him a peck on the cheek. 'You do look well, dear.
Happy Christmas, Eric.'

Lucy arrived, taking no notice whatsoever of Eric,
who sat down helplessly at the table, not knowing what
to do or say. Mrs Sanderson bustled about, bringing in
the food and pouring the wine. She toasted the occasion
and they all settled down to enjoy their meal.

After three glasses of wine Eric felt his head spinning
a little, but he felt warm and relaxed. He was dimly
aware that the food tasted rather nice. The main course
finished, Mrs Sanderson and Lucy sat and chatted,
giving themselves a chance to digest the turkey before
clearing away the plates and bringing in the Christmas
pudding.

Suddenly, a terrific commotion came from the direction of Eric's bedroom. There were shrieks and shrill
squeals of animals in agony. Mrs Sanderson and Lucy
were transfixed with horror and Eric stood up so violently that he knocked over his chair into the sideboard,
breaking a serving-dish.

Tearing upstairs at top speed, he threw open his
bedroom door to be met by a scene of total chaos. The
chilla rat had opened all the other rodents' cages and
had devoured the lot, leaving, fur, heads, tails and claws
all over the room. Eric went in and closed the door. The

chilla rat sat in the middle of the bed, licking its paws, its powerful incisors gleaming menacingly.

Eric stood and watched it.

Without any warning, the chilla rat leapt at Eric's throat and bit through the jugular vein. A jet of blood spurted into the air and Eric fell unconscious to the floor.

Then the chilla rat settled down to the best meal of his life.

Downstairs, Mrs Sanderson and Lucy began to relax and Mrs Sanderson poured them each another glass of wine.

'Well, dear, Eric seems to have sorted out everything upstairs. He's so clever with those animals, don't you think?'

Lucy said nothing.

'I'll just bring in the Christmas pudding', said Mrs Sanderson, 'and then I'll call Eric down.'

A few minutes later Mrs Sanderson returned, bearing the Christmas pudding with the sprig of holly burning merrily in the middle. She placed it on the sideboard and returned to the door of the dining room.

'Eric!' she called, 'Come along now, Eric! I've just brought in the Christmas pudding. It looks ever so pretty.'

From upstairs there was total silence. The chilla rat was devouring Eric's brain.

The Stag Do

Standing on its own at the end of the village, the Draper's Arms was built in *faux* Elizabethan style, complete with sloping beams and whitewashed walls. The interior mirrored the outside in reverse. The walls were of dark oak panelling; the low black beams and diamond-paned windows let in little light. The living-gas fire was on full, sending flickering shadows around the small room, making it oppressively stuffy. Despite the cramped interior, the pub was popular with the locals, especially at weekends.

On a gloomy evening in early December a scrubbed pine table was laid for eight in the dining area. There was no pretension, no fuss, just a knife and fork, one glass and a gaudy orange paper table napkin at each place. The chairs were pine, hard and uncomfortable, as if the landlord had no wish for his diners to linger. From the saloon bar next door came the chink of glasses and raucous laughter as a regular told another lewd joke. Outside, the fog thickened and the rain increased.

Greg was the first to arrive. Tall lean and gangly, his clothes too small, he walked with a drunken gait, which helped to disguise his frequent bouts of excessive alcoholic consumption. He had barely sat down at the table when Dean entered, short red-haired and bespectacled.

'Hi, mate! No sign of Nige?'

'No sign of anyone yet.'

Dean sat down next to Greg and began to fiddle with the cutlery.

'Known Nige long?'

'No. Met him in the Bull and Bear last Saturday.'

'I was in school with Nige. We was in the same class. For a bit.'

'Was you, then?'

The door opened with a blast of chill air. A fat young man stood uncertainly in the doorway.

'This Nige's party?'

'It could be. I was told the Draper's Arms. But there's no Nigel. He ain't here yet.' Greg sounded puzzled.

'I'm Mick,' said the fat young man, closing the door and joining Greg and Dean at the table. 'Known Nige long?'

'Dean 'ere 'as. They was at school together.'

'Just for a bit,' said Dean.

'Nige should be here,' said Greg. 'After all, it *is* his party.'

Suddenly there was a commotion outside, growing louder as the door of the pub was flung open. Two young men staggered in, one supporting the other, who collapsed on the floor, sobbing loudly. Dean ran forward and knelt on the floor beside the prostrate figure.

'Hey, Nige! What's up? You're drunk already and your stag party hasn't even started.'

Nigel looked up, tears flowing down his cheeks.

'It's off. Marlene's fucking left me!'

Early Morning Tea

Mary knocked gently on the door.

'Good mornin', your ladyship.'

There was no reply. Mary knocked a little louder.

'Good mornin', your ladyship. I've brought yous a nice cup o' tea...'

As there was still no reply Mary put the tray down on the landing table. It was nicely laid with a lace cloth, silverware and a fine bone china cup and saucer. She opened the door gently, picked up the tray and carried it into the room. A sound of harsh snoring came from the bed in the corner. Mary put the tray on the dressing table and tiptoed over to the bed. Leaning over the substantial bundle propped up on several pillows, covered with a thick pile of bedclothes, she spoke gently.

'Good mornin', m'am. Are yous after waking up now? It's gone past eight o'clock and I've brought yous a nice cup of tea.'

The mountainous figure in the bed turned to face the wall, snoring even louder. Mary leaned a little closer.

'Your tea's getting cold m'am. You know how yous hate cold tea.'

The figure grunted, rolled back again to face her and opened her eyes.

'Good morning, Mary. I assume another day must have dawned or you wouldn't be tormenting me like this. And what o'clock is it, pray?'

'It's gone after eight o'clock, m'am, and a lovely spring mornin' it be too, if I might remark.'

'You may remark, Mary', replied Lady Crockford-Browne tartly. 'You always remark, whether I wish it or not. Kindly open the curtains. I wish to see a little more of the lovely spring morning.'

Mary went over to the window and opened the curtains.

'Is that enough m'am?' Mary enquired, opening the curtains almost to their full extent.

'Not so much, Mary!' her ladyship gave a gasp of horror. 'The bright light does so hurt my eyes.'

Mary closed the curtains to about half way.

'Will that do m'am?'

'A little more, please, Mary.'

Mary closed the curtains almost completely.

'Is that all right, m'am?'

' No. A little more light, please, Mary. You know how I like it. It's the same each day.'

'If I might remark, m'am, it's quite different each day. It depends on whether it's rainin', whether the sun is shinin', or whether it's June or November.'

'Exactly. I always require the same amount of light each day. Therefore the curtains need to be adjusted according to the weather. On a dark day they should be almost completely open. On a very bright one, such as this appears to be, they need to be rather more closed.'

Mary readjusted the curtains. 'Like this, m'am?'

Lady Crockford-Browne heaved a deep sigh. 'That will have to do, Mary. I thought you were becoming slightly more skilful of late but today I fear you are just off the mark.'

'I do my best, your ladyship'.

'Are the birds singing today?'

'They are indeed, m'am. And beautiful singin' it is too.'

'I rather fancied I heard bird-song. Please pour my tea, Mary.'

'Yes, m'am. And how would her ladyship like her tea today?'

'What are the options?'

'You can have tea with milk, or without milk; with sugar or without sugar.'

'Indeed. How did I take my tea yesterday, Mary?'

'Yesterday I believe you took sugar and no milk.'

'Then today I shall take milk and no sugar. You know how I like a change, Mary. My life in here is so monotonous I must do what little I can to ring the changes.'

'Yes, m'am. Shall I pour the milk or the tea in first?'

'Let me give the matter some careful consideration, Mary. If the tea is poured in first it's easier to ascertain how much milk is required. On the other hand, if the milk is served first it facilitates the judgement of the appropriate amount of tea needed.'

'Of course, m'am, I understand you exactly', said Mary uncomprehendingly. 'So what have you in mind?'

She picked up the silver teapot in one hand and the milk-jug in the other.

'What do you deem to be more important, Mary, the amount of milk or the amount of tea?'

'I suppose the amount of tea, m'lady, seeing as it's a cup of tea you're about to be havin'. Unless of course, you'd prefer a cup of milk with some tea added?'

'That might make a change, mightn't it, Mary?'

Mary dutifully poured a cup of milk and added a little tea.

'Would her ladyship care for some sugar?'

'Did I take sugar yesterday, Mary?'

'Yes, m'am. But yesterday was different.'

'In what way, Mary? I am not aware that any day is different. In fact, I find all the days painfully similar.'

'Yes, m'am. I quite understand. But yesterday you took a cup of tea without milk. Today you are about to take a cup of milk with a little tea; which leaves the way open to havin' sugar or not.'

'I see, Mary. I fear this requires a little more thought. I think some sugar would be quite nice.'

Mary picked up the silver sugar-tongs and delicately placed two lumps in the china cup. She glanced around the room.

'Where will you drink the tea, m'am?'

'Out of the cup, I presume.'

'Yes, m'lady. 'What I mean is do you wish to drink the tea in bed or shall I place it on the table by the window?'

'Where did I take it yesterday, Mary?'

'I believe you had it in the chair by the window, m'am.'

'Then this morning I shall take it in bed. But before I drink it I must ask you please to tidy the bedclothes.'

'Of course, m'am.'

Mary set the cup down on the bedside table and started to rearrange the vast quantity of blankets underneath the hand-crocheted lace coverlet. She helped Lady Crockford-Browne to heave her huge frame slowly into an upright position, emerging from the covers like a whale encased in lace-trimmed silk lingerie, her head adorned with a similarly trimmed night bonnet.

'Don't forget the pillows, Mary. They all need plumping.'

'Yes, m'am. I haven't started on the pillows yet.'

Mary picked up the top pillow from the considerable pile and beat it ferociously, as if she were beating her tyrannical employer.

'Not so hard, Mary.'

'And why not?'

'It damages the feathers.'

'But aren't they dead an' all?'

'Dead they may be but I don't want them turned into pulp.'

Mary finished plumping and rearranging the pillows and helped Lady Crockford-Browne to settle herself more comfortably in the capacious bed. She placed the cup of milky tea within easier reach.

'What day is it, Mary?'

'I believe it's Wednesday.'

'And what month are we in now? Judging by the amount of sunlight outside this morning I imagine I must have survived another winter.'

'Indeed an' you have, m'am. Isn't that wonderful?'

'Wonderful? Is it wonderful to continue surviving at my age?'

'Indeed an' it is, your ladyship. And I'm sure you'll go on livin' to a ripe old age.'

'A ripe old age? I don't know that I want to go on living to a ripe old age. I'm probably a ripe old age already. I don't really recall exactly how old I am. I'm just old... old... and withered...'

'I don't know about withered, m'am...' Mary looked at the huge, bloated form in the bed with some amusement. 'Withered people tend to be... you know...' She indicated with her hands '... not quite so rounded. Almost on the thin side, in fact.'

'Oh, I'm not thin! I wouldn't want to be thin! At my age it could be rather dangerous to be thin, don't you think? But I'm withered in mind and spirit. One can be withered and not thin.'

'Yes, your ladyship.'

'We haven't settled what month it is, Mary.'

'No, indeed an' we haven't.'

'And what month is it?'

'It's April, m'am. The nineteenth of April.'

'Is that so? Then it will be May next month. My birthday's in May. I used to enjoy birthdays and getting presents and being taken out. Now no one gives me presents because I've got everything I want and no one takes me out because I can't walk. It's no fun growing old, Mary. You must always try and stay young.'

'Yes, m'am.'

'How old are you, Mary?'

'Twenty three last August.'

'Indeed? You don't look more than sixteen.'

'Thank you, m'am.'

'Did you come straight from Ireland to this house?'

'Yes, m'am.'

'And do you miss Ireland, Mary?'

'Not so much as I did, your ladyship.'

'And how long have you been in service here?'

'Going on five years now.'

'Really? So I must have been here at least five years. Five years in this house full of other old people, whom I never see, thank goodness, and who are probably withering and wasting away or who have gone to seed, swollen and bloated as I am. People who may have led happy, active and fulfilled lives in their youth, but now that they're no longer young they're empty husks, waiting for death to claim them at last. Don't grow old, Mary. Keep your youth and your looks and make the most of every precious second of your life while you are still young enough to enjoy it. Keep young! Keep young! And spend your time with other young people as much as you can. It's a pity we old people are so entirely dependent on the young. But I can't do anything for myself any longer. It's all I can do to drink a cup of tea.'

She picked up the cup and took a little sip. 'Oogh! It's disgusting! What on earth is this, Mary? Is this what you call a cup of tea?'

'Well, no, your ladyship, it's a cup of milk with a little tea added.'

'But it's cold.'

'It would be by now. It's been sittin' there awhile.'

'And there's too much milk.'

'That's how you wanted it today. For a change, you said.'

'I can't drink this, Mary. Please bring me a cup of coffee.'

'Yes, m'am.' Mary prepared to leave the room.

'And Mary...'

'Yes, your ladyship?'

'Please open the curtains a little bit wider. I would like to see the sunlight and hear the birds singing more clearly before I ... before I ...'

Her voice trailed off as Mary went to the window and opened the curtains a little bit more. Returning to the bedside to collect the untasted cup of cold milky tea, she glanced at the bloated figure lying motionless against the pillows, her face ashen grey. In some alarm

Mary set down the cup and took the old lady's wrist. The arm and hand were limp and lifeless.

Lady Crockford-Browne had died peacefully in her ninety-sixth year.

Wine Tasting

'Mum! Come here!' Sebastian's voice was urgent.

'What is it, darling?' called Veronica from the dining room.

'The label's come off the bottle!'

'Well, stick it back on. You know how busy I am.'

'I can't reach it. It's too high up.'

'Oh, all right.'

Veronica came into the kitchen, wearing an apron, her hair in curlers. She reached on tiptoe and took the wine bottle off the mantelpiece.

'Yes, it was rather high up, wasn't it, darling? Will you stick it back on for me?'

'Yes, of course I will. Shall I use some super-glue?'

Veronica laughed. 'I think that'd be a bit over the top. A bit of Bostick will do.'

Sebastian got to work with enthusiasm. At nine years old he loved sharing in the preparation for any event. It was often more enjoyable than the event itself.

'Mum, what do you enjoy most: waiting for something, or the moment when it actually happens?'

'What sort of thing?'

'Well, like Christmas, for instance.'

'Christmas?'

'Yes. Do you enjoy the preparation and the excitement of waiting or do you prefer the day itself?'

'Oh, I prefer the day itself, of course. Don't you?'

'I like both. But don't you find that sometimes waiting for the day is better than the day itself? Like the time Jonathan invited me to his birthday party. I was ever so pleased and excited. What with us going to different schools we hadn't seen each other for simply ages. I was so looking forward to it. And then when I got there I didn't know anybody so I didn't really enjoy it at all.'

'Yes, I know what you mean.'

This evening was almost certainly going to be difficult. Evenings with Heinz and Isabel invariably were. Isabel was sweet, charming, and most attractive. Heinz was bellicose, aggressive and tended to dominate the conversation in his high-pitched, whining tenor voice, with a heavy guttural German accent. He was insatiably curious about where she had bought the food, the wine, the new dining suite, or the new fridge and always insisted on knowing the price of everything. He could invariably tell you where you could have bought your new acquisition much more cheaply. He knew people who knew someone who had obtained the latest hi-fi at cost, or a washing machine which had just fallen off the back of a lorry. He would launch into a long story about how he had just met someone who knew exactly where to obtain the very same item that Veronica had bought in John Lewis last week for a fraction of what she had paid.

'You should have asked me first, Veronica,' he would say.

'But I can't ring you up each time I plan to go shopping.'

'That would be too much a pleasure. Then a long chat we can have and that is so nice.'

That was the trouble. One could never get him off the phone.

It was unfortunate that Isabel had married someone like Heinz. Veronica was appalled when Isabel had brought Heinz to dinner just after they had become engaged. Isabel was a close friend. They had been at school together and Isabel had been one of the bridesmaids at Veronica's wedding. Having known Isabel for so long, Veronica realized they were now stuck with Heinz.

Isabel and Heinz were food and wine buffs. Isabel was an excellent cook who had taken a *Cordon Bleu* cookery course and then gone into hotel management. She had met Heinz at a food fair and their great mutual interest had drawn them together. After her marriage Isabel had given up hotel management and instead gave frequent and elaborate dinner parties. She was a perfectionist and only served food cooked to the highest standards, never using frozen or pre-prepared foods. She had been known to throw away nine chocolate cases out of every ten because they were not quite regular in shape. Although she had known Isabel from childhood, Veronica always felt a little intimidated in inviting her to sample her own much simpler culinary fare.

Up till now they had always invited Heinz and Isabel with at least one other couple, so that Heinz's overpowering personality would be somewhat diluted. But they were now running out of friends who were willing to put up with Heinz. When Veronica mentioned Heinz's name on the phone to one of the prospective guests there was often a complete change in the tone of voice.

'Oh, Veronica, darling, I'm just looking at my diary. Did you say Saturday the 7th? I thought you said the 14th. I'm so sorry, but Tony's got one of his Lodge dinners then. I'm afraid we won't be able to make it.'

Sometimes a friend would actually enquire if Heinz and Isabel were to be among the guests.

'That awful German isn't coming too, is he? Ze Bakéd Bean. Look, I'm sorry, Veronica, but I just couldn't go through another evening like that again. The man's quite impossible. Leave us out this time, there's a dear. A pity. His wife's so sweet.'

So now they were forced to endure an evening with Heinz and Isabel on their own. This was certainly one of those occasions where the preparation was more enjoyable than the actual event.

'Why are you playing this trick on Mr. Kohl, Mummy?'

'It's not a trick, darling. It's a joke. Well - a sort of test as well.'

'What are you testing him on?'

'His knowledge of wine.'

'So you've pretended that the wine that you and Daddy cooked up with your Boots kit is a *Château Pichon-Longueville-Lalande*.'

He read the name hesitantly off the bottle.

'Yes. Just for fun. Mr. Kohl is a *Tastevin* and insists that he knows a great deal about wine. But we've never been able to test him. He snoops around the kitchen before the meal is served and manages to see the label on the bottle even if we hide it. So this time we thought we might catch him out by changing the label.'

'And you're making the test more interesting by putting home-made plonk in it.'

'Exactly. It's just a little game.'

Sebastian decided he would definitely find some pretext on which to appear downstairs in the middle of the party.

Everything was going exactly as planned. As usual Heinz had several whiskies before dinner and smoked one of his heavy, aromatic cigars. Isabel, Ian and Veronica sipped dry sherry. Isabel knew that whisky dulled the palate. The first course was a delicate fish mousse, which Veronica served with a light, dry *Pouilly Fuissé*.

'You are spoiling us, Veronica,' drooled Heinz. 'The pâté it is so excellent and the wine it is perfect: so light and dry. Of course, I don't agree that you should chill it so much. With a great wine of this quality is better you haf it not quite so cold. You agree with me, of course, my darling little Isabel? My Isabel and I we always agree together, do we not, my love?'

Isabel sighed. 'Not always, Heinz. This time I think Veronica is quite right. The wine seems perfectly chilled to me.'

The recipe for the fish mousse having been thoroughly dissected, and some suggestions for improvement made by Heinz, Veronica cleared away the plates.

'Now, Heinz, we are really going to spoil you,' declared Ian, coming into the dining room with the bogus bottle of claret on to which Sebastian had carefully stuck the label from the bottle of *Château Pichon-Longueville-Lalande*.

'What is it this time?' Heinz started to get out of his chair in enthusiasm.

'No, no, Heinz,' said Ian laughing. 'I'm not going to let you see the bottle until you've tasted it. I'm going to make you guess what it is.'

'Guess?' Heinz sounded a little nervous. 'I don't know if I could guess exactly...'

'But you're a *Tastevin*, aren't you?'

'But that was some time ago. Over thirty years. It is a long time'.

'But you've had plenty of practice in between, and at least you've got something to go on by the shape of the bottle.'

'Ze shape of ze bottle. But of course!' Heinz seemed relieved at having something concrete to grasp. 'Ze shape of ze bottle! Of course, a *Bordeaux* it is.'

'Well, now we're making progress,' said Ian, pouring the top half-inch of the bottle into his own glass before serving everybody else.

'Cheers, everyone. *Salut et bon appétit.*'

At that moment Veronica brought in the main course, feeling a little nervous as she always did before serving one of her dishes to Isabel.

'What haf we got here?' enquired Heinz, lifting the lid off the end of the casserole dish and trying to take a peep.

'Now then, Heinz,' admonished Ian, 'Let Veronica see to the food. I want you to concentrate on the wine.'

Veronica began to serve and passed the first plate to Isabel.

'Help yourself to the veggies, Issy.'

'I at least can ask what is it,' protested Heinz a little huffily.

'Of course you can, Heinz,' rejoined Veronica soothingly. 'It's *Cuisses de Canard Braisé à la Brunoise de Pistaches.*'

'Goodness' murmured Isabel, 'Wherever did you get that from?'

'It's from my new recipe book,' said Veronica proudly. '*Les Recettes Préférées d'Hubert.* It's to go with the...the special wine.'

'Marvellous!'

Isabel didn't sound too enthusiastic. She'd eaten many of Veronica's exotic French recipes in the past and some had been a complete disaster.

The vegetables were passed round and as Veronica helped herself to the duck there was complete silence round the table. Everyone was watching Heinz. He fingered his glass nervously, picked it up, put it under his nose and inhaled deeply.

'What a wonderful aroma! What a beautiful bouquet!' He took a sip and rolled it carefully round his tongue. 'Delicious! Quite delicious! A warm, fruity taste, but not bland. Of course not! A wine of great character and depth. A fine example of *Bordeaux* from one of the most illustrious vineyards it is.'

Ian was watching him closely. 'But which vineyard?'

'You want me to name the vineyard?' Heinz sounded worried.

'Well, if you can't, the region will do.'

Veronica kept her eyes on her plate. She didn't dare look up at Ian.

'Let's eat shall we? Otherwise the food'll get cold.'

Heinz sipped the wine, trying to conjure up some of the great *Bordeaux* names. The other three ate and attempted some half-hearted small talk. All eyes were furtively on Heinz.

'It could be a *Château Lafitte*.'

Ian shook his head.

'No, I didn't really think it was. *Château Latour?*'

'No.'

'It's not a *Château Mouton-Rothschild,* of course? It's much too distinguished for that.'

'You're quite right there.' Ian felt uncontrollable laughter welling up inside him.

'*St. Estèphe?*'

'No.'

'I was thinking it might possibly be a *Château Montrose* or a *Château Clos d'Estournel*'.

'No.'

'Then it must be a *St. Julien,*' said Heinz triumphantly, taking another sip. 'The bouquet is so similar to that of the *St. Julien*'.

At this point Isabel picked up her glass and took a sip. 'Very good. Very warm, rich and fruity.' She sniffed the glass delicately.

'How strange. There is no bouquet whatsoever. Now all the great wines of the *Bordeaux* are famous for their bouquet. I wonder if, after all...' She looked closely at Ian.

'Is this quite a...'

In the hall, listening carefully through the door, which had been left ajar, Sebastian had been following the conversation. He felt a rescue operation was imperative.

'Mum, I feel awful! I've just been sick!'

There was general consternation round the table as Veronica took Sebastian upstairs. When she returned, things had become much more animated and Ian had opened another bottle of wine. 'I'm sorry it's not the same as the one we've just had. We only had one bottle left which we saved for you both as a special treat. This one is nice but more ordinary. Want another guess, Heinz?'

'I haven't guessed the first one yet. Tell me'.

'Well, it was a *Château Pichon-Longueville-Lalande.*'

'From the *Pauillac* region?'

'Yes.'

Well, I didn't do too badly with *Lafitte, Latour* and *Mouton-Rothschild*,' said Heinz sulkily.

'No. But I expected someone of your great knowledge and skill to be more specific.'

'Give him 5 out of 10,' said Veronica gaily, relieved that nothing worse had happened. She wondered if Sebastian had really been sick.

Heinz sipped the new wine and carefully sampled the bouquet. 'Excellent. Excellent. Eminently drinkable. But not a patch on the first bottle of course.'

The evening progressed with increasing ease and enjoyment. In the end they consumed nearly two bottles of wine apiece.

Heinz phoned the next day to thank them for such a delightful evening. He was gushing in his praise of the mystery wine.

'*Château Pichon-Longueville-Lalande?* I write it down. How you spell *Longueville?* Now you must give me the vintage and of course the shipper. I will order a case or two and then you come to try.'

Three weeks later Isabel invited them to dinner. It was curious, mused Veronica, that they were always invited to Heinz and Isabel with much greater alacrity than she displayed in inviting Isabel and Heinz to their house. There were eight guests altogether and Heinz was in a state of high excitement.

'I haf six cases of the great *Château Pichon-Longueville-Lalande,*' he confided to Ian and Veronica as he took their coats in the hall.'

'Six cases?' Ian sounded rather aghast.

'Yes, six. We try one to-night.'

Only a case and a half each, thought Veronica. That should do.

They went into dinner. The first course was soup, which required no wine to accompany it. Clever Heinz and Isabel, thought Veronica. They're saving our taste buds for the special treat. Four bottles stood on the sideboard already opened. Eight more, still unopened, stood in reserve beside them. Heinz filled the glasses with great ceremony.

'Now, I must explain. This wine is most special. When we last dined with our dear friends, Ian and Veronica, they served us a bottle of this most exceptional wine. Isabel and I were so impressed and overwhelmed by the great quality of the wine that now I haf six cases ordered. We try one whole case tonight if we like. Cheers, everyone.'

'Cheers. Cheers'.

They all raised their glasses. Isabel took the first sip and made a face.

'Oh dear! This wine is corked.'

'Corked! What you mean, corked?'

Heinz was shouting in consternation. He took a quick sip. 'Yes, Isabel, my darling, you are quite right. Isabel is usually right about wine. Change the glasses, Isabel. We try the next bottle.'

The next bottle was also corked.

They sampled the four open bottles with the same result. Opening the fifth bottle, Heinz now really concerned. He had five more cases. Surely they couldn't *all* be corked. The sad process continued. Each time Heinz opened a fresh bottle he poured half an inch into his own glass and then poured Isabel the first full one. He waited carefully until Isabel had tasted the wine and made a sign of disapproval before he took a sip from his own glass and joined her in condemnation of the bottle.

'Corked, also, I think Isabel, yes?'

'Alas, yes.'

It wasn't until they reached the fifth bottle that Isabel looked up from her first sip, relieved and happy. Watching his wife closely, Heinz quickly took a sip.

'I think we are all right, do you not think, my Isabel? This somehow seems to be a good bottle.'

'Yes. This is an extraordinarily good wine.'

Heinz turned to Ian, beaming. 'I am most relieved. I was beginning to think I had ordered the wrong wine. But this is certainly every bit as good as the one to us you served.'

They drank their way well into the second case and everyone declared it had been a most successful evening.

Veronica phoned Isabel the following day to thank her and Heinz for such a splendid evening.

'A shame so many bottles of the *Lalande* were corked,' remarked Isabel. 'Were all your bottles all right?'

'Oh, I think so.'

'How many bottles did you buy?'

'I can't really remember,' said Veronica cautiously. 'I think Ian bought that wine some time ago - or maybe we received a few bottles as a present. Tell me,' she continued, trying to distract her friend from any further probing into the matter, 'why does Heinz always wait until you have tasted the wine before he makes any comment? Is it true that he's a *Tastevin*?'

'Oh yes. He bought his *Tastevin* many years ago, before we even met. I believe it's just a matter of eating the right number of dinners with the appropriate people - and drinking the wines to go with the food. Poor Heinz. He had a nose operation about fifteen years ago and he has quite lost his sense of taste and smell. That's why he waits for me to taste everything first. It's a shame really.'

'Oh, dear!' Veronica was glad that Isabel was unable to see her blushes over the telephone. Their trick on Heinz had been completely wasted.

And she did feel a little bit mean.

The Reluctant Window Cleaner

Bill Baines dipped the sorbo rubber mop into the bucket of soapy water and drew it across the top of the large Victorian window. He shook it, hung it on the side of the ladder and peered into the room. It was a drawing room, with a settee along the opposite wall and a piano in the far right hand corner. Bill finished the window and reversed carefully down the ladder. He suffered from vertigo and was most unsuited to the calling of window cleaner. But casual jobs were hard to come by these days and Bill disliked full-time employment.

It was almost four o'clock in early November. The day had been cloudy with intermittent drizzling rain and already darkness was closing in. He would have to hurry if he were to finish all the windows before it became too dark. He picked up the ladder, carried it to the gate at the side of the house and went along the narrow passage to the back. No light came from either of the neighbouring houses and without the aid of the street lamp which illuminated the front, very little was visible. Bill laid the ladder carefully on the York stone patio and decided to call it a day. He took out the note-pad, which he always carried for these occasions, and searching for a pencil in the pocket of his overalls, he looked around for something to lean on. Placing the note-pad on the curved lid of a dustbin, he wrote slowly and laboriously: *Deer Liddy, I cud knot finnish the wendows bicos of the darck. I wil cum bak termora, Bill.* He tore off the page and placed it under the jam jar containing the money on the kitchen windowsill. Better not take the money now. Better to wait until he had finished the job. After all, it might rain tomorrow.

As he stepped back and looked up at the house, the windows stared back at him, dark and silent. What secrets did the house hold? Who were the people who lived here and what did they do with their lives? Although he often wondered about the occupants whom he had never met, he actually preferred it that way. Anonymity made things easier.

Bill walked slowly across the deserted patio and surveyed the ground floor carefully. There were three doors at the back of the house. Three possibilities of gaining entry. He tried the kitchen door first but to no avail. It was bolted top and bottom. Next he tried the door that led directly from the hallway down three stone steps to the patio. No joy there. The third door was that of a handsome Victorian French window, also opening onto the patio. No luck there either. Bill gave the house one final glance. Yes. By the side of the neighbouring fence, a casement window had been carelessly left open. Bill stepped into the flowerbed, scratching himself on some prickly bushes. The window had been left unlatched and the horizontal brass rod hung loosely. With evidently practised skill, he squeezed his hand through the small gap and lifted the rod noiselessly off the base of the window. Now it was decision time. Should he rearrange the window as he had found it and return tomorrow to finish his job, or should he do the house over and scarper? If he did decide to return tomorrow he would be able to case the place in daylight, which would be much easier. If the lady of the house were to arrive home now and find lights on she would be alarmed and probably call the police. On the other hand, if he were to return tomorrow, in all probability the unlocked casement window would have been secured and he would have missed a golden opportunity. It seemed a shame to look a gift-horse in the mouth.

Bill decided to go in.

He found himself in a spacious well-furnished living room. The walls were lined with books and several paintings. He flashed his torch around. Paintings, he mused. He'd heard there was a great deal of money in paintings. But specialist knowledge was essential; and even then they were difficult to dispose of. No. Not paintings. Much better to stick to cash and jewellery. Jewellery was usually easy to dispose of in the right places. Cash, of course, was quite perfect. The sitting-room door was closed. As he turned the handle the thought occurred to him that it might be locked, but it turned easily and he stepped into the hall.

All was silent, dark and eerie.

For a moment panic seized him. He wondered if there was a dog. Bill was frightened of dogs. But surely, if there were a dog, it would have started barking by now.

Suddenly something brushed against his legs and he stood transfixed with terror. His heart thumped louder, his mouth went dry and his knees began to shake. The 'thing' rubbed against him again and he heard a soft 'mieow'. In a brief flash of light a passing car in the road outside lit up the hall. Reflected in the beam was a pair of cat's eyes staring at him. He almost laughed out loud with relief. I must be losing my bottle, he thought. I'll have to retire soon. Maybe I can make this the last good haul.

The cat left him and slunk off towards a room at the back of the house; probably the kitchen. The kitchen was no use to him. What Bill was looking for was usually kept upstairs in the master bedroom. He padded cautiously along the hall, flashing his torch on the banisters. This was the worst part. Once upstairs he was trapped. With no head whatsoever for heights there was no way he was ever going to try and escape through a first floor window. He paused for a moment at the bottom of the staircase and switched off his torch. He could still go back. He hadn't as yet reached the point of no return. Bill was no hero. Nevertheless he decided to go on.

Having made the big decision Bill now acted with all the speed he could muster. With the aid of his torch he bounded up the stairs two at a time. Here the staircase divided in two and another four steps on either side led to opposite wings of the house. Should he go right or left? He turned right and immediately found a closed door on the left. He opened it cautiously and flicked his torch around. It was a child's nursery. The wallpaper was patterned in pink and blue animals with matching curtains. In one corner stood a baby's cot with a white crocheted coverlet, covered with soft toys. A nursing chair stood at the end of cot. In the corner was a white chest-of-drawers with a pile of snow-white terry-towelling nappies. The lady of the house was obviously expecting a baby.

Bill left the nursery, closing the door silently, and in a trice he was up the few stairs that took him to the opposite landing. Here too the doors were closed. He opened the nearest one on the right that turned out to be the bathroom, so he made for the door straight ahead of him. Hurrah! It was a bedroom. A king-sized double bed opposite the door was flanked on either side by capacious built-in cupboards. On the right, in front of the window, stood an elegant exquisitely-made rosewood dressing table, inlaid with walnut marquetry. It was undoubtedly the master bedroom. Bill made straight for the dressing table. With practised skill he opened the top drawer, which yielded nothing. Neither did the second, which held only safety pins. But on opening the third drawer his luck changed. It held three small boxes, each containing one ring. In the first one lay a solitaire diamond set in platinum, nestling on a bed of dark blue velvet. Bill took it out, put it in his pocket and returned the box to the drawer. The second box contained a large richly-hued sapphire surrounded by small diamonds, also set in platinum or white gold, lying on a bed of red velvet. The sapphire joined the solitaire diamond in the pocket of his dungarees. In the third box was an eternity ring: a narrow gold band in which were set small emeralds alternating with diamonds of a similar size. Bill thought guiltily of the nursery, feeing sure this was a present to celebrate the forthcoming birth of the baby. He hesitated a second before putting it in his pocket with the other two trophies, but he reckoned his need was greater than that of the lady of the house. Feeling more than satisfied he left the room, closing the door carefully behind him. He prided himself on leaving everything just as he had found it, except of course for a few small missing objects. But that was only to be expected in his calling.

He padded swiftly down the staircase, flashing his torch into the hall to make sure he didn't fall over the cat. In order to make a quick get-away, he had left the door of the living room ajar. He scrambled out of the casement window into the flowerbed beneath, rearranging the window as he had originally found it and shone his torch onto the patio.

Damn! The ladder! He'd completely forgotten about it. That would make his exit much more difficult. But he couldn't leave it where it was. It was an absolute give-away. Picking up the ladder, he heard voices in the hall. A light was switched on, bathing the patio and the front part of the lawn in a brilliant pool of light. The lady of the house had returned home. He had no time to waste. As he passed the corner of the house a light went on in the kitchen, illuminating the side passage that was now his only means of escape. Two female voices were just audible from the kitchen.

'A cup of tea would be wonderful, Miranda!'

'Just get two mugs out of the cupboard over there, would you, Charlotte, while I put the kettle on.'

Bill thought of his note under the jam jar on the kitchen windowsill, wondering if he ought to retrieve it, but decided it would be too risky. Anyhow, it wasn't conclusive proof that he had stolen the rings.

A speedy departure was now vital.

The passage at the side of the house went past a second kitchen window. In the bright light he could see a female head bobbing to and fro as the tea was being prepared. The light from the kitchen window lit up a small part of the passage. Beyond its orbit, still some distance from the side door to the front of the house, all was pitch black.

He had just reached the comparative safety of the dark area when he stepped on something soft, which let out a piercing screech. Now totally unnerved, Bill lost his balance and let the ladder fall to the ground with a crash. He fell heavily, landing on the cat, which gave him a ferocious scratch as it escaped from underneath him and ran off down the garden.

From the kitchen came the sound of broken china.

'Heavens above, Charlotte! Whatever was that?'

'Sounds like a cat to me. Do you have a cat, Miranda?'

'Yes. We have a tortoiseshell called Raffles. She's ever so gentle. She wouldn't hurt a fly, let alone another cat. I think I should go and investigate.'

Bill heard the clip-clop of a lady's high-heeled shoes in the hall and the sound of a door being unlocked. Throwing caution to the wind, he ran the remaining length of the passage to the front of the house without even pausing to shut the side door. He tore down the street, turning left, right, and left again to where he had parked his ramshackle old wreck of a car. Thank goodness he had stuck to his principle of never leaving his car outside the house where he was working. He strapped the ladder onto the roof rack and drove off at high speed.

Miranda walked out onto the patio and looked up at the house. The light from the kitchen drew her eye to the windowsill, where the jam jar containing the money still stood, with a note underneath. At eight and a half months pregnant, Miranda had difficulty in reaching the jar. Making a final effort she retrieved it, letting the note fall unnoticed into the railed off area beneath. At the same moment she felt a warm rush of water in her lower regions. The rush finally became a tidal wave as she staggered back into the house.

'Charlotte! I think I've started! The waters have broken! Ring for an ambulance right away!'

As Charlotte dialled the number and waited anxiously for a reply, Miranda sat down limply on a chair by the hall table still clutching the jam jar.

'What's the jar for, Mandy?' asked Charlotte quizzically.

'Oh that?' Miranda put the jam jar down on the hall table. 'That's the money for the window cleaner. I was expecting him today but obviously he couldn't come. His movements are very irregular.'

Gloria

'Hanger or bag, Mr. Swaddle?'

'Oh, hanger, please. The wife saves the hangers. She likes the shirts hanging all uniform on the same kind of hangers. She says they must all be the same shape and size. No mix and match. The wife's very organised.'

'You can tell that from the way she dresses.'

'Of course you can. She wears her clothes like they were on the hanger. All stiff and straight.'

'But very becoming, Mr. Swaddle. Very proper - and orderly.'

Gloria put the trousers on a wire hanger and hung them up under the large roll of plastic sheeting. She pulled the sheeting down and a metal bar descended, cutting the sheeting off at the top, shaping the plastic cover over the hanger. The trousers were now protected from dust or contact with dubious objects in Mr. Swaddle's capacious shopping bag. Each time she covered a newly cleaned garment with plastic sheeting Gloria felt a slight thrill of satisfaction. One clean item duly protected.

'Does Mrs. Swaddle keep the plastic covers as well?' she asked.

'Indeed and she do. Everything in the cupboard is covered in plastic to keep it all clean.'

'But this plastic isn't very strong. It tears very easily. She'd do much better to buy some of those covers with zips. They don't work out expensive if you buy a dozen. You see them advertised in all the colour supplements.'

'A dozen wouldn't do her, said Mr. Swaddle, 'She's got that many clothes.'

'I know she has. Don't I see most of them in here at one time or another?'

Gloria loved her job at the dry cleaners. It wasn't just the satisfaction of returning clean garments in the plastic covers or even in a brown paper bag. It was meeting the customers that gave her such pleasure and satisfaction, sharing their troubles and enjoying their jokes.

There was gentle Mrs. Honey, who must be well into her seventies by now. Gloria thought how aptly named she was with her fading honey-coloured hair faintly tinged with beige-grey streaks and soft hazel-coloured eyes, smiling kindly behind thick spectacles. Even her skin was honey-coloured, smooth and creamy as if artificially tinted every morning with some magical substance from a bottle. Gloria couldn't remember Mr. Honey. Maybe he was honey-coloured too? He had certainly taken the appropriate wife to wed; but maybe she had grown like that, married to Mr. Honey. Even her clothes appeared to Gloria to be predominantly honey-coloured, as Mrs. Honey dressed only in muted shades of brown, beige, camel and cream; never in bright colours.

Then there was Miss Murgatroyd, headmistress of the local girls' high school, looking every inch the imposing spinster teacher with her grey hair plaited on each side and curled in two buns just above each ear. She was tall, very thin and leaned backwards slightly as she walked. She only wore suits, all of a rather similar style with long, well-cut jackets and either straight or box-pleated skirts. The colours were muted: black, navy, grey, brown, heather-mixture flecked tweeds, or herring-bone. Gloria knew each one like a friend.

Then there were the gentlemen who worked in the City, wearing almost identical well-cut grey suits. Luckily the tickets were clearly marked; otherwise the gentleman in question might not receive his own suit back. This certainly would have had unfortunate consequences, as Mr. Tibbitt was tall and very thin, Mr. Palgrave was short with a protruding stomach and Mr. Wynne was very large and fat.

Gloria always knew when the local day Prep School had its half term, as the counter was piled high with grey shorts and the distinctive burgundy blazers trimmed with orange braid. All had to be ready by closing time on Saturday. This was Gloria's busiest moment, her shining hour. She could not let down the mothers or the boys of St. Jude and St. Just's Preparatory School. Any boy returning without his uniform on Monday morning could face a detention. Gloria always hoped that her other customers wouldn't bring in too many garments which were urgently needed just before half term. But she never refused a request and always tried to please everyone.

Working in a dry cleaners was not how Gloria had expected things to turn out. After her divorce, she had gone to work in Morrison's just along the street. But she was shunted around from pillar to post, stacking shelves, directing customers or working the till at the checkout. She felt no identification with any particular part of the store. She would just begin to feel an involvement with stationery or confectionery when the supervisor would move her to kitchenware or household plants, all of which had to be completely rearranged somewhere else. As she loaded plants or pots and pans onto a trolley in order to wheel them to the farthest part of the store, a customer would ask the way to stationery or confectionery.

'Of course,' said Gloria helpfully, 'you'll find confectionary down the third aisle on the left.'

Invariably the customer would return a few moments later.

'There ain't no sweets down there, miss. It's all chemicals and stuff.'

Another assistant had been detailed to move *her* confectionery, to spoil *her* careful arrangement and set up another one of their own in a completely different part of the store. It was too discouraging.

Then there was her stint at the checkout. It wasn't the customers purchasing the goods who were the problem. It was the customers returning the faulty items, which they had purchased by mistake, who caused all the hassle. In particular there were people who were insistent to the point of being rude that they should have a full refund, even though they had lost the receipt. Gloria stuck out Morrison's for nearly three months. When she saw an advertisement for 'assistant wanted' in the stationers across the road she had no hesitation in applying.

At first it was a welcome change from Morrison's. The shop was small, cramped, and extremely old-fashioned with little on display. Most of the goods were concealed in dark oak cupboards, stretching from floor to ceiling, the top ones so high up they could only be reached by ladder. Items which could not be accommodated in these cupboards were stored in unwieldy cardboard boxes, stacked haphazardly around the shop floor and in the small room at the back, euphemistically called the stock-room. As the newly arrived assistant, Gloria was given all the worst jobs. There were four other ladies who worked in the shop on a rota and a strict hierarchy prevailed. Unofficially Mrs. Wadge was in charge. As the oldest and longest-serving assistant she had taken it upon herself to organise all the others and made quite sure she did most of the serving. While engaged with a customer, she would send a colleague to the stock room or ask her to scale the treacherous ladder to retrieve a heavy packet of old-fashioned foolscap paper, which had lain unrequested for years.

Mrs. Wadge had a particularly unpleasant servile manner. 'Of course, madam, that is quite the best in stock. I thoroughly recommend it. You would rather have it in blue? Of course. Gloria will see if there's a blue one, won't you, Gloria? I should think you will find it in that bottom box over there,' indicating a pile of five large cardboard boxes.

One day the ladder slipped and Gloria fell, badly bruising her shoulder. Mrs. Wadge was totally without sympathy. She said it was entirely Gloria's fault for placing the ladder badly. Feeling bruised in more ways than one, Gloria left and was without a job for nearly three weeks.

The rest was certainly enjoyable. It was now mid-May. The weather was beautiful, the sun shining constantly from a Mediterranean blue sky. If only there were no need to work at all, thought Gloria, as she spent each day in her delightful little garden, tending her plants or just lazing in a deck chair. She was enjoying her leisure so much she couldn't even be bothered to read. With simple goals and horizons, her material and physical needs were modest. Unfortunately one of her needs was food and after two weeks of perfect leisure, Gloria's diminishing bank balance forced her to admit that she must find another job.

She scanned the local paper each morning in a desultory manner. At first there was no urgency. Her enforced holiday was so pleasant that she felt there was no need to rush into another job. Then as the end of the second week approached she felt she really ought to make a bigger effort at finding employment. Perhaps she could get a job in London? It would mean travelling up by train every day, but it would make a change from Chorleywood, the small suburban town near Watford where she had lived for nearly ten years. Maybe she should go up to London tomorrow and have a look at the shops to get the feel of the place.

She looked up the timetable, discovered that the trains left every half-hour and the journey took only 29 minutes. She decided to catch the 9.13, arriving at Marylebone Station at 9.42. In the morning she set off in high expectation, wearing her new suit, which she hoped would do justice to the sophistication of the great metropolis. Walking briskly down the High Street towards the station she saw an arresting notice in the dry cleaners:

'Assistant wanted. Must be reliable and of good appearance and ready to start at once. Salary by negotiation.'

It must be a good omen, thought Gloria, and went in. Reg Wallis, the owner, took to Gloria right away. She was just the type of person he needed. Someone of pleasant appearance and agreeable manner who would get on with the customers and would be able to run the shop on their own if he wanted a holiday or a day off.

Although her main duty was to serve the customers, Gloria soon became so adept at doing the bookkeeping and working the machines that she often found herself running the shop single-handed. Her expertise with the steam iron and above all her charming and courteous manner with all the customers boosted sales so much that after two months Reg put her on a percentage. He gave her time off on the really sunny days so that she could enjoy her garden and she took over the shop on Mondays so that Reg could spend a long weekend with his family. She had never felt so happy and fulfilled. She got on with Reg so well that after five years he mooted that she might become a partner. Being essentially quite a simple-minded person Gloria couldn't fully grasp the implications of this generous suggestion. Although the partnership deal failed to materialise, she was horrified two years later when Reg told her that the shop was for sale.

For sale! It was quite some time before the full realisation dawned on her. It wasn't merely the fact of being unemployed again. There were other jobs and she would have glowing references. There wouldn't even be any urgency to get another job, for in addition to the splendid references Reg had promised her a handsome golden handshake when the sale of the business had been finalised. The real agony for Gloria was parting with the customers to whom she had given such good service. The thought of no longer being able to chat across the counter to Mr. Swaddle, Mrs. Honey, Miss Murgatroyd or Mr. Tibbitt plunged her into deep gloom.

Since her husband left her fifteen years ago, Gloria had led a very quiet life. Their marriage had been a childless one, which was just as well considering the fact that he had walked out one day leaving her quite penniless. In the divorce settlement she had won possession of their house but had spurned his offer of maintenance, feeling it wiser to sever the connection completely. Coming from a small family, most of whom lived in Scotland, she had found herself very much on her own. Understandably, the customers at the dry cleaners had formed the backbone of her social life. And now all that was about to change.

Of course she could get another job in some other shop along the High Street, except not in Morrison's or the stationers. But that still left plenty of choice. There was the baker, greengrocer, opticians, shoe repairs, travel agent and Sainsburys. She ruled out Sainsburys straight away. It was a very large branch and she knew she would become quite lost among the endless aisles of beverages, cereals, confectionery, dairy produce, meat and poultry.

Working in a baker's shop didn't appeal to her. The assistants all seemed to have the same doughy, pasty complexions and faded streaked hair that looked as if it had been dusted with flour. Most of them had a tendency to go to fat after a few months, nibbling the broken biscuits and sampling the fresh scones. Gloria was proud of her trim figure, her smooth complexion and her shining raven-black hair.

She didn't relish the thought of working in the greengrocers either. Handling all the unwashed fruit and vegetables would make her hands course and grubby unless she wore rubber gloves all day. And then there was the unwelcoming cold in an open shop-front in the winter to contend with. A great contrast to the pleasant warmth of the dry cleaners. The opticians? That would be far more demanding. She was sure considerable training was needed to adjust spectacles and understand the complexities of 'vari-luxe' and contact lenses. Not at her age.

That left the shoe repair shop and the travel agent. She ruled out the former. She hated the smell of old, decaying leather and smelly feet were much worse than smelly bodies. She would enquire at the travel agent the following morning.

'No. There's no vacancy at the moment,' said the manager. 'Business is a bit slack.'

That was it, then. She would have to try and get a job in London. At least it would be an adventure. She scoured the 'situations vacant' in the Evening Standard and applied for a job in Selfridges, Oxford Street.

Gloria found herself working in the china department in the basement. She had never worked in a basement before. It was an odd feeling; going indoors out of the pale early-morning sunshine and down the escalator to a subterranean level where there was no daylight. Her lunch break was only forty-five minutes, so there wasn't really enough time to go out and find somewhere along Oxford Street for a light lunch and get back for the afternoon shift. She had morning and afternoon breaks as well, of course, but they were only twenty minutes each, which gave her no time at all to go out and seek daylight. Now in early September, the evenings were still light when she left the store at 5.30 but she wondered what it would be like once the clocks went back and the winter evenings drew in. She would hardly see any daylight at all during the winter months.

Then there was the train journey to contend with. In order to be at her position by 9.15 am for the first customers arriving at 9.30, she had to catch the 8.13 from Chorleywood, arriving at Marylebone Station at 8.42. If she was lucky she could hop on a bus going down Baker Street, but more often than not the buses were full. The return journey was equally tiresome. She had to leave the store very promptly at 5.30 in order to catch the 5.55, arriving at Chorleywood at 6.24. If she missed it there was no train until 6.30. This was a slow train, which didn't get to Chorleywood until 7.19. There were certainly drawbacks to working up in London.

The first few weeks passed pleasantly enough. Going to work in the capital city made her feel special and as she boarded the train she experienced a faint tingling of excitement in case one of her customers should turn out to be Someone Really Important. She had a great deal to learn about selling china. There were so many new names to learn: Spode, Wedgwood, Aynsley, Royal Doulton. And the china was really beautiful to handle, much more pleasant than clothes which needed cleaning. Finding the work quite tiring, she often dozed on the return journey.

Each morning she took to standing on the same part of the platform and always got onto the same part of the train. She found it odd she should do this, but on looking round at the other passengers waiting for the train she discovered that every day they were positioned on exactly the same part of the platform and got onto the same part of the train. It was quite different on the return journey. She never saw any of the people who waited for the 8.13 from Chorleywood. They had all dispersed throughout the metropolis only to reassemble the following morning in the same place as on the previous day.

One morning a newcomer appeared in their midst. He was about fifty years old, tall and striking, with greying hair beginning to recede at the temples. Gloria was surprised and rather taken aback as he followed her into the carriage, which already had its full complement of regulars. Where would the gentleman sit who usually joined them at Rickmansworth? Gloria felt vaguely upset and wondered if she should say anything but decided not to. After all, none of the seats were reserved. As she sat, without book or newspaper, looking out of the window, she noticed the newcomer's eyes kept straying towards her from the far corner of the carriage. On Friday at the end of the week she felt a twinge of regret that he wasn't on the platform. However, on boarding the train, she was startled to find that he was already there, seated in the opposite corner to where she usually sat. As she entered the carriage he half got up, bowed slightly, gave her a quizzical smile and returned to the Financial Times. Trying to concentrate on the objects flying past the window, Gloria could feel his eyes upon her over the top of his paper. This continued for the next three days. On the fourth day he bowed and smiled as she entered the carriage, resettling himself in the seat opposite her. He bade her 'Good-morning' and they started up a conversation. He explained he now boarded the train two stations earlier as he was more likely to get a seat. With each successive journey they began to know each other better. She told him about her job in Selfridges and he told her about his work as a partner in a big law firm. By the middle of the following week his offer of lunch was regretfully declined due to lack of time, but was replaced by an invitation to have a drink before the journey home. From then on they met regularly after work, sometimes at the station, more often in a pub. The pre-dinner drink stretched into dinner, which then turned into a night in a hotel.

Having no ties, no one to whom she owed an explanation for her absence, Gloria acquiesced readily to his suggestion that they should spend the nights together. He was the perfect lover: strong, yet sensitive and caring, touching her where she yearned it most, entering her body at just the right moment, coming to his climax just as she was coming to hers. After their lovemaking he lay panting in her arms, stroking her body gently and murmuring: 'Oh, Gloria! Wonderful, wonderful Gloria!'

And she would kiss and caress him, hoping to arouse him again as soon as possible.

His name was François Duval. His father, now dead, was French; his mother, in her eighties and living in Bath, was English. He made no mention of a wife and children, so Gloria assumed he was unmarried and childless. They dined together every evening after work and spent the night together in his small flat, a pied-à-terre overlooking Regents Park. She had no idea whether he owned the flat and she didn't think to ask. She was wildly, hopelessly in love with him. The evenings and nights seemed an ever-flowing river of joy spent in sublime lovemaking interspersed with delicious dinners and witty, sparkling conversation.

The strange thing was they never saw each other at weekends. They met on the train, always in the same seats of the same carriage on Monday mornings and on Friday evenings, after a drink at the station he saw her on to the 7.55 to Chorleywood. Once she enquired as to how she spent the weekend.

'Oh, mother, you know. She's elderly now and has become more demanding.'

A couple of times he told her that he'd spent the weekend in Paris visiting his father's family. Gloria was so utterly happy and fulfilled by his companionship during the week that she felt that she should not intrude on the privacy of his weekends.

Then one cold Monday morning in mid-January she boarded her usual carriage on the 8.13 train and he wasn't there. The corner seat was empty. Gloria felt shattered but consoled herself that there was a simple explanation. He was ill or had missed the train or perhaps his mother had died. She struggled through the week in a torment of anguish. She even broke a most valuable china dish, but her supervisor was most understanding about it. 'You don't look well, dear,' she clucked. 'Why don't you take a few days off?'

The following Monday there was still no sign of François on the train. After work Gloria went to the flat over-looking Regents Park where they had spent so many ecstatic nights. No, the caretaker hadn't seen Mr. Duval for ten days and he had no other address for him. He was sorry he couldn't be more helpful.

Gloria was distraught. There had been no sign of François for a week now and she began to realise how tenuous their relationship had been. She didn't know where he worked and she didn't know where he lived. Their only meeting place had been on the train at Chorleywood Station and the only place they visited regularly together was the flat over-looking Regents Park, which maybe wasn't his at all.

Gloria hadn't really worked out for herself how she expected the relationship to progress. She hadn't consciously thought about marriage. She only knew she had been wildly, passionately in love with François, that each moment with him, in or out of bed was filled with ecstasy. Now he had gone, disappeared out of her life and her whole body ached for him.

Four more weeks passed and still François hadn't appeared. Gloria's life became total drudgery. She had been moved to the haberdashery department on the second floor. She found that selling needles, threads, buttons, bows, hooks and eyes was extremely boring after the comparative delight of selling beautiful bone china. There was no daylight on the second floor either. It seemed the whole store was lit only by artificial light. It was mid-February and extremely cold. It was just as she had feared. She left home in the dark and returned in the dark. Sometimes she didn't see daylight for as many as five or six days on end. The train journey was quite the worst part of the day. Out of habit and living in hope of seeing François again, she always boarded the same carriage and sat in the same seat. But he never reappeared.

She stuck haberdashery for three weeks and then asked to be transferred to another department. The following week she found herself in hosiery on the ground floor. It was too much to bear. She gave in her notice and left at the end of the week.

The dry cleaners where she had been so happy for nearly eight years had stood empty for five months. She passed it every day on her way to and from the station always with a feeling of sadness and longing. On her second to last morning, hurrying along in the chill March air, she noticed a hoarding had been erected round it and building work was in progress. A prominent notice on the centre board read:

'These premises will re-open as a dry cleaners on March 21st. Spring discounts available. Assistant wanted. Experience not necessary. Please phone 01927 839 835.

Her heart sang as she boarded her usual carriage.

Two days later she went into the newly refurbished dry cleaners and approached the manager. He was a young Greek Cypriot, a complete contrast to Reg, but they took to each other at once and Marios engaged Gloria on the spot.

Gloria now felt her life had come full circle. Her husband had left her and her lover had completely disappeared. She had lost the only job she had ever really enjoyed but had now regained it. The shop had new machinery, a completely different layout and was always flooded in daylight. Marios and Eleni were kind and friendly and really valued Gloria's experience. The counter faced the street and the sun shone directly on to her in the summer months. But best of all, all the old customers returned: Mrs. Honey, Miss Murgatroyd, Mr. Tibbitt and Mr. Swaddle. Mr. Swaddle, in particular, was delighted to see her.

'How nice to have you back, Gloria.' he said. 'Good to have the shop back too. It was real inconvenient having to go right up the hill past the Post Office just for a bit of dry cleaning.'

'Shall I leave the hanger for your wife's collection, Mr. Swaddle?' asked Gloria.

'No thanks, Gloria. No need for them hangers any more. You see, they wouldn't give us the hangers at the other place. They said it was too expensive to let the customers have the hangers even though they charged more for the cleaning. So the wife went up to London on a bit of a shopping spree. She bought a lot of new hangers, all matching like. And she bought some of them plastic covers with zips, like you was talking about. So all her clothes is covered up now on matching hangers. It looks ever so nice.'

'I'm sure it does indeed,' said Gloria pleasantly. 'And where did Mrs. Swaddle buy her hangers and covers, if you don't mind my asking?'

'To be sure I think she bought them in Selfridges. Do you know Selfridges? It's a great place. They seem to sell everything. But it's a long way in the train. I wouldn't want to do it too often.'

Gloria smiled to herself.

'Well, so long, Gloria. Have nice weekend. I'll be in next week with the winter coats. It's good to have you back.'

'It's good to be back. Good-bye Mr. Swaddle.'

Joe's Spanish Adventure

'Please phone us as soon as you arrive in Seville,' said Ruth.

'Of course I will, Mum. Don't worry!'

Ruth gave him a hug. 'Good luck! Enjoy yourself!'

On arrival in Seville, the fourteen-year-old pupils were dropped off in groups of twos and threes at their host families. As the bus wound its way out of the town Joe and Sam were the only boys left on board. Joe stared out of the window, his heart thumping.

'We're not staying in Seville at all! We'll be miles away from all the others!'

Finally the bus stopped beside a bleak expanse of anonymous high-rise apartments. Mr Garcia got off the bus and accompanied them to the door. Looking at his sheaf of papers he read out: 'block M, apartment 968.' As the swing door was unlocked they walked into a dank hallway painted battleship grey, reeking of garlic.

'Shall I let you two boys take the lift up on your own or would you rather…?'

He sounded a bit uncertain. It wasn't what he had expected. His opposite number at the school in Seville had given him to understand that all the pupils would be staying near each other at homes in the town.

'Don't worry, sir. We'll be fine, won't we Sam?' said Joe, trying to sound jaunty and nonchalant.

The boys took the lift up to the 9th floor. Hesitating for a second outside apartment No 968, Sam plucked up courage and rang the bell. The door opened a crack and an elderly female voice croaked in Spanish:

'That my two little English boys?'

'*Si, señora,*' replied Joe in hesitant Spanish.

The door opened wider to reveal a little old lady, thin, bent and wrinkled, her grey hair tied back in a bun. She wore an apron, pince-nez and bedroom slippers.

'*Buenos dias.* Come in.'

The two boys followed the old lady along a dark narrow passage to a room at the end of the corridor. It was shabbily furnished with three easy chairs, a sofa with a large black cushion in the centre and a Zimmer frame at the side. Straight ahead was a dining table covered by a garish wax cloth, surrounded by six non-matching, uncomfortable-looking straight-backed chairs.

'Please sit down,' said the old lady. 'You must be hungry.'

Still in their coats, feeling scruffy and travel-stained, the boys sat down at the table.

'I need the toilet,' said Sam.

'The toilet! Of course! Follow me.'

The old lady led the way back along the corridor towards the front door and indicated a door on the right. She returned to the kitchen and a few moments later Sam reappeared in the dining room looking shocked. He said to Joe *sotto voce:* 'it's awful! It smells, the chain won't pull and the door doesn't lock.'

At the table the old lady served soup into two bowls from a chipped tureen. A hard grey roll lay at each place. Joe picked up his spoon and cautiously dipped it into the soup while the old lady poured herself a large glass of beer.

'So you go to Spanish school tomorrow with your English friends. Yes? That is good.'

'That'll be very...' Sam looked up and noticed that the black cushion on the sofa was moving.

'*Señora!* What on earth's that? The cushion... on the sofa...'

The old lady gave a wild cackle of laughter. 'That's no cushion! That's my mother. She's a hundred and three years old...'

The 'cushion' rose slowly off the sofa and a hand groped around for the Zimmer frame. Then the apparition moved very slowly towards the dining table.

It wasn't until break at the school the following morning that Mr Garcia had a chance to speak to Joe and Sam.

'Everything all right? How's the family? Is there a boy of your age?'

Joe gave a slightly hysterical laugh. 'No boys, sir, just two very old ladies. The one who cooked our supper is eighty-four. Then there's her mother who's a hundred and three...'

'Are you sure you're all right, Joe?' Ruth said anxiously over the phone. 'What if the old ladies should fall ill – or have an accident...?'

'Nothing'll happen, Mum. Don't worry. We're fine.'

'What's the apartment like? Is your bedroom OK?'

'Well, it's all very Spanish...'

Just two more days to go, thought Joe, as he snuggled down under the heavy duvet. It hadn't been too bad.

Carmen, the eighty-four-year old who did all the domestic chores, was really quite sweet and very patient with his and Sam's Spanish. The food was a bit of a struggle: heavy, strongly spiced and full of garlic. Luckily the school lunches were more edible.

Suddenly Joe sat bolt upright in bed. There was an odd smell, slightly acrid. Perhaps something had been left on in the kitchen? After all, at the age of eighty-four... Joe got out of bed and made his way along the passage, through the living room into the kitchen. Switching on the light, he checked there was nothing burning in the oven. Then he heard a crackling noise. It wasn't in the kitchen. It was outside. He opened the window, craned his head round and looked up. Flames were shooting up from the apartment block next door.

A fire! He raced back down the corridor into Sam's bedroom and shook him.

'Wake up! There's a fire! We've got to get out!'

'A fire? Where?'

'Next door. We'll have to be quick. We must wake Carmen and get her to organise her mother...'

'Oh, Gawd! The old ladies! We'll never get them out...'

'We've got to try. You wake Carmen. I'll get Granny...'

Joe rushed into the old lady's bedroom without knocking and hauled her out of bed. Looking blank, the old lady mumbled something unintelligible and reached out for her Zimmer frame.

The frame! thought Joe. How can I carry her down nine floors with the bloody frame?

Joe joined Sam and Carmen by the apartment's entrance door. Terrified, Carmen struggled with the rusty bolts, finally wrenching the door open. Along the corridor came the dull 'thump, thump' of the Zimmer frame. Joe went back to try and speed up the old lady. Out on the communal landing the empty staircase stretched endlessly below them, all nine floors. Realising that it would take the old lady a good half hour to get down the stairs by herself, Joe picked her up and threw her over his shoulder, her withered frame belying her dead weight. Startled, the old lady let go of the Zimmer frame, letting it clatter down the stairs.

Half way down they heard an even louder crackle of flames and smelt the acrid smoke. The fire had crossed over into their apartment block. Clutching the old lady tightly, Joe started running down the staircase.

'Come on! Hurry!' He called to Sam and Carmen as they followed after him.

The stairs seemed endless but in fact it took Joe and Sam only three minutes to get the two old ladies out of the building. A group of residents and the Fire Brigade had already gathered outside.

A middle-aged man rushed up and hugged them.

'What bravery! What exceptional boys! I'll make sure the mayor hears about this.'

A year later Joe and Sam returned to Seville and were presented with its highest honour: the freedom of the city.

Scotch Eggs

A white council van drew up to a jerky halt outside No 20 Sudeley Square. A short plump lady, hair well coiffed and wearing a fluorescent jacket, climbed out of the driver's seat. She opened the door at the back of the van, rummaged about in an assortment of differently shaped boxes and selected two small plastic containers. Clutching them tightly, she made her way down the narrow wrought iron staircase to the basement area. Jabbing fiercely at the doorbell, she waited a few minutes before trying the bell again.

'C'mon, Edward! I ain't got all day!'

Shuffling footsteps approached. Three heavy bolts were drawn back and an elderly man, shabbily dressed in unfashionable clothes, opened the door. His bow tie was askew, one of the leather elbow patches on his jacket hung by a thread and bare toes peeped out through the holes in his slippers.

'Good morning, Marlene. Have you brought my breakfast? Or is it lunch? I never know the time any more – or what day it is.'

'It's eleven o'clock on a Friday, Edward. Yesterday I told you it was a Thursday. I'm only 'ere to give you your lunch – not to give out lessons on the day of the week. 'Ere…' She held out the two plastic containers. 'Your lunch.'

Edward made no move to take the proffered boxes. 'What is it?'

Marlene inspected the labels. 'Chicken tikka, ratatouille and potato soufflé. Then for pudding it's stewed apple with meringue.'

'They do make it sound fancy these days.' Edward took the containers with reluctance. 'Thanks, Marlene. See you tomorrow.'

'Not tomorrow, Edward. Tomorrow's Saturday. See you Monday. Enjoy.'

Clutching the boxes, Edward watched the meals-on-wheels lady make her way up the staircase to the council van. At the top Marlene turned and waved. She had a soft spot for Edward. He was such a gentleman. His clothes had seen better days, but there still remained an aura of elegance, of happier times past. She often wondered about him. Did he have a family? Why did he live on his own in a basement flat? But she never enquired. She didn't want to get involved with any of the elderly people to whom she delivered meals-on-wheels. That was up to the social services. She started up the engine and drove on to her next delivery at No 5 Coleman Fields.

Edward padded back into the flat and placed the two containers on the kitchen table. Returning to the small entrance hallway, he pulled the three heavy bolts across the front door. Security was of paramount importance. Being burgled was one of his greatest fears. Back in the kitchen he inspected the two lunch boxes, which, being plastic, were microwavable. He loosened the lid of the box marked 'chicken tikka, ratatouille and potato soufflé', placed it in the microwave, setting the time for three minutes. He laid the kitchen table with a mat, knife, fork and napkin, saying, as always: 'Juliet would be proud of me for not letting standards slip.'

From the cupboard he selected a plate and placed it on the counter beside the microwave, which suddenly emitted two shrill pings, making him jump. He opened the door, carefully removing the container with a tea towel, put it unopened on the plate and carried it to the table. Gingerly lifting off the lid, he examined the contents. The pungent smell was indecipherable; he couldn't detect any chicken – or ratatouille or potato soufflé. He tipped the food onto the plate and picked up his knife and fork. The first mouthful was crucial, as it was often his last. The hot food burnt his tongue but tasted of nothing at all. He tried another mouthful; then deciding to abandon the dish altogether, he dumped the entire contents in the bin.

Picking up the second container, he studied the label: stewed apple and meringue. He smelt it, but deciding against trying even one mouthful, he consigned it also to the bin. He opened the fridge and surveyed the contents consisting mostly of Scotch eggs. He took out two packets each containing two Scotch eggs and checked the sell-by dates. In his head he heard his son James's voice: 'always check the sell-by dates, Dad.' There were still three days left to go on both packets but perhaps there were others at the back that should be eaten first. He hadn't been shopping for almost a week. What with his rheumatism and the treacherous English winter weather he hadn't felt up to going out.

Again he heard James's voice: 'always put the new purchases at the back.' Reaching to the back of the fridge he found three more packets, also containing two Scotch eggs. Two packets were well past their sell-by-date, so they joined the meals-on-wheels lunch in the bin. He put the packet with today's date on a plate on the kitchen table. Thinking it looked rather bare, he placed a bowl of tomatoes and grapes beside the plate. He took a wine glass out of the top cupboard and returning to the fridge he took out an open bottle of Chablis, always at the ready. He poured a glass of wine and started on the first Scotch egg. Half way through the second one he realised he would be unable to finish it. That's tonight's supper, he thought, and wrapping the remaining portion of egg in cling-film, he returned it to the fridge. He nibbled at a plum tomato, poured the remaining wine and took the glass next door to his small sitting room. Comfortably settled in his favourite armchair, he finished the wine and fell fast asleep.

It was a cold Saturday December afternoon. Edward was seated in his favourite armchair watching Spurs play Everton. He was totally absorbed in the match, particularly as Spurs were winning 3 -1.

Thump, thump, BANG. Thump, thump, BANG. Thump, thump, BANG.

The noise coming from upstairs was getting louder. It was distracting and ruining his enjoyment of the match. Edward didn't want to interrupt the match to go upstairs, asking them to be quiet. Of course they were just children – but even children didn't have the right to make so much noise that they spoilt an adult's pleasure. He wondered if they had been left on their own again. The parents seemed a rather incompetent lot, hanging around on weekdays when they should be working, out gallivanting in the evening when they should be supervising homework and putting the children to bed. That's today's world, thought Edward, a feckless, louche world. *We* never did that. Juliet and I were responsible parents who took good care of our children. We made sure they did their homework and went to bed at the proper hour.

Thump, thump, BANG. Thump, thump, BANG.

I can't stand this, thought Edward his eyes still on the television screen. Oh, great! Another goal for Spurs. He got up slowly and with difficultly, leaning heavily on his cane. I'll try banging on the ceiling. Perhaps that'll stop the noise. He put one hand on the back of the armchair to steady himself, attempting to lift his cane in the air. But his rheumatic joints were too stiff to enable him to straighten his arm and the cane waved about aimlessly, almost causing him to fall over. Returning to his chair, he decided he would finish watching the first half and go up at half time.

When Gary Lineker and three other pundits began to dissect the play, the players and the managers, Edward went into his bedroom to fetch his coat, hat, scarf and gloves. Struggling slowly up the metal staircase, he opened the wrought iron gate, stepping cautiously onto the pavement. Holding tightly onto the railing surrounding the basement area, he walked up the four steps to the main front door. The Victorian bell-pull was still in the same place as it had been when he and Juliet had bought the house over forty years ago. He pulled the brass handle, now dull and unpolished, the bell jangling loudly across the quiet square. No one answered. He waited a few moments and then tried again. Still no answer.

'Well, there's obviously someone there,' he said aloud. 'I'll give it one more try.'

The bell jangled again as loudly as before and a couple came up the steps.

'You looking for someone, mate? That's my house.'

'Oh, are you the new tenants?'

'That's right.'

'I do hope you are enjoying the house.'

'Why do you ask?'

'Well, it used to be my house – and my wife's, of course.'

'Ah, you must be the old codger who lives in the basement. The estate agent told me that once you lived in the whole house. It was the family's house, he said, where your children grew up.'

'That's right.' Edward brightened a little. 'It was a splendid family house – but now, of course... with me on my own...'

'It got too big. Well, Mr Houghton, if you'd like to come up for a cup 'o tea one day.'

'That's most kind of you I'm sure...'

The man put one foot on the first step. 'And now if you'll excuse us, Mr Houghton, we must see what our kids have been up to. I hope they haven't disturbed you...'

'N...no, of course not.' Edward couldn't rightly remember why he had come out in the first place. He opened the gate of his basement. 'Good bye Mr...'

'O'Leary.'

'Good bye Mr O'Leary, and thank you for inviting me to tea.'

'*And* a one, two, three; *and* a one, two, three. Arms forward, stretch and relax. That's right, Ada! Very good! You're not having your best day, but you're trying very hard. Not quite, Edward. You need to stretch forward - more like this. Now we'll do the kneeling exercise. Stand in front of your chairs and hold on firmly...'

'Oh, no! Not the kneeling exercise!' moaned Edward quietly. He was exhausted already and the class had only been going twenty minutes. And whose stupid idea had it been in the first place? He couldn't rightly remember. Nevertheless, he struggled through to the end of the class, thankful when it was all over.

'Well done, Edward!' The instructor came over to congratulate him. 'I thought after Christmas I'd send you to another class. There's a nice one on a Tuesday – with music.'

'Music?' murmured Edward. 'Music would be nice.'

He walked round the corner to the bus stop. He felt he deserved a taxi home after the class but he worried about over-spending. It was a short bus ride, just three stops, but then came a rather challenging walk. To a younger and more able-bodied person it was only ten minutes, but it took Edward a full half hour. His route took him past the local corner shop. He couldn't remember what food he had in the flat so he went in and stood in front of the chilled food section for a few moments, finally selecting a litre of milk, six free range eggs and four packets of Scotch eggs.

Back in the basement area at No 20 Sudeley Square something underneath the stairs caught his eye. It was his meals-on-wheels lunch which Marlene always left on a Wednesday while he was out at his exercise class, his 'dancing class', as she called it. He took the containers into the flat and closed the door, forgetting to bolt it.

Squinting at the labels with his short-sighted eyes, he read with difficulty: 'pork with prunes and pommes Dauphinoises,' on the larger container, and on the smaller one: 'chocolate mousse.'

Suddenly he felt extremely tired – too tired to battle with the microwave. He put both containers, unopened, in the bin and unpacked his new purchases. Opening the fridge he found three more packets of Scotch eggs, so selecting a packet at random, he put it on a plate on the kitchen table. Returning to the fridge for a glass of Chablis, he suddenly felt dizzy. Holding onto the counter, he lost his balance and crashed to the floor, hitting his temple against the sharp edge of a cupboard, knocking himself out completely.

He lay on the floor, unconscious, for almost half-an-hour. Then he stirred, gradually becoming aware of a small metal object by his collar bone. He put his hand inside his shirt and felt a ribbon hanging round his neck. Of course, he thought. Thank goodness! The telephone alarm button that his sons had insisted on his wearing constantly, even in the shower. He struggled to sit up, but it made him feel dizzy. Lying on the floor, he pressed the alarm button. It rang twice and was answered by a sympathetic male voice.

'Mr Houghton? Are you OK?'

'No. Not really. I've had a fall. I'm lying on the kitchen floor. I can't get up.'

'Don't try, Mr Houghton. Just stay where you are. We'll be there in ten minutes.'

Then secure in the knowledge that help was at hand, Edward dozed off.

Going to the Dogs

Nathan Solomon rang the doorbell of a shabby end-of-terrace Victorian house in one of the poorer districts of Hackney. He waited a few moments and rang the bell again. Shuffling footsteps came along the hall and the door opened a crack.

'Who is it?' enquired an elderly, querulous male voice.

'It's Nathan Solomon, Mr. Toombs. I've come to see you about the insurance.'

'The insurance? What insurance?'

'The house insurance, Mr. Toombs.'

'I ain't got no house insurance. I ain't paid it for ages.'

'That's why I've called, Mr. Toombs. May I come in? I've called to see how I can help.'

'Help? You can help by just going away,' said Mr. Toombs crossly. 'I'm too busy watching the telly to see people nowadays. It's East Enders on at the moment.'

He tried to close the door but Nathan pushed against it and forced it open a little wider. 'Now, Mr. Toombs, please let me in. The man from the Pru is here to help. A nice property like this needs some insurance cover, you know.'

Grudgingly Mr. Toombs opened the door and Nathan stepped into the hall. There was a chill on the place and a dank, musty smell. The wallpaper was cracked and peeling and the carpet was threadbare, old Victorian tiles showing through the holes. Certainly not a nice property as it stood but its potential was enormous. Of course it should be insured.

'Better come into the kitchen. We don't want to disturb the telly, do we?'

'No, of course not. Is there someone else here, then? Someone else watching the telly?'

'No, of course there ain't, but it interrupts the programme to turn it off, don't it?'

'Oh, does it? Let's go into the kitchen.'

He followed Mr. Toombs along the dingy corridor and almost fell down the three steps at the end. 'You need more light around here.'

'I can't afford no more light. All me money goes on the tea and the telly and some on the gas fires in the winter.'

'Gas fires, eh, and not insured? Dear me, that won't do at all. May I sit down?'

He looked round rather helplessly at the kitchen table with the stained, crumb-strewn oilcloth and the rickety cane-seated chairs.

'Yes, yes, take a pew.' Mr. Toombs shuffled round filling the electric kettle from the solitary tap in the cracked stone sink. 'Cup o' tea? But I better warn you: I ain't got no sugar, nor no biscuits neither. Can't afford them things these days.'

Nathan protested. 'No thanks. I won't have any tea.' He patted his stomach and gave a little laugh. 'I've just had my dinner, you know.'

'Dinner! It's lucky for some! Bread and Flora is all I can afford with the tea - and the odd slice of Spam. I'll just make meself a cup, if you don't mind. It's thirsty work watching all them soaps.'

'Please do.' Nathan set his briefcase on what he hoped was the cleanest part of the table. He took out a bundle of papers from the top of the pile and began to read them through. 'Now, as I understand it, Mr. Toombs, this house was left to you by your sister, Mrs. Nellie Crankshaw.'

'That's right. It were her husband's house and when he died she asked me to move in to keep her company, like. In them days this were a deal nicer than the council flat I were in.'

'I'm sure,' said Nathan with feeling. He'd been in plenty of those.

'Her husband had left her a little bit of money and we was quite comfortably off in them days.'

'And your sister kept up the insurance payments regularly.'

Nathan flicked through the bundle of receipts.

'Yes, she was most particular.'

'I can see that. After Mrs. Crankshaw died the pay-ments continued regularly for over two years.'

'Well, there was still eleven months to go on the payment after she died and I managed to pay the next one myself and then ... and then...' his voice trailed off.

'Yes, Mr. Toombs? What happened after that?'

'I just found it difficult to keep up the payments. I had other expenses at the time... like...'

'Like what, Mr. Toombs? Do you quite realise the importance of keeping up the insurance payments on a valuable property such as this? Perish the thought, but if there were a fire, you'd lose everything and there would be no compensation whatsoever.'

Mr. Toombs looked up, bleary-eyed, from his mug of tea. 'Who would compensate me for the loss of all me memories? Me whole life's in this house. I would lose all me past if the house burnt down. There's no compensation for losing the past.'

'I dare say, Mr. Toombs, but at least you would have somewhere to live and a handsome cash payment to boot. That is... er... that is, of course, if you were to pay up the extra premium stated here, which would give you an immediate cash payment of £10,000 if you were to be left quite destitute.'

Mr. Toombs' eyes widened and he brightened up a little.

'£10,000? There's a lot I could do with £10,000. When would I get that?'

'When you've paid the insurance premium of £200 with the added bonus for the cash of £75. Just a mere £275.'

'I ain't got £275.'

'You can always pay in monthly instalments.'

Nathan reached for his calculator. '£275 divided by 12 comes to £22 and ninety-one pence with six recurring.'

'Six recurring?' Mr. Toombs sounded puzzled.

'Yes. But we'll round it up a little to cover the administrative costs. Let's say £24 per month. I'm sure you can see your way to paying £24 per month to insure a pretty little property like this, Mr. Toombs.'

'Well, yes of course. But not right at the moment. I've got some other pressing expenses...'

'I understand, Mr. Toombs.' Nathan was trying to be patient. He had two more calls to make that evening. 'If you could just let me have a cheque now for £24. You can date it as of yesterday and then you'll be completely covered.'

'I can't do that!' replied Mr. Toombs in some alarm. 'I ain't got no bank account. Me money's in a Building Society. That way I get the interest, see?'

Nathan was becoming more and more exasperated.

'In that case, I'll call back tomorrow evening and you can give me the cash.'

'Not tomorrow. Come the day after tomorrow. I'll have lots of money by then.'

'Why the day after tomorrow? Why not tomorrow?'

Mr. Toombs leant across the table confidingly and lowered his voice almost to a whisper.

'Because the day after tomorrow I'm going to the dogs!'

'The dogs?'

Mr. Toombs gave a cackle of laughter. 'Down Walthamstow Stadium. It's me livelihood now. I bet on the dogs.'

Nathan was fascinated. 'You live by betting on the dogs?'

'Yes, it's great. You get out, see your mates. And often there's big money at the end.'

'Do you always win?'

'No. You win some. You lose some.' He gave a chuckle. 'I'd better win on Thursday, though. I'm right down on me uppers.'

'Best of luck, then.' Nathan gathered his papers and stood up ready to leave. 'See you Friday.'

Mr. Toombs accompanied him along the narrow, badly lit passage and opened the front door.

'Bye, then. Thanks for calling. See you Friday.'

'Good night.'

Nathan wasn't the least bit interested in selling insurance. As his basic salary wasn't very high, he had to work hard to earn sufficient commission to maintain his wife's extravagant life-style. Nathan had no aspirations for an extravagant life-style. His only ambition was to retire early and become a writer. It was a secret. He had told no one, not even his wife. Miriam wouldn't understand. She was too practical, too down-to-earth and totally involved with meals-on-wheels, Neighbourhood Watch and the local synagogue.

Nathan kept a notebook, well, an exercise book, in which he jotted down phrases, odd names and ideas for stories. In the evenings, when he had finished his calls and his wife was either out sitting on one of her committees, or watching the television, he would go to the small room upstairs over the hall, which he called his study (although it was no larger than a box-room), unlock the great mahogany roll-top desk left to him by his father and get out his most prized possession: his collection of exercise books containing notes, jottings and half-finished stories. He hadn't, as yet, actually succeeded in finishing anything. He always seemed to get stuck somewhere along the line, usually after the first three or four pages. He blamed this on the fact that he didn't have sufficient time. As so many of his clients were out at work during the day, he rarely got home much before nine o'clock in the evening He took a dinner-break of course, around six o'clock. He wasn't a workaholic by any means, but being a sociable and friendly chap his calls usually took a great deal longer than the demands of duty required.

Once seated at his desk he would start by reading through what he had written the night before. Sometimes he felt really optimistic and he would try to continue with the same chapter or idea until fatigue finally drove him to bed. What gave him most pleasure was starting something new. Beginnings were exciting, full of promise and could start in so many different ways. The reader could be eased into the story with a poetic description. He could begin with a simple everyday conversation or be shocked from the outset with an explosion or violent accident. These were some of his favourites.

'The night was completely still. The full moon threw her opaque and translucent light onto the terrace, contrasting with shadows of inky, wicked blackness. Lucy threw open the French windows and walked out onto the balcony overlooking the terrace. She was clad only in the barest of shimmering shifts. She leant on the balcony rail and heaved a deep sigh. If only he would come again. It was many nights since they had lain together and now she waited for him longingly with a dull ache of desire in her loins.'

That was his favourite. He'd become very fond of Lucy. But pithy conversation made a good opening too.

'Cut it out Chuck'.

'Cut what out?'

'Cut the crap.'

'What crap?'

'The crap you keep talking.'

'I ain't talking no crap.'

'You talk nothing but crap, Chuck.'

'You're full of crap yourself, Bert."

Then there were the violent openers.

'The aeroplane plummeted straight from the sky; its big flat shining belly just missing the motor-way and blowing up on impact as it landed on a council-house estate. Over 300 passengers perished in the ball of fire. The vermillion flames licked their way high into the black, velvety darkness and the enormous explosion was heard for several miles around. Nancy's father had been among the passengers.'

'Good stuff,' he murmured appreciatively as he finished reading the last passage. Now which one should he try to go on with? Fond as he was of Lucy he didn't know quite at which moment he should allow her lover to appear. There was something so poignant and beautiful about the waiting, the yearning, the unrequited desire, all the stronger for having been satisfied so recently. Who was Lucy's lover? What did he look like? Maybe he should attempt a description of him. Should he give him a name straight away or let the name slip out in the course of the writing. Or should he be nameless such as the famous heroine of 'Rebecca'?

Something like this perhaps.

'The tall, dark stranger padded his way softly along the petal-strewn path, skirting the petunias now past their full bloom. He was dark-haired, of medium build and walked with lithe springy steps, as if anticipating some joyous event.'

Nathan wrote slowly and laboriously, pausing to re-read as he reached the middle of each sentence. 'His breath came in short pants and his heart-beat quickened as he rounded the corner and saw...'

'Nat! You're not still up are you?'

Miriam's strident voice on the staircase rudely interrupted his creative flow. He tidied away his writing materials hurriedly, locked the roll-top desk and went out onto the landing.

'Hello! Nice committee meeting?'

'Excellent. Most constructive. I got them all sorted out and forced Hannah and Rachel to resign.'

You would, thought Nathan. The only two decent beings among the lot of them.

'It's time for bed, dear. It's well past your bed-time.'

Nathan found it difficult to sleep. He quite often found sleep eluded him when he had been interrupted in the full flow of his creativity. His thoughts returned to Lucy and her handsome dark-haired lover. Was he being too fanciful, he wondered? Should he try and base his writing more on his own experiences of life? After all, he'd never seen a thinly clad woman on a balcony and he'd never walked past fading petunias in the moon-light. In fact, he'd never dated any girl except Miriam. They had met at her cousin's Bar mitzvah when he was nineteen and she was seventeen. They had started going out together and from then on Miriam took charge of everything. It was she who decided which film they would see and which fish and chip shop they would visit afterwards. It was even she who hinted that it was time he proposed. Well, maybe she had a point; they had been going out together for nine years.

Their marriage had been happy enough. Miriam was a practical and well-organised housewife who took good care of him. They had a couple of nice grown-up children and three splendid grandchildren. What more could a chap want? And yet he felt there was some dimension missing in his life. He didn't seem to have done anything really interesting, nothing really worth writing about. Maybe it was because he hadn't been to India. India seemed to produce some great writers and some great books: V.S. Naipaul; Salman Rushdie; and EM Forester's 'A Passage to India,' to name but a few.

That was his goal. He would somehow manage to get some extended leave and go to India. Miriam wouldn't want to go with him. She was far too busy with all her committees and Hazel was expecting her second baby in six weeks. Anyway Miriam hated the heat, physical discomfort and poverty. He'd worked a long time with the Pru. He was sure to get some extra holiday - even if it was unpaid. Ah! That was the nub of the problem: money, as always. He would have to forego his commission on new policies. He would get his basic salary for his legitimate holiday but would that be enough on which to travel to India and leave Miriam adequately provided for during the time he was away? He made some calculations. No, he certainly wouldn't have enough. India was a large country. To see it all properly he reckoned he would need to be away at least four weeks. There wouldn't be enough money to maintain Miriam's current life-style if he were to forego four weeks' sales commissions.

How on earth could he finance his trip?

To-morrow was Thursday. He ran through the various calls in his head. Two house-hold insurances, four cars, one a Rolls-Royce and a payment to be made on a boy's bicycle, which had been stolen from outside a newsagents' in the High Street. Pity about that. The company never liked compensating its clients. It only enjoyed accepting the premiums. Maybe he could persuade the boy to spend the money on another bicycle, which would need to be insured.

Then on Friday he had arranged to go and see Mr. Toombs to collect the first monthly instalment on his house. Mr. Toombs would have been to the dogs on Thursday evening at the Walthamstow Stadium and he would have...

The dogs! Why hadn't he thought of it before? He would place a bet on the dogs. Not all on one dog, of course. He would spread it around a bit. Lots of people made money on the dogs. Mr. Toombs was living off them. Nathan had a little bit of money put by. Not a great deal: just over £800 in the Abbey National for a rainy day. Well, the rainy day had arrived. He felt quite justified in risking the money in order to finance his trip to India. After all, it was going to further his career as a writer.

The next morning he stopped off at the Abbey National and withdrew £800, leaving the account open with £41.79p remaining. Fortunately it was not a joint account but in his name only. Another little secret he had withheld from Miriam.

That evening Nathan hurried through his dinner in order to be at Walthamstow Stadium before 7 o'clock, in good time to study the form and hopefully pick up a few tips. He drove along Chingford Road and paid £1 to leave his car in the large car park opposite the Stadium. As he waited to cross the busy main road he looked up at the imposing white building bordered in red lights with 'Walthamstow Stadium' emblazoned along the top. He had passed it often enough but had never felt any real urge to go in. He couldn't decide which of the two entrances to use. At the right hand end was a sign saying 'Popular Entrance' and at the far end another one saying 'Main Entrance'. He decided on the latter.

He paid the £5 entrance fee, was given a programme and went through a turnstile into a pleasant entrance hall with a sweet kiosk in the corner. Beyond the open door he could see the racetrack. He followed the 'Way In' signs down a passage, through several swing doors, passed Lou's Bar, turned right and went outside to the front of the covered seating area. He found himself halfway along one side of the Stadium. Mounting the steep steps he took a seat about halfway up which gave him an excellent overall view of the track. He was pleasantly surprised at the scene that met his eyes. The oval Stadium was beautifully laid out with fountains playing in well-kept flowerbeds in the centre, the track with lush green grass curving round the outside. At the extreme edge was an electric rail - presumably for the clockwork hare. Although it was now almost a quarter to seven the stadium was still fairly empty. The bookies were gathering down below, putting out wooden boxes to stand on so that they could be seen above the crowd, and erecting the blackboards with the name of the firm above. Names like Kelly, Power, O'Grady and Sullivan seemed to Nathan to have an evocative ring.

He studied his programme. Each race had six entrants with their previous wins and losses, plus and minus points and their form clearly listed in abbreviations that were explained in the front of the programme. At the far right-hand end of the Stadium was an enormous scoreboard setting out the predictions for the Tote betting. Along one side was a column stating how many people had placed a Tote bet on which particular dog. He decided to use this as a yardstick for his own bets.

It was now two minutes to seven and the first race was due to start. He noticed several men wearing white gloves, standing in prominent places on the terrace, gesticulating wildly. There was a flurry of activity among the bookies as six greyhounds were led along the racetrack by stewards wearing white coats. As the dogs disappeared at the far end, the activity among the bookies increased. Figures were being scrawled on the black-boards with such speed that it was almost impossible to read them. Punters coolly handed over large wadges of money to receive a small card in exchange bearing a number and the name of the firm.

Suddenly there was a harsh rattling noise as the furry clockwork hare appeared and tore along the metal track at high speed. The dogs were released from their traps and sped after the hare to the subdued cheers of the small crowd. No.2 was in the lead; No.2 was winning until just at the end when it was overtaken by No.5. No.5 had won.

Nathan glanced up at the Tote Scores. Yes, more people had backed No.5 than any other. That was the way to do it. He had missed the first race but he was learning fast.

The next race started at 7.15. In order to place his bet on time, Nathan decided to take a walk around the concourse where all the bookies stood. The Stadium was slowly filling up. At first the small crowd seemed to consist mainly of older men. Now they were joined by youngsters with prominent tattoos, in torn jeans and leather jackets, middle-aged men in office suits and women of varying ages, some dressed to kill.

Nathan sat down on the lowest step, neatly covered in a well-washed rubber coating and studied his race programme. No.5 seemed to have the most chance this time. No.5 wore the orange coat with the number emblazoned on it in white. He glanced at the Tote figures. Yes, certainly No.5 must be the favourite. Already 725 people had placed their bets on it. He walked along the row of bookies. All the odds seemed very short 9-4, 7-2. No, wait a minute. Here was a longer one. Tyler gave

4-1. Nathan handed over fifty pounds and received a little card in exchange.

The same pre-race routine took place. A man in jodhpurs and a bowler hat appeared on the track and blew his horn. The six dogs, wearing their little numbered and colour-coded coats, were led round by the white-coated stewards. No.5 stopped just in front of Nathan and relieved himself. The man beside him laughed.

'That's the one. That's the winner. You'll see.'

'Why is that?' asked Nathan, curious.

'Cos he's more comfy when he's 'ad a pee and he's that much lighter for it.'

'Oh! I'd never have thought of that.'

'You'll see,' said the man again and moved away.

The clockwork hare appeared and the dogs were off. Nathan climbed up a few steps to get a better view. The race was over in thirty seconds. No.5 had won and Nathan won £200. The dog had also been the favourite.

Nathan couldn't decide whether to pick the dog that relieved itself or the one tipped as the favourite. He could only hope that both factors would coincide. In the next two races this happened and he won another £400. In the fifth race No.4 was the favourite but No.6 was the most impressive lavatorial performer. He went for No.6 and won again.

Now the Stadium was really filling up. Brimming with confidence, Nathan went to Lou's Bar and bought a pint. Races 6 and 7 were over hurdles. He marvelled as the dogs swished their way through the white nylon brushes. They also had higher stakes as the jackpots had come into action. Success followed success. Nathan was by now delirious with excitement. By the tenth race he had won over £2,000 and he was on his third pint.

The eleventh race, the penultimate one of the evening, had the largest jackpot. By now Nathan was quite convinced that a good bowel and bladder action just before the race was the key to success. He no longer paid much attention to the numbers of people betting on the Tote. He just watched carefully as the dogs were led on before the race. He had already won enough to travel to India, but if he could double it he could do it in style. According to the Tote, No.1 seemed to be the favourite although the bookies' odds appeared to be pathetically short. He watched carefully as the dogs were being led round. People were laughing as dog No.6, in the black and white striped coat with the bright scarlet number stopped for a major lavatorial performance. No.6 it was then.

Nathan hid behind a pillar and counted all his money: £2,300, all in £50 notes. With a jaunty step he passed down the line of bookies. There was Power with 10-1 on No.6. He handed over his thick bundle of notes. The bookie looked up in surprise.

'You sure, guv?'

'Of course I'm sure.'

'O.K. then'. The bookie took the money and handed Nathan his card. In a state of mounting excitement and growing confidence Nathan took a seat high up at the back of the Stadium. The clockwork hare appeared and the dogs were released from their traps, No.6 well in the lead. Nathan became hoarse from cheering as his dog maintained its position. Then, horror of horrors, a few yards before the finish, it tripped and fell. No.4 had won. No.6 struggled to its feet and finished last.

Nathan had lost everything.

He took a different route home. As he drove along the street where Mr. Toombs lived in the end-of-terrace house he heard the wailing siren of an ambulance or fire engine. At the end of the street he saw smoke belching out from the last house on the right. Two fire engines were already in action, squirting their powerful hoses on the now steadily blazing building. The third fire engine had just arrived. Nathan slowed down and cautiously drove a little nearer. It was Mr. Toombs' house all right. No mistaking a house at the end of the terrace. Poor Mr. Toombs, thought Nathan: all his memories gone up in flames and no insurance to fall back on. He wondered whether he had perished inside or whether he was still at the dogs. And if so, had he won anything?

Nathan would never know. He had decided it would be insensitive to call back tomorrow. Even if Mr. Toombs were still alive he had nothing left to insure. As for him, Nathan, he had lost all that he had put by for a rainy day. There would be no trip to India after all and no novel or stories based on the Great Indian Experience.

With a heavy heart he reversed the car and took a side turning. Perhaps after all he should try and base his writing on some of the events in his own life.

On arriving home to find that Miriam was out he went straight upstairs and unlocked the roll-top mahogany desk. He selected a brand-new exercise book and picked up his Parker fountain pen. He wrote the date laboriously in the margin followed by the title: 'The Aspirations of an Insurance Salesman'.

Nathan looked at it for a minute or two and then crossed it out, replacing it with: 'Going to the Dogs'. He started to write: 'Joshua Rosenberg rang the door-bell of a shabby end-of-terrace house in one of the poorer districts of Hackney...'

Nathan was away.

The Beach Hut

As Fred opened the door of the beach hut the hinges creaked. Inside, the cobweb-covered windows shrouded the room in semi-darkness. Fred placed his plastic carrier bag on the small rickety table and looked around. Except for the dust, nothing seemed to have changed. It looked exactly the same as it had done all those years ago. He unpacked the carrier bag and placed the contents on the table: tea, sugar, milk, two slices of ham, two hard-boiled eggs, a tomato and a Danish pastry. That should be enough for lunch. There was a small cupboard in the corner containing plates, mugs and cutlery. Fred rearranged these on the top shelf, placing his fresh provisions neatly on the shelf below. He was meticulously tidy.

How should he fill in the time before lunch? Take a walk along the beach or just relax and finish reading the paper? Having decided on the latter course, he took a folding chair outside and opened it. A few earwigs ran out onto the sand. Ugh! Horrible things! He sat down and looked around at the deserted beach. Dorset in August! The height of the holiday season with almost no one in sight. He took the paper out of his pocket and started to read, as two gulls circled overhead calling for the remains of the lunch he hadn't yet eaten. He could hear the gentle swish, swish of the waves as they broke on the shingle at the edge of the shore. Each wave seemed to be a little louder than the last, so the tide must be coming in. In spite of the peaceful silence, he found it difficult to concentrate. A couple walked along the edge of the water, arm in arm, their jeans rolled up to the knee, carrying their trainers. The sight of the young people so happy and absorbed in each other gave his memory a painful jolt. Everything would have been so different if it hadn't been for that terrible accident.

Hoping for good weather on the south coast, Fred had booked two rooms with breakfast and evening meal at a boarding house in Swanage, Dorset for the middle two weeks in August. The first year they went down by train. Alan and Paul were seven and five and Rosie was nearly three. It was a most enjoyable holiday. A complete change from inner-city life in their small house and garden in Hackney. Full of fresh air and exercise, the children returned home with bright eyes and glowing cheeks. Fred booked again for next year for the same two weeks in August.

By the third year he was able to afford a car. Noticing that other families came well-laden with holiday items, they followed suit and slowly acquired buckets and spades, bats and balls, folding chairs, a collapsible table and a couple of lilos. Even with a car it was a major operation to pack up all the gear every morning only to unload it a few minutes later on the beach. Hospitable and friendly though Mrs. Rundle, their landlady was, she liked her guests out of the house by 9.30 each morning so that she could 'get on.' In practice this meant they were forced to spend the entire day out of doors, however inclement the English weather. They lunched on the beach, often shivering with cold, swathed in extra jumpers, anoraks and bathing towels; though if it rained, they all squeezed into the battered old Ford. Afternoons were spent in the amusement arcade, which Fred discovered could be rather expensive.

Glancing inside the beach huts with open doors, they envied the families who owned or rented one. Although they were really quite small, a great deal could be packed into them. Some were used merely for storage and were over-flowing with tables, chairs, sun-beds, fishing tackle, snorkelling gear and rubber dinghies. Others were more homely and had the appearance of a weekend cottage. They gave the impression of being a safe-haven, a place into which one could retreat and hide from the crowds of people on the beach or the cold blustery English summer weather.

For in those days the beaches on the south coast were usually crowded. The post-war boom of cheap flights and package holidays had not yet arrived. Every year the masses poured out of the towns and cities and converged onto the English beaches for two weeks in August. They sat huddled together in their winter clothes, sipping hot drinks and telling each other how lovely it was to be on holiday. Brighton was perfection before the discovery of Benidorm.

The following year Fred managed to secure the use of a beach hut for two weeks in July. The hut was a delightfully warm cosy place to return to after a chilly swim or a walk along the shore. They lunched there, passing the time with cards and board games if it rained and at the end of the day they could turn the key in the lock, leaving all their belongings inside.

The convenience of the hut prompted them to buy even more equipment. They bought basic furniture, cups, plates and cutlery; even a camping-gas stove. With the roof rack piled high, the journey home to London at the end of the holiday was more than a little hazardous.

Finally Fred bought a beach hut outright. That year the weather was exceptionally good and they spent a perfect holiday. As their large quantity of beach furniture and equipment no longer fitted into the car, it was a huge relief at the end of the season to stack everything neatly in the hut and lock the door.

They spent two more happy holidays, fully appreciating the comfort, convenience and privacy of their own beach hut.

The children were growing up fast. Alan and Paul were now sixteen and fourteen and Rosie was nearly twelve. The boys were very active and keen on sport. They organised games of cricket on the beach; they played football and volleyball. They were both excellent swimmers and sometimes swam round the headland out of sight. Fred thought his family should have the opportunity to take part in all the holiday activities available, so he bought a rubber dinghy with an out-board engine. The boys spent endless happy hours in the dinghy fishing for mackerel, often catching enough for supper.

Tuesday the 18th of August dawned like any other day. The holiday was now in its second week and the whole family was determined to make the most of every minute. At nine thirty they arrived at the beach hut just as the sun came out. Alan and Paul gathered a group of friends together for a game of cricket, while Fred set up the folding chairs on the sand, rolled up his trousers and his shirt sleeves and settled down to read the paper. As Jean and Rosie returned from their trip to the supermarket, laden with goodies for lunch, Alan and Paul wandered back to the beach hut after their game of cricket.

'Let's go fishing,' suggested Alan.

'Good idea,' replied Paul. 'Let's take a picnic and go off for the whole day.'

'Dad, come with us.'

'Well...' Fred looked doubtfully at Jean. 'I don't know whether ...'

'Oh, do. I'm sure Mum won't mind.'

'Please stay here, Dad,' pleaded Rosie.

'Yes, of course I will, darling,' Fred reassured his daughter hastily. 'You boys'll have much more fun on your own.'

Fred, Jean and Rosie spent a perfect day. They swam, lunched on the beach and walked along the shore. It was only when the boys hadn't turned up at the boarding house for seven o'clock supper that Fred became anxious. When they hadn't arrived by nine o'clock, he phoned the police.

'Not to worry, sir. Boys will be boys, I'm sure. It's 'appened 'afore, sir. They'll just turn up. You mark my words.'

The gruff voice of the officer on duty crackled over the wire, trying to sound reassuring.

Three days passed with no sign of Alan and Paul. Fred and Jean were distraught; Rosie couldn't stop crying. Fred blamed himself entirely for allowing them to go off for the whole day on their own. A full air and sea search was mounted. Kindly Mrs. Rundle, equally distressed, offered to let them stay on free of charge at the boarding house as long as they wished.

A week passed. Fred and Jean were numb with grief and shock, although they hadn't yet given up hope.

Three days later a phone call came from the Sussex police. Two bodies answering to the description of Alan and Paul had been washed up in Bognor Regis. Would Fred please come down and identify them. They were an appalling sight: swollen, disfigured and almost unrecognisable.

Fred and Jean tried hard to keep life as normal as possible for Rosie's sake but there was no longer any sanity or coherence in their lives. They went on a camping holiday to France but the year after that Rosie said she wanted to see if the beach hut was all right, so they returned to Swanage in August. It rained most of the time and they went home early.

After that life seemed to go steadily downhill. Fred was made redundant and was out of work for nine months. Rosie married young and went to live in Canada. Jean took a job as a waitress in a café and five years later, waiting for the bus to take her to work, she was killed by a motorcycle. Fred worked as a night watchman at Ford's in Dagenham and became a recluse.

Every year he returned to Swanage for a few days around August 18th. Mrs. Rundle was long since dead. Another link with the past gone. So, preferring not to make any more strong ties, he stayed at a different place each time, revisiting old haunts in the town and spending solitary hours in the beach hut thinking of happier occasions in the past.

With a heavy sigh Fred stood up and walked down to the edge of the sea. He felt the water with his big toe: not too cold. A swim might help to give him an appetite for lunch. He changed into his bathing trunks in the beach hut, remembering with nostalgia the cosiness, convenience and warmth and the joy of having his family around. Returning to the water's edge, he walked in slowly. The water got deep quite quickly and soon he was swimming strongly and evenly, thrusting through the silky, smooth water with a regular rhythm, on and on, further and further out to sea.

The Doorman

Helen got off the bus at Bank and turned left along Threadneedle Street. It was mid-March and during the night most of England had been besieged by violent storms, leaving havoc in their wake. Scurrying along, drenched and bedraggled, Helen glanced at her watch. She would only just be in time for her class. The bus stop in Threadneedle Street was further than she thought and there was no shelter to protect the hapless passengers from the rapidly worsening weather. A few feet from the bus stop was an empty doorway. Helen stepped thankfully inside and folded up her umbrella. The doorway was discreet and anonymous without any sign to state its function. Standing just inside was a young man in his early twenties, smartly dressed in a pale grey frock coat, narrow pinstriped trousers and bow tie. He wore a label on his lapel with the name 'Michael.'

'Oh! I'm so sorry! I didn't see you. May I shelter here? It's terrible weather.'

'The weather it is too bad. Please to share with me.'

'Thank you. What is this place? A bank?'

'No. Not a bank. A hotel it is.'

'A *hotel!* There's nothing to say it's a hotel. What's it called?'

'The Fred Needle Hotel.'

'Threadneedle Hotel? I've never heard of it.' What's more, I've never known a hotel that doesn't have its name emblazoned on the front. What sort of hotel is it?'

'Very good hotel. Is five star.'

'I see. And you work here?'

'Yes, I am to open door for guests.'

'Have you been working here long?'

'I am in London since two years.'

'Where do you come from?'

'Poland.'

'How long do you have to stand here?'

'I am standing eight hours.'

'Eight hours! But you do have a break.'

'Yes. A half-hour break after four hours.'

'How many more hours do you have to do today?'

'Just one.' He laughed.

'Oh, that's good.' Helen stepped out and glanced down the narrow street. 'I've been here ten minutes. Even the buses seem to have been badly affected by the weather.'

'What number you want?'

'Number 26.'

The young man stepped out onto the pavement and looked in the direction of an approaching bus. 'Here is number 26.'

Helen boarded the bus and took a seat by the window. She waved to the young man, who waved back.

The following week the day of Helen's class dawned bright and sunny. As before, she got off the bus at Bank and walked towards the bus stop in Threadneedle Street. Just past the doorway was the nameless Threadneedle Hotel and in the doorway stood Michael.

'Hello,' he said, sounding both surprised and pleased. 'You back again for your 26 bus?'

'Yes. But it's a lovely day. I can stand at the bus stop and leave the doorway free for your five star guests.'

'No. Please to stand in doorway with me. You such nice lady. Where you go on your number 26 bus?'

'I go to Covent Garden.'

To Opera House?'

'No. More's the pity. I do a class at a college.'

'What you learn in your class?'

'Italian.'

'Italian! Why Italian? You must learn Polish. Then to Poland come and I will show you everything...'

'Well... Perhaps one day I'll go to Poland. But at the moment I'm learning Italian...'

A tall portly man with a bulbous whiskey-drinker's nose appeared in the doorway. 'Morning, Michael.'

'Good morning, sir.' Michael held the door open for him as he went into the hotel lobby.'

'One of your guests?' asked Helen.

'No! He no guest. He other doorman.' Michael looked at his watch. He relieve me in half an hour.'

'Looks as if he likes his whiskey.'

'He like the whiskey more than he like people. Especially he no like me.'

'Why ever not?'

'He call me dirty foreigner and say I must go back to Poland. I say I live in London. He say: "one day I make you leave..."'

At that moment the number 26 bus approached. 'I see you next week,' he said. I arrange same duty time.' Helen boarded the bus and turned to wave. Michael waved back and blew her a kiss.

The following week was the last day of Helen's Italian class. Getting off the bus at Bank, she turned left into Threadneedle Street, her heart thumping. Why was she, a woman in her fifties, so taken with a young Polish boy in his twenties? Approaching the featureless Threadneedle Hotel she slowed down. Perhaps he wouldn't be there this time... Perhaps he hadn't been able to arrange the same duty slot. She stopped by the bus stop to regain her breath. He was just a few feet away now... She strolled towards the hotel entrance as a well-dressed couple, oozing opulence, left the hotel followed by the doorman, arm raised to hail a taxi. Helen glanced at the doorman. It wasn't Michael after all. It was the other doorman who didn't like Michael because he was a foreigner. Helen let a number 26 bus go by and waited as the cab drew up by the hotel entrance. The doorman opened the cab door and the lady got in. The gentleman tipped the doorman, thanking him in a strong American accent. As the taxi drove off, Helen walked up to the doorman.

'Has Michael finished?'

'Michael? You a friend of his?'

'Well... sort of. Is he coming on duty later today.'

'He's not coming on duty ever again at this hotel. He got the sack last week – caught with his hand in the till.'

'Oh! How awful! I am sorry...'

'I shouldn't be sorry, m'lady. We're better off without him.

Too shocked and distressed to speak, Helen turned and walked slowly back towards Bank Station.

Christmas Pudding

Violet added a little more rouge to her cheek-bones. Too much? Perhaps. She took a Wet-One out of the packet and rubbed a little of the rouge away. That looks better, she thought. Mustn't overdo it. Now. Eye make-up. She took the black marker pencil out of its case, turned the hand-mirror round to the close-up view, carefully drawing a line over her eye-brows and round the top of her eyelids. That's fine, she thought. Especially as I wear glasses. She picked up her glasses from the make-up shelf and put them on. 'Perfect,' she said out loud. 'Now all I need is some lipstick to show off my pretty pink top.' She rustled around in the cupboard, picked up three lipsticks and inspected them. 'Yes. That's the one. Now I'm ready.'

She put her make-up away carefully in the bathroom cupboard, arranging it all in height order. Closing the door she went into her bedroom, picking up her handbag and the wrap that were lying on the bed. Once in the living room she sat on the sofa looking out of the window at the pale winter sunshine falling obliquely onto the garden square below. I hope the cab won't be late, she thought. Then something else occurred to her. Why have I ordered a cab? Why don't I take the tube to the in-laws? She made a move towards the telephone to cancel the booking when the entry-phone sounded.

There it is! The cab has arrived so I can't cancel it now. Taking the lift down to the ground floor, she walked the short distance to the main gate of the apartment block. The driver got out of his seat and opened the rear door for her.

'Happy Christmas, madam!'

'Christmas? Is it Christmas today?'

'Yes, madam. Today is Christmas Day.'

'Oh! I didn't realise. So that's why I ordered the cab.'

'Yes, madam. There's no public transport on Christmas Day.'

'Oh dear! I've forgotten the presents. My Christmas presents for the family. I've left them behind. Will you wait while I go back for them?'

'Of course, madam. That's part of my job.'

He hopped out of the driving seat and opened the rear door.

'I'll be as quick as I can.'

'Of course. But please don't rush.'

Forty minutes later the cab pulled up outside the wrought-iron gates of a large imposing house in Hampstead Garden Suburb. The driver got out of his seat and opened the passenger door. Violet gathered up the two large carrier bags of Christmas gifts and began struggling out of the back.

'Please allow me, madam,' said the driver holding out his hand for the carrier bags. As they walked towards the wrought-iron gates, they opened as if by magic. Crossing the driveway they stood by the front door as Violet rang the bell. When the door opened she held out her hand for the carrier bags, thanking the driver pro-fusely for his trouble. As the front door closed Violet waved good-bye. The cab driver remained on the door-step, a little non-plussed.

He had expected to be paid. He would have to call his controller.

'Violet! Why are you late?' Lutetia spoke in her habitual haughty tone as she led her daughter's mother-in-law across the opulent marble-floored hallway to the spacious living room, past three large over-decorated Christmas trees.

'Sorry. The cab was late.'

'Perhaps you should have ordered it earlier. Anyway – Happy Christmas!'

'Happy Christmas!'

Following Lutetia into the living room, Violet paused a moment to survey the scene. There was holly everywhere. It curled around the lamps and paintings, wound up the sides of the bookcases and stretched along the top of the books. There was a Christmas tree in each corner and one by the fireplace, the gleaming red balls and golden tinsel sparkling in a profusion of fairy lights. Three children sat on the floor in front of the log fire. Hearing voices, the oldest one stood up and came running towards her.

'Hello, Granny! Happy Christmas!'

Violet wished she were younger and strong enough to pick up her eldest granddaughter as she had done in better days. Instead she bent down and gave the ten-year-old a big hug.

'Happy Christmas, Hermione!'

The two younger girls looked up. 'Happy Christmas, Granny!'

'Holly! Hope! Aren't you going to get up and give Granny a hug?' Lutetia's tone was strict.

The two younger girls stood up and walked towards Violet. 'Happy Christmas, Granny!'

Violet bent and gave each of them a hug. 'Happy Christmas, my darlings!'

Lutetia indicated a seat on the low wide sofa. For a fraction of a second Violet wondered if she should sit so low down. Would she be able to get up again? Perhaps an armchair higher up would be more suitable? Saying nothing, she lowered herself cautiously into what she felt was the depths of the earth.

'A glass of champagne?' suggested Lutetia gaily.

Violet thought longingly of the champagne she and Miles had enjoyed on so many occasions. But Miles had been dead now for almost ten years. The champagne seemed to have died with him. 'I'll be quite happy with a glass of water.'

'Well! That's no problem. Perhaps Hermione...'

'Of course, Grandma.' Hermione was up and out of the room in a flash. As a door opened, the sound of laughter and the crashing of cooking pots wafted across the hall.

'Oh! Is someone preparing lunch?' asked Violet.

'They certainly are. Christmas lunch. Turkey with all the trimmings.'

'Who's doing it?'

'Well, Adrian, of course.' Violet thought hard. Adrian...? 'As master of the house he's the person in charge.'

Violet nodded. 'Of course.'

'David and Melanie are helping him.'

'David? You mean my son, David?'

'I certainly do.'

'I haven't seen David for ages. I'd like to go and say 'hello.' Violet struggled to get up from the imprisoning sofa.'

'No, no! Stay where you are! I'll ask David to come in here.'

Violet leant back thankfully against the soft cushions. In a moment David appeared in front of the sofa. Now in his late forties he was still slim and handsome with a full head of dark hair. He sat down beside her and gave her a big hug.

'Happy Christmas, Mum! You look great! Just as good as you did yesterday.'

'Yesterday?'

'Yes. We all went out to dinner yesterday at your favourite local Italian Restaurant. Remember?'

'Oh, yes! Of course.' By now all dinners seemed to have merged into each other. Rather like the champagne evenings with Miles.

'How long will lunch be, David?' Lutetia didn't want any involvement in Violet's increasing memory loss.

'About ten minutes.' Getting up from the sofa, David paused by the living room door. 'No champagne, Mum? Perhaps a glass of wine with lunch?'

Violet nodded. 'That sounds lovely.'

A few minutes later a bell sounded in the hall. 'Lunch.' Lutetia's voice sounded more commanding than the bell. Violet struggled to stand up but the sofa springs and the deep cushions seemed to pull her further down. 'I can't...' she mumbled. Lutetia came towards her and held out her hand.

'You should have sat on an armchair, Violet. It's not a good idea to sit so low down.' She nearly added 'at your age' but thought better of it. Standing up, Violet felt a little more in control, though she refrained from pointing out that it was Lutetia who had indicated the sofa in the first place.

Festooned in decorations, the large dining room across the hallway looked less austere than usual. There were two Christmas trees; one at each end, the decorations similar to those on all the other trees. By this time Violet had lost count of how many trees there were. The table was elegantly laid for eight with solid silver cutlery and Waterford cut-glass crystal. A tall grey-haired man in his early seventies stood by a large expensive-looking mahogany sideboard, brandishing a large carving knife and fork.

'Violet! How lovely to see you! Happy Christmas! Now, why don't you sit here...' indicating a chair at the side of the table near where he stood. 'Then you and I can have a good little natter about all the interesting things you're up to... Lutie, perhaps you and Melanie could organise the girls down that end,' pointing towards the door. 'Then David and I will do the serving.'

The girls started arguing. 'No! You go there!' 'I don't want to!' 'I want to sit next to Granny!' 'So do I!'

'You can't both sit next to Granny. She's sitting next to Grandad. There's only one other seat next to Granny.' Melanie tried to take control and finally the three girls were seated as David placed several dishes of vegetables on the table.

'Sprouts for Christmas.'

'I don't like sprouts,' Hope piped up. 'They're stringy.'

'That's OK, Hope. We've got broccoli...'

'That's stringy too..'

'Never mind. We've also got peas, broad beans, carrots and parsnips...'

'Sounds like a greengrocer's shop.' Violet felt she should lighten the situation.

'Now, Violet, would you prefer leg or breast or a little of both?' Adrian was busy carving away like a professional chef.

'Just a little of each, please, Adrian. But not too much.'

'No. Of course not. And bacon, sausage, stuffing and Yorkshire pudding?'

Adrian placed a plate piled with food in front of Violet.

'Good heavens! What a plateful!'

'Just eat what you can.'

'I hope that goes for the rest of us,' said Lutetia, apprehensively eyeing her over-loaded plate.

Bringing his highly piled plate to the table, Adrian sat down and raised his wine glass. 'And here's to a very Happy Christmas, everyone!

'Happy Christmas!' 'Happy Christmas!'

'More drinks, girls?'

'Yes, please.'

'Coke or orange juice?

'Some of each please.'

'In the same glass?'

'Yes. Why not?'

David moved round the table filling up glasses. Violet put out her hand pointedly over her half-filled glass. 'Oh, no thank you, David. I've really had plenty for the moment. I have to get home, you know.'

'But not on your own.'

'Oh, no. I'll take another cab.'

'Don't worry, Mum. I'll drive you home.' David refilled his own glass.

'Not if you have much more wine, darling,' objected his wife succinctly.

'I'll be fine. All the patrol car drivers will be having their own Christmas dinner. Sorry, lunch. Let's clear away the plates and I'll bring in the Christmas pudding. Would anyone like some cheese?'

'Yes, please.'

'Before or after the pudding? We've got some Stilton – with a lovely Port.'

Murmurs of appreciation went round the table. 'Stilton and Port would be a treat. Perhaps after the pudding?'

'*After* the pudding! That's not very French.'

'We're not in France, David.'

'No. Of course we aren't. I'll bring in the pudding first.'

David went into the kitchen to prepare the Christmas pudding. There was plenty of thick cream and brandy sauce but he felt the pudding needed some more brandy before he set it alight and served it in the dining room. Now standing up, he realised he had had quite a bit to drink. Perhaps I'll call a cab for Mum after all, he thought. Goodness! The kitchen was a right mess! He and Melanie would have to do the clearing up. After all, Adrian had done all the cooking and he'd had a few drinks too. David took the pudding from the fridge, where it had stood for a good three months and carefully upturned it onto a plate. He stuck a sprig of holly in the centre and looked around for the brandy. He lit up the pudding and just as he was leaving the kitchen he slipped on an invisible patch of grease. Despite clutching at the side of the working top he lost his balance and fell over. The lighted pudding fell on top of him setting his hair on fire. Screaming, he fell flat on the floor. 'I'm burning! I'm burning!'

Then he passed out.

Hearing David's screams from the dining room, the family rushed into the kitchen. They were appalled to find him lying on the floor, eyes closed, his hair still smouldering. The three girls sat down on the floor beside him, sobbing uncontrollably.

'Daddy! Daddy! What happened?'

Violet stood in the doorway, shaking with shock.

Melanie was the only person who retained any self-control. 'I'll call an ambulance,' was her only comment, as she walked towards the telephone in the hall.

'*Twas the night before Christmas, when all through the house*
Not a creature was stirring, not even a mouse.
The stockings were hung by the chimney with care,
In hopes that St Nicholas soon would be there.'

Six-year-old Hope cuddled up beside her mother on the sofa.

'But it's not Christmas *tomorrow*, Mummy. It's not till next week.'

'But this is the poem. I didn't want to alter it. I wanted you to hear it as it was written. There's a lot more. Shall I continue?'

'Yes, in a minute. So you and Dad have a week to plan it all. I hope there won't be any more accidents. Not like last Christmas.'

'Last Christmas was very difficult. But we're all over it now, thank God and Daddy is fine.'

'Where will Christmas be this year?'

'Right here.'

'Oh, good. I'd much rather be at home for Christmas.'

'Me too.'

'Will Granny, Grandpa and Grandma be coming here?'

'Oh, yes. I think so. It wouldn't really be Christmas without them, would it?'

'No. I suppose not.'

'Will Granny remember?'

'We'll remind her. And Daddy will pick her up so she won't need a cab.'

'How old is Granny now?'

'She's over 80. Perhaps 83? Ask Daddy. He'll know.'

'Gosh! That's old!'

'Mum, I'll pick you up on Christmas Day about 11.30 am so you won't have to order a cab.'

'That's lovely, darling. Thank you so much.'

As she replaced the receiver Violet began to think hard. About Christmas. Another Christmas. Could I go through it all again, she thought. Last Christmas was frightening. Hopefully this year there won't be a Christmas pudding. Certainly not set alight. Thank goodness David had almost completely recovered from his horrible burns.

On Christmas morning Violet set her alarm clock for 8.30 am. She needed time for breakfast, a shower, dressing and make-up preparations. At 10.30 she was ready. All the presents for the family were in two carrier bags by the front door so she wouldn't forget them. Not like last year. What will happen this year? Would she enjoy it? She adored her son David and the three grandchildren. But then she had Melanie, Adrian and Lutetia to contend with. In-laws could be a pain. She needed more time to think about it all.

Then there was the problem of Christmas presents. Melanie insisted that Granny gave presents that the children could unwrap and hold in their hands. Every year towards the middle of November Violet received a long list. A few years ago she suggested that a 'financial gift' would more aptly fit the bill. But Melanie was having nothing to do with such an impersonal gesture. It had to be something solid wrapped in Christmas paper.

Then there were the presents that Violet herself received; one from each family member. Now over 80 years old Violet had everything she needed. Nevertheless, every year she received a scarf, a stole, bedroom slippers, a box of handkerchiefs, perfume or make-up. She was well-known at her local charity shop for donating her excess Christmas gifts. Christmas was certainly a challenge, especially for the elderly.

Perhaps a walk would help to straighten out her thoughts – and anxieties. A walk around the square and even into the park beyond. Violet donned her coat and her outdoor shoes. She decided not to take any money or her travel pass. The shops would be closed and there was no public transport. She didn't even take her door key. Leaving the front door of her apartment unlocked, Violet went out, quite unprepared for any eventuality.

As arranged, David arrived promptly at 11.30 am. Inserting his key into the front door he was surprised to find the door unlocked. Just behind the open door were two carrier bags containing brightly wrapped parcels. Closing the door quietly he called out: 'I'm here, Mum! Happy Christmas!'

There was silence. Violet's bedroom was immediately on the right with the bathroom round the corner. David stood in the doorway of the bedroom and called out again: 'I'm here, Mum! Are you in the bathroom?'

Silence. David walked down the hallway to the spacious living room at the end. Perhaps Violet had fallen asleep on the sofa. After all, at 82... But the living room was silent and empty. Perhaps Mum's gone for a walk in the square, he thought. It's a lovely day. As the Christmas presents were neatly packed by the front door she couldn't have forgotten it's Christmas Day. Even so I'll try and persuade her to have some memory checks in the new year. Perhaps her memory loss is more serious than we imagine. But for the moment he put aside any sinister conjecture. It was, after all, Christmas Day. His main responsibility now was to find his mother and take her to his house for lunch. He opened the sliding door to the terrace and stood by the railing, looking out on the large well-kept garden square. But it was empty. There was no one there at all. Returning to the living room, he picked up the phone and dialled his home number.

'Melanie, it's David. I'm in Mum's apartment but she's not here and she's not in the square either. I'll go out and see if she's in the park. I've got my mobile with me so I'll keep in touch. Don't worry, I shan't be late for lunch.'

He took the lift down to ground floor level and walked around the square. But there was no one there. He left the apartment complex by the large imposing entrance gate and walked up the road to the park. Inside the park he walked past a holly bush bowed down with berries. How Christmassy, he thought. Then turning a corner he saw someone sitting on a bench in the sun.

As he approached he realised that 'someone' was an elderly lady, fast asleep. His heart started to beat fast when he realised the person was Violet. He sat down very quietly on the bench and stroked Violet's hand gently.

'Mum, it's David, your son. Happy Christmas!'

Violet shuddered and opened her eyes. 'David! Where am I? Why am I here?'

'Well, you went for a walk. Perhaps to get up an appetite for Christmas lunch.'

'Christmas? Again? We've just had Christmas. And there was that dreadful accident with the pudding…'

'Yes, Mum. But that was last year… We're not having a pudding this year. Melanie has bought a Yuletide Log. Come. My car's outside and I'll take you to our house for Christmas lunch. The family is looking forward to seeing you.'

Bells

The bell was loud and seemed to ring for ever. What on earth is that bell for, thought Hannah, glancing up at her bedside clock. 7.00 am. I'm never awake that early. She rolled over, pulling the coarse sheet and thin blanket over her head. A few minutes later a hand shook her and a girl's voice spoke urgently.

'Hannah! You must get up! Now!'

Hannah pulled the blanket down a little. 'Why so early?'

'It's breakfast at eight o'clock.'

'But that's almost an hour away. Why do I have to get up now?'

'It's the rule.'

'Where am I?'

'Hawkhurst Hall.'

Confusion as well as exhaustion assailed Hannah. 'Hawkhurst Hall?' She couldn't remember where that was. Or why she was there.

'Try to get up and get dressed. Then I'm sure you'll feel better. I'll be back in ten minutes.'

The girl moved away to her own bed in the far corner. Hannah sat up, rubbed her eyes and glanced round the bleak dormitory. There were nine other iron-framed narrow beds, all with the same coarse bedding as hers. The wooden floor was scuffed and stained.

There was no carpet, not even a rug. The walls were painted a pale lime green, without any pictures. To Hannah it appeared to be a large prison cell. Girls in various stages of undress were chatting to each other in subdued voices, rather as if they were afraid of being overheard. Hannah got out of bed and went to the bathroom next door. She remembered it from the night before, containing a toilet and a grubby wash hand basin. Nothing else. Returning to the dormitory she searched in her bedside locker for something to wear.

Fully dressed in her new school uniform of dark green tunic, white blouse, black bow-tie, white ankle socks and black buckled shoes, Hannah sat down on the end of her bed. She had folded the covers back, not knowing what to do with them. She was completely at a loss. The girl who had woken her earlier came over.

'Hello! You must be Hannah, the new girl.'

Hannah nodded.

'I'm Nicola. I'm head of the dormitory and I've been asked to look after you until you settle in. But you can't leave your bed like that. A prefect comes round to check that everyone has made their bed. If they're not made they're stripped and the owner gets an order mark'

Hannah felt sobs welling up. 'Oh, I'm sorry. I didn't know.'

'That's OK. I'll help you. Then we'll go down for the run.'

'The run?'

'Yes. We all have to run twice round the quad every day before breakfast.'

'Why?'

'To get us going, I suppose.'

Hannah followed her mentor downstairs and outside. Other girls, dressed exactly the same as she and

Nicola, were jogging round the quad. Hannah set off on her own at a brisk pace, leaving Nicola far behind.

Joining Hannah at the end of the run, Nicola sounded rather envious. 'Wow! You're a good runner. Are you good at games?'

'It depends on the game. Is it breakfast time now?'

'In ten minutes. After the BBC 8 o'clock radio news.'

After breakfast another bell rang as the girls walked to the classrooms at far end of the quad. They were in what looked like a large temporary pre-fabricated hut. Hannah followed Nicola into the nearest one and was shown to a shabby old-fashioned desk.

'That's yours – entirely yours. Do you have a pen and a pencil-box?'

'Yes. But they're in my trunk. I haven't unpacked yet.'

'No, of course not. Miss Hollow will supply you with essentials.'

'Who's she?'

'Our form mistress. She'll be here in a moment.'

The other girls filed into the classroom, standing silent and erect by their desks as a tall thin lady with grey hair, wearing thick glasses, followed them.

'Good morning, girls.'

'Good morning, Miss Hollow.'

'Please sit down. You all have a copy of the week's timetable in you desk. If you'd like to get it out we can read through it together.'

At 11.00 am a bell rang for morning break. This was held in the gym, a large building at one side of the quad, resembling a greenhouse. At one end tables were laid with biscuits and fruit juice, dispensed by older girls. 'Sixth formers,' explained Nicola. As they queued up two girls in their age group came up and gave Nicola a hug. 'Nicki! Hello! How are you? Who's your new friend?'

Nicola turned to Hannah. 'These are two of my best friends, Ann and Pat. This is Hannah Compton. She's new and I'm looking after her until she settles in.'

The taller girl, slim with red hair, extended her hand. 'Hello, Hannah. And welcome to Hawkhurst Hall. I'm Pat. This is Ann.' The shorter girl with dark, very curly hair gave a warm smile. 'Hello, Hannah. I'm sure we'll be great friends.'

As the three girls arrived at the table to collect their snack, the bell rang. Ann laughed. 'That always happens. I don't care if I'm late. I'm hungry. What's your next lesson, Hannah?'

'Latin.'

'Latin! Oh, poor you! But you must be clever to take Latin. I'm not doing it. I'm too stupid. Are you in the top stream?'

Hannah turned to Nicola. 'Am I?'

'Yes. You are. So'm I. C'mon on. We'd better go to our Latin class. It's with Miss Greedy. She's never late.'

The wooden strip was very narrow and seemed endless. The instructor helped Hannah up and held her hand for a second. Then she let go.

'What am I supposed to do now?' asked Hannah, totally confused.

'Walk along the beam.'

'I can't. It's too narrow.'

'The other girls manage it.'

'I'm not the other girls,' Hannah mumbled under her breath.

'Go on, Hannah. Walk! We've haven't got all day. The bell will be going soon.'

I hope it goes now, thought Hannah and took a step forward. It was like walking the plank. Even one step was too much. She fell off, hitting her shoulder hard on the solid wooden floor. In those days there was no matting in a school gym.

The instructor said nothing. She didn't even help Hannah up.

'Now it's time for the rope,' said the instructor.

Hannah looked up at the rope. What happens now, she thought. Am I going to be hanged?

'What do I have to do?' she asked the instructor.

'Climb up.'

In her earlier childhood days in Ireland Hannah had climbed an endless number of trees. In the huge house where they had lived on the outskirts of Dublin there was a wild valley where she and her sister had spent more time up trees than they spent on the ground. But she had never climbed a rope. What was the point? She had no idea how to start.

'Perhaps you could show me what to do?' she asked the instructor. The instructor looked round the class. Although they were all twelve-years-old, they were of varying height and weight and certainly of different ability. The instructor picked a girl at random. 'Have you climbed a rope before?'

'Oh, yes. We've got one in our garden.'

And up she went like a trapeze artist, right to the top. She swung the rope, let go of one hand and waved, as the class clapped.

'Now you try, Hannah.'

Hannah grasped the rope in both hands and, copying her class mate, put her knees on either side and pulled herself up. As the girls started to cheer, she made it to about three feet off the ground. But the rope was rough and coarse. Her knees lost their grip as she slid, helpless, down to the bottom, the palms of her hands covered in blood. Nicola came over to help her up.

'Are you OK, Hannah?'

'I will be in a minute.'

The gym instructor went to the side and pushed a large wooden object with a leather cover into the middle of the gym. It stood on four splayed out wooden legs with two parallel handles the same height in the centre.

'Right girls! Queue up for the vaulting horse! Who'd like to go first?'

A tall slim girl with red hair put up her hand.

'Thank you Pat. Just vault however you want to.'

Pat ran up to the vaulting horse, put one hand on one of the handles, swung round the end of the horse and landed neatly on the far side with her feet together.

'Excellent!' called the instructor. 'Very well done, Pat.'

Several other girls followed suit, all vaulting slightly differently. Hannah tried hiding behind a taller girl at the back but the gym instructor spotted her right away.

'You have to try,' she insisted.

'But I might break my glasses!'

'Take them off.'

'Then I won't see where I'm going.'

'Oh!' said the instructor, now at a loss herself. 'There goes the bell. I'll let you off this time. But I suggest you mention your short-sightedness to the school doctor at your medical check-up.'

For the moment Hannah's gym torture was over.

Hannah followed Nicola into the dining room for lunch. 'We're at the same table,' explained Nicola, going to the far side of the room.

'How do you know?'

'A table list goes up every week on the hall notice board. I'll show you after lunch.'

Hannah pulled out a chair and was about to sit down.

'No, no! You mustn't sit yet!' exclaimed Nicola. 'We've got to wait until the staff come in.'

As she spoke about a dozen teachers entered, each one going to a different table. The oldest girl at Hannah and Nicola's table held out a chair and an elderly plump lady with greying hair sat down. The girls remained standing until Miss Greedy came in and took a table by the door. Hannah recognised her from the Latin class. Short, thin, grey hair in a bun by each ear, she leant backwards as she walked.

'For what we are about to receive may the Lord make us truly thankful,' intoned Miss Greedy. Then everyone sat down and the chatter started as the maids came around serving the food.

'Do you live far from here?' asked the girl sitting on Hannah's left.

'No. I'm from Ireland'

'*Ireland!* That's a long way from Kent. How long was your journey?'

'All of twenty four hours.'

'How exhausting. Did you fly? I've never been in an aeroplane.'

'Nor have I. I came by boat. My father thinks aeroplanes are too expensive. I left home at seven in the evening and took the boat from Dublin to Liverpool, which sailed at eight o'clock, taking ten hours. I had to share a tiny cabin with a lady I'd never met before. Then I had a five hour train journey from Liverpool to London where I was met by an escort from an agency that specialises in that sort of thing.'

'Another lady you didn't know.'

'Yes. We had four hours to fill in before I had to take the school train from Charing Cross Station at four o'clock, so she took me out to lunch. The restaurant was called Lyons Corner House.'

'Was it good?'

'Much better than I expected. Especially as England is still being rationed.'

'Isn't there any rationing in Ireland?'

'No. Ireland wasn't in the war – officially.'

'Oh, I didn't know that. So what did you do after lunch?'

'We went to a huge shop. A department store where the lady looked at reams and reams of material to recover her sofa. It was dead boring.'

'I bet it was. *And* exhausting. And at the end of term you'll have to do the whole thing in reverse.' She giggled. 'My name's Tamsin Webb, but I'm always called Tammy. And you're...'

'Hannah Compton. And where do you live, Tammy?'

'Sevenoaks. It's not far from here. Have you been to the Festival of Britain?'

'No. But I've heard of it. A cousin has promised to take me round when she meets me in London sometime.'

'Good. There's a marvellous concert hall called The Royal Festival Hall. That's where I want to sing when I'm grown up. Do you sing?'

'Yes. And I play the piano.'

'What grade are you?'

'I don't know. I've never taken any exams.'

'You'll find out soon. This place is very exam bound. Who's your piano teacher?'

'Miss Strangeways.'

'Oh, good! She's nice.'

Lunch was over and the maids came round collecting the empty plates. There was a scraping of chairs as everyone stood up and Miss Greedy intoned another grace. 'For what we have received may the Lord make us truly thankful.'

Silence engulfed the dining room as the girls filed out.

'What happens now?' asked Hannah in a loud voice.

'Shush.' Nicola put her fingers to her lips. 'It's silence in the corridors at all times. And no running. Follow me.'

Hannah followed Nicola up the four flights of stairs to the dormitory. 'Rest time. I bet you could do with one.'

'Do I get undressed?'

'That's up to you. I always take off my outer clothing. It's more comfortable. I'll come and get you in an hour.'

Hannah sat down on the hard unyielding bed, took off her shoes and outer clothing and climbed into bed. In two minutes she was fast asleep.

An hour later the bell rang. In three minutes Nicola appeared, dressed quite differently. 'It's games now for an hour-and-a-half.'

'What games do we play?' enquired Hannah.

'Netball and lacrosse.'

'I don't like netball and I've never played lacrosse. We played hockey at my last school. I was in the team. Left wing.'

'We never play hockey here. It's forbidden. Miss Boswell, the head, thinks it's bad for our posture. If you've never played lacrosse, why not give it a try? Miss Meldew, the sports teacher, will give you a stick.'

Hannah's heart sank as they walked towards Miss Meldew, the teacher she had had to face that morning in the gym.

'Miss Meldew, Hannah, the new girl, needs a lacrosse stick.'

'Of course. Just follow me.'

They followed Miss Meldew to a hut filled with sports' equipment. The teacher selected a stick and handed it to Hannah, who held it with some bemusement. She had never seen anything like it in her life before. It was about three feet long with a leather net at one end and a support underneath. Miss Meldew picked up another stick and started explaining the game.

'You hold the stick upright with the net at the top. You watch out for a member of your team who will throw you the ball provided you are not 'marked' by an opposing team member. You catch the ball in the net and either run with it towards your 'home goal,' or throw it to another team member who is 'unmarked.' Like most team games each side tries to score as many goals as possible. I suggest you stand on the sideline and watch for a bit.'

Hannah stood on the sideline as the other girls, including Nicola, took their places for a game. To Hannah it looked difficult and rather dangerous, even vicious, particularly for someone who had to wear glasses all the time. She was just wondering if she should join in when a ball came hurtling towards her. She lifted up the stick to protect herself but it was too late. The ball hit her right in the face, smashing her glasses, knocking her out completely.

Miss Meldew stopped the game and walked towards her.

As in most English private schools, usually known as public schools, there was a house system. At Hawkhurst Hall there were four houses; York, Lancaster, Tudor and Stuart. The houses were made up of girls of different ages throughout the school, with a sixth former as head of house. There were endless house competitions. The houses competed with each other in lacrosse, netball, athletics, tennis and rounders. Marks for good academic work were entered as 'plus house marks.' Clever girls were prized by the head of house; the less able were frowned upon. Music also played a part. Those achieving a merit or distinction in their Royal Schools of Music exams gained a good house mark; those who failed received a black mark.

Behaviour was taken very seriously. Rudeness, disobedience or breaking one of the endless school rules was punished by bad marks, which went against the house. The smallest demeanour was punished by a careless mark, which meant one bad mark against the pupil's house. Next up the ladder was the penalty mark, earning three bad marks. More serious was the order mark, with five bad marks. For really bad behaviour there was the conduct mark, earning fifteen bad marks. A girl with a conduct mark received further punishment by a strict telling off from the headmistress in her study. Two conduct marks usually meant expulsion. There were no marks for good behaviour, only bad marks. It was a totally negative system.

'No, Miss Greedy. That's not quite right, Miss Greedy.' Hannah put down her pen and looked up.

'What do you mean, Hannah? That's what it says here.'

'But you're using an *English* textbook to teach us Irish history. I learnt Irish history in Ireland from an *Irish* textbook. The Irish textbook must be correct. Henry II invaded Ireland in 1171 and the Irish suffered greatly under British rule until the Irish Free State was created in 1922.'

There were giggles round the classroom. Looking quite bemused, Miss Greedy closed her textbook. She was quite at a loss. This upstart, this foreigner, who was top of the class in almost all subjects was now teaching the teachers. The bell sounded across the quad. Saved by the bell, thought Miss Greedy. She reopened her textbook. 'For prep read pages 96 – 112 for a test next week. That will be all for today, girls.' She stood up and the girl seated nearest the door opened it for her.

Most of the girls in Hannah's class disliked biology. The teacher, Mrs Joseph, was short, ugly and very domineering. She had warned them that in the next class they would dissect a rabbit. No one liked the idea. Several of the girls had pet rabbits at home and the idea of cutting one up was extremely unpleasant. When the bell rang for class it sounded like a death toll as they made their way to the science lab in the main school building. They filed silently into the room.

'Good morning, girls.'

'Good morning, Mrs Joseph.' The reply sounded like a funeral chant. There on the large table down the centre of the room, lay a dead rabbit still with its fur on.

As the custom was, the girls put on overalls and rubber gloves. Any blood on their uniforms was unacceptable. Attired and ready, most of them turned to face the table. A few were unable to look.

'Who would like to make the first cut?' enquired Mrs Joseph. 'Sarah? I think you're good at this sort of thing.'

'OK. I'll try. Where do I start?' Mrs Joseph handed her a sharp knife.

'Start with cutting the fur off.'

Sarah walked closer to the table brandishing the knife, feeling sick. She started to cut the fur round the rabbit's stomach but nausea overwhelmed her. She laid down the knife and vomited all over the dead rabbit. A few of the other girls screamed. Others cried. They all swore they would give up biology at the earliest possible moment.

At the end of every school year exams were held towards the end of the summer term. Coming top, or near the top of her class in most subjects Hannah was confident she would come top of the class when the exam results were announced. Except in art. Even as a small child at her Dublin day school Hannah had never been able to draw or paint. The whole process bored her. What was the point? Nowadays most people had a camera. All you had to do was line up the person or the object and just press a button. Simple. And as cameras improved so did the result.

Painting or drawing needed equipment. A sheet of good quality paper the correct size and a well sharpened pencil were essential for drawing. The requirements for painting were more complicated. In addition to the suitable paper was the question of paints. Paints could be bought for very little from a stationary or art shop in a tin box all arranged in a certain order. But the art teacher, Miss Gomferts, disapproved of this option. As a painter of some talent herself, she insisted that all the colours should be mixed in the art room from the three primary colours: red, blue and yellow. There were two art exams. The first took place in the art room where Hannah struggled to mix the paint correctly, never mind paint a good picture. The second exam took place out-of-doors. This time the paints were already mixed so all the girls had to do was paint an outdoor scene of their choice, based on the view in front of them. They were seated in pairs on the benches overlooking the valley and the games field beyond. Hannah was paired with Alice, considered one of the best painters in the class. Hannah watched, fascinated, as her companion sketched in the view with a pencil and slowly painted in the details. Hannah knew perfectly well that she was quite incapable of doing anything even remotely similar. Suddenly she had an idea. I'll paint a fog scene, she thought. With no pencil drawing to distract her, she picked up a paint brush and covered the whole sheet of paper in mid-grey.

As she watched, Alice laughed. 'At the worst you could get an Order Mark for that.'

'I don't really care.' Hannah added some darker grey at the top.

She received a D Minus for her art exams, which pulled down her average exam mark to A. She had expected to receive A plus.

The plus side was that the following term she was allowed to drop art. 'It will leave more time for your music at which you excel,' said the headmistress generously.

A plump young teacher in her early twenties sat at the piano in the school hall playing chords to accompany the choir as they sang scales, a semi-tone higher for each new scale.

'Doh, ray, me, fah, soh, la, te doh… ' Miss Holden sang along with them until they reached top G in the treble register. 'Want to try A Flat?' she suggested. 'Perhaps you'd like to give us a solo, Tamsin?'

Tamsin stepped forward confidently and sang the scale up to top A flat. Everyone clapped. 'That's excellent,' said Miss Holden admiringly. 'I'll probably give you a solo in one of our set pieces.'

She stood up from the piano and faced the choir.

'Those of you who have sung before at the Hastings Music Festival know that the choir has to perform two set pieces and one of our own choice. Then there's a separate section for soloists. For those of you who play a musical instrument there are entries at several different levels. The level isn't decided by the entrants' age but graded according to the level of the Associated Board of the Royal Schools of Music. As most of you probably know the grades are one to eight. I'll go through it in more detail with my piano pupils in their lesson. And I'm sure Miss Strangeways will do the same.

'Now girls, please open your scores at page seven and we'll go through the Coronation Anthem.'

There was a rustle of paper as the girls found the page in their music books. Then the bell sounded harshly outside in the corridor.

'Oh, dear! There goes the bell! What a shame! Sorry girls but we'll have to leave it there.'

'Have you noticed that Miss Wilson seems to spend an inordinate amount of time in Norma Burns' room?'

remarked Pat as she Ann, Tammy and Hannah walked round the quad one sunny day at break.

'Why does Norma Burns have her own private room?' asked Tammy.

'I suppose it's because she's in the sixth form.'

'But the other sixth formers don't have their own rooms,' objected Ann.

'Maybe it's because she's working for a place at University.'

'Aren't any of the others trying for Uni?'

'Not that I've heard of. But the point I'm making is that Miss Wilson is in Norma's room for *simply ages*. And sometimes when I pass by to go to the dorm I hear moaning noises.'

'Moaning? Is one of them in pain?'

'No, I don't think so. I think the moaning is of pleasure – sexual pleasure.'

'*What!* But they're both female.'

'That's the point I'm trying to make. I think they're lesbians.'

'*No!* Do you mean…they have sex together.'

'Exactly.' Pat sounded smug, as if she knew all about lesbianism.

Steven pulled up her skirt and stroked her stomach. 'You *are* allowed down in this valley, aren't you, Randy Mandy?'

'Yes, of course I am. You know I'm in the sixth form. I'm allowed to do a lot of things that the younger girls aren't allowed to do. But I'm not allowed to do this.'

She rolled over on top of him and gave him a long deep kiss, curling her tongue around his mouth. 'But you're not allowed to do it either, are you Steven Prank?

You've certainly got the right surname. How many of your other pupils do you treat like this?'

'None here, Mandy. Not at this school. I've only got five pupils. I'm only here for half a day.'

'So, where are most of your other pupils then? How many other schools do you teach in?'

'Three in Sevenoaks, two in Tunbridge Wells and one in Tonbridge.'

'That doesn't leave you a great deal of time to perform, does it?'

'No. It doesn't. But I don't want to play in a symphony orchestra. I'm hoping to form a string quartet.'

'Cello in a string quartet. That sounds good. Will we hear the bell from down here? My next lesson is at midday. History with Miss Greedy. Know her?'

'The old thin one with grey buns round her ears who leans backwards when she walks?'

Mandy laughed. 'They're nearly all old. Except you, Miss Holden and Miss Strangeways.'

'Who is your piano teacher?'

'Strangeways.'

'Is she good? Do you like her?'

'Oh, yes. She's very good and I like her. I'm taking Grade Eight Piano next term.'

'And Grade Eight Cello this term.'

'Stevie, there's the bell. I must go to my history lesson.'

'And practise the cello. I'll see you next week.'

Steven gave Amanda another passionate kiss. Then she fled up the slope and went to her history lesson. Steven folded up the rug and followed her slowly back to the school.

'Those bells are driving me mad,' remarked Hannah as she and Ann walked back to the classroom after break.

'There's nothing much we can do about them. We would have no idea what to do when if it weren't for the bells.'

'That would great. I could do with a break.'

'It's OK for you. You're top in most subjects. It's the idiots like me who have to learn.'

Hannah smiled mischievously. 'I've had an idea.'

'About what?'

'Bells. I'll explain later.'

Later that evening, after supper, Hannah explained her idea to Ann.

'When the bell sounds for lights out we'll pull on the rope. Hopefully that'll lift the teacher who's ringing the bell off the floor.'

Ann laughed. 'Great idea. I love it.'

Just before nine o'clock Ann and Hannah went up to the first floor where the bell rope could be spotted on it's way up to the top. Precisely at nine o'clock the bell started ringing. Ann and Hannah pulled the rope up hard. The bell stopped ringing and there was a screech from the ground floor.

'What's happening?' yelled the teacher.

Pealing with laughter Ann and Hannah went to their respective dormitories to get undressed for bed.

The next morning at assembly Miss Greedy made an extra announcement.

'Yesterday evening at nine o'clock someone pulled on the bell rope and Miss Hardy was lifted off the ground. I have already interviewed the domestic staff who all assure me that they took no part in this most unfortunate event. I assume it was one of you girls. So we shall all remain in the hall until the culprit owns up.'

There was a deathly hush. No one moved.

Hannah put up her hand. 'I'm sorry Miss Greedy, it was me.'

Then Ann's hand went up. 'And me, Miss Greedy.'

A gasp went round the hall. Then the bell sounded.

'All right, girls. You may go now. But Hannah and Ann must remain behind.'

As the whole school filed out in silence Miss Greedy turned to the two miscreants. 'You will go and see Miss Boswell in her study. You will most certainly each receive a Conduct Mark. Go now.'

The visit to the headmistress's study was short and to the point. Both girls received Conduct Marks and five hundred lines to write out. It was a close shave and they both knew it. They realised they could have been expelled with the probability of finding no other school to go to.

'I'm going to be very nervous, Miss Strangeways. I've never played in public before.'

'You'll be fine, Hannah. You play really well. There's always a first time. They say that's the worst.'

'Have you played much in public?'

'Oh yes. Quite a few times. It was part of the course at the Guildhall School of Music. I'm sure you'll go on to study at one of the three big London colleges of music. This will be good practice for you.'

'Shall I play from memory or take the music? I'd need someone to turn the pages.'

'Whatever you prefer, dear. I'll turn the pages for you, of course.'

'I'll try from memory now.'

Hannah put her music at the side of the piano and played the whole of Beethoven's *Appassionata Sonata* from memory. It was an outstanding performance for a thirteen-year-old. Miss Strangeways was lost for words.

Hannah's older musician friends explained that the hardest part of the whole procedure was playing to the headmistress, Miss Boswell, in her study. All the other entrants for the Hastings Music Festival were also there, performing and listening to each other. Two girls, playing without music, had serious memory lapses. Miss Boswell suggested they play from music. 'Miss Holden or Miss Strangeways will turn the pages for you.'

In addition to another outstanding performance of Beethoven's *Appassionata Sonata*, Hannah played Bach's *Prelude and Fugue in B Flat Major* from Book One. At the end of each work she received resounding applause.

On the great day two coaches collected the young performers from Hawkhurst Hall and drove them to Hastings. The entrants included four choirs from different age groups. The pianists were the first to perform. Hannah won both her categories and was told she would be expected to play again at the winners' concert at the end of the week. It seemed that her public performances had got off to a very good start.

Every day except Sunday the whole school filed into the hall at 7.50 am to listen to the BBC 8 o'clock radio news. Everyone sat cross-legged on the floor except the sixth formers who were sufficiently privileged to sit on chairs. Precisely at 7.55 the member of staff on duty switched on the radio. As the dulcet tones of the BBC 'weather man' read out the forecast, the girls took out their notebooks and pencils. Taking notes was mandatory. Every Sunday there was a compulsory current affairs test. Each girl was assigned marks out of ten, which were added to the house points.

Precisely at 8.00 am the six radio pips sounded. All pencils were poised. The BBC's news-reader's voice was smooth, clear and expressionless. 'Here is the news for Thursday the sixth of February. It is with great regret that Buckingham Palace has announced the death of King George VI.'

A gasp of horror broke out across the hall.

'His Majesty passed away peacefully during the night at the royal home in Sandringham, Norfolk. Although suffering from a short illness, his death came as a great shock. Out of respect to His Majesty it is expected that the nation will be in mourning for six weeks.'

Some of the girls began sobbing. No one was capable of taking notes. The teacher on duty switched off the radio as she realised that no one could absorb any more news after such a shocking announcement.

The entire school wore black armbands until the end of the term.

On Friday 1st June 1953 there were few girls remaining at Hawkhurst Hall. The Coronation of Queen Elizabeth II was scheduled to take place the following day and would be televised world wide. Most of the girls had already gone home to enjoy the ceremony with their families and the only ones who remained behind were those who lived too far away. These included Nancy, whose parents lived in India; Sarah, whose parents had emigrated to Spain; Hannah and about ten or twelve others whose parents lived in various remote countries around the world.

The school staff had made a great effort to help the girls forcibly left at school feel as comfortable as possible for the Great Occasion. Even Miss Greedy tried to be friendly, an emotion rather foreign to her personality. On the day before the coronation she made an announcement during breakfast to the few girls left remaining.

'For the next few days, until the other girls return, there will be no bad mark system. Nor will there be any bells.'

The remaining girls in the dining room cheered and clapped.

The following day they awoke to pouring rain. The weather forecast for the Great Day was not promising. After a particularly good breakfast the fifteen or so girls took their seats in the hall in front of the large television screen. The Coronation Ceremony took all of eight hours. A break was made for lunch and mid-way during the afternoon they reached the highlight of the ceremony: the Coronation Oath. This included the Queen's vows to serve her people, maintain the laws of God and defend the Protestant religion. The most moving part of all was the anointing of the Queen with holy oil by the then Archbishop of Canterbury, Dr Geoffrey Fisher, who ended the ceremony by placing Saint Edward's crown upon her head. This was so over-whelming that some of the staff and the older girls were on the verge of tears.

Everyone was emotionally involved except Hannah. She felt rather non-plussed and a little detached. Although impressed by the gravity and enormity of such a special event, she found it difficult to be completely part of the scene. After all it wasn't *her* Queen who had been crowned. Elizabeth II was the Queen of England not the Republic of Ireland. The ceremony made Hannah feel even more strongly that she wasn't English. At school she was Irish. However, when she returned to

Dublin for the school holidays she was no longer Irish. She was a foreigner. She had no friends in Dublin and she had lost her Irish accent. Perhaps after another three years at Hawkhurst Hall she would finally become English?

Only time would tell.

Butter

Gustave lifted the piping hot toast out of the toaster and put it quickly on his plate. He reached for the glass butter dish, set it down beside him and cut off a liberal wedge. He spread it as rapidly as its solidity would allow, the hot toast melting the butter as he smoothed it out. He picked up the slice without cutting it in half and as he bit in noisily, a large rivulet of melted butter ran down his chin.

'Mm,' he murmured appreciatively.

Ruth looked up, horrified. 'Gus! That's far too much butter!'

Taking no notice, Gustave took another mouthful of the succulent toast, replaced it on his plate and smothered the remainder with marmalade.

'I can't taste it unless I take a decent amount.'

'I call that an indecent amount.'

'What's sauce for the goose isn't necessarily sauce for the gander.'

'I'll have to start rationing you. An ounce a day.'

'That's not much!'

'It's a hell of a lot more than people had during the war.'

'So what? Why do you bring in the war each time I eat too much? You weren't even born during the war.'

'My mother always brought up the war each time I didn't scrape my plate clean. She said I was lucky not to remember the war but I should think of all the children round the world who were still starving. I said they were welcome to the liver, brains and bread and butter pudding she tried to make me eat and suggested she put it all in a jiffy bag to send to them, instead of putting it in the dustbin.'

Gustave laughed. 'You must have been a dreadful child. No wonder you've grown up into such a monumental bully.'

'Gus, I only speak for your own good.'

'What's good about not getting what I want if it doesn't hurt anyone else?'

'Who said your vast butter consumption wasn't going to hurt anyone else?'

'As I see it, it's only boosting the dairy trade.'

'There's plenty to boost the dairy trade. It's your health I'm thinking of - and my widowhood.'

'How idiotic! Why should eating too much butter lead to my demise? Fat lubricates the system. And you can't accuse me of being over-weight.'

'No. But surely you've heard of cholesterol?'

'Isn't that some complaint that elderly men are prone to? Like gout?'

Ruth laughed. 'You're hopeless. There's no connection between gout and cholesterol.'

'Oh, good. That's something, anyway.'

'Actually, I don't know how you can taste the butter with all the other things you pile on top of it. Why, at breakfast you can't see your slice of toast for all the marmalade you slosh on it... So greedy – and unnecessary.'

'Not at all.'

I'll have to think of a cure, thought Ruth.

'I've booked a different sort of holiday for this year.'

'Oh, yes?' Gustave was barely audible through his toast.

'It's a cure.'

'A cure for what?'

'Butter addiction.'

Ruth was feeling weary. Dressed in the regulation pale, buttercup yellow overalls, cap and similarly coloured rubber boots she followed the little group of visitors round yet another dairy. This was their seventh visit on the tour planned to give dairy produce enthusiasts every insight into the fabrication of butter, cream and cheese. The 'activity' holiday was centered on daily visits to the more prestigious dairies in the region. It also included Devon cream teas at every possible stop and nights in hotels specialising in local butter and cheese. Ruth hoped that such a superfluity of dairy produce, butter in particular would eventually make Gustave sick of the sight of anything remotely connected with the cow.

As for Ruth, well, she was just feeling sick.

But where was Gustave? Ruth looked round at the select little band of visitors. Gustave was here a moment ago. He was always up at the front asking tiresome questions, like teacher's pet. The whole boring tour had been organised specially for him. It would be too infuriating if he had just sloped off.

They were nearing the end of the tour - thank goodness! It was always the same routine. All the employees in their butter-coloured uniforms lining up to say 'goodbye' and presenting the same gifts of butter and cheese, which Gustave usually demolished in the car while Ruth drove on to the next stop for a cream tea.

Where was Gus? Ruth walked down the line of employees, shaking hands. At the end stood a familiar figure.

'Good-bye, Ruth. Thank you for a arranging such a wonderful holiday. I've found my true vocation now. I'll visit you in London when I can get away.'

Judgement Day

'Oh, Clive, that's really wonderful news. I'm delighted - and so proud of you, darling.'

'Yes, of course. I knew you would be.' Clive poured milk into his coffee cup with a slightly shaking hand.

'But darling, you don't seem to be really happy about it. You're surely not worried are you? After all, it's just the final step up the ladder of your tremendous achievement and success.'

'Yes, I suppose so.' Clive's voice was flat and expressionless. He sounded tired.

'It's what every barrister aspires to, surely.'

Clive gave a short laugh. 'Well, not every barrister. Otherwise there would be more judges than barristers. But I suppose the more able ones...'

'And you're so able, Clive. You've always been exceptional: head and shoulders above the rest.'

'I've had every opportunity. I just made the best of everything that was on offer.'

'You mustn't be so modest, dear. You've had such a splendid career. Your diligence and integrity are the admiration of everyone. To be made a High Court Judge is a tremendous honour. And at such an early age too! Why, you're bound to be knighted one day. Sir Clive and Lady Montague. Doesn't that sound wonderful? Lady Montague. I really like the sound of that. Lady

Antonia Montague. It trips off the tongue so easily, doesn't it, darling?'

Antonia got up from her chair, glided gracefully round to the other side of the breakfast table and gave her husband a light peck on the cheek. 'Congratulations, Sir Clive'.

'Oi, hold it,' protested Clive. 'I'm not knighted yet. I'm merely Judge Montague.'

'Yes, darling, I know. But it won't be long before we are Sir Clive and Lady Montague.'

Before we are, thought Clive. Antonia had always been very ambitious for him. Or was it solely for herself - so that she could bask in his reflected glory? People who didn't have sufficient talent or ability themselves were often forced to find fulfilment in the success of others.

Clive looked at his watch. 'I must be off. I'm in court again to-day.'

'Your last case from the courtroom floor?'

'I don't know.'

'But you'll soon be in the seat of judgement, won't you?'

'I'd prefer to call it the judge's seat. The seat of judgement sounds - well - too omnipotent.'

'But judges are supposed to be omnipotent, aren't they?'

'Omnipotent means all-powerful, almighty. I don't think judges are supposed to have total power. They are meant to guide the court - and of course, to pass sentence at the end of the trial.'

'Even so, they must be of impeccable character - or at least give the impression of being so - even if they do lead double lives.'

'Do you think some judges lead double lives?' asked Clive in some amazement.

'Heavens, no! I'm only joking. Judges must have extremely high moral standards to inspire public confidence. After all, they have to stand in judgement over others - like Solomon.'

Standing in judgement over others: like Solomon. Clive felt a twinge of uncertainty, tinged with fear. Who was he to stand in judgement like Solomon - over anyone?

Clive Montague had only known success. From his earliest days at school he stood head and shoulders above his peers: in the classroom and on the sports field. Although undoubtedly aware of his abilities, Clive began to realise, as he grew older, that the greater his achievements, the more was expected of him. A high mark for an exam or a piece of homework would often be greeted with:

'Well done, Montague, but I'm sure you'll do even better next time'.

In the Public School system pupils of high academic ability are usually expected to shoulder extra responsibility. The theory, though often erroneous, is that those with fine minds generally make fine leaders. So Clive was always elected class monitor and in his final year, head-boy. Due to his high ability and the responsibility thrust upon him, Clive found himself set apart from his peers. He wasn't expected to join in any prank for fear of the consequences, although he hated being excluded and longed to be part of the crowd. There was one occasion in particular which he always remembered with sadness and misgiving. A midnight raid on the tuck-shop had been planned. At least eight boys were involved and Clive begged to be allowed to join them. With great reluctance the others finally agreed. The little band left the dormitory just after midnight, made its way stealthily along the corridor and down the stairs into the quad. The idea was that they would break into the rear window of the tuck-shop, steal what they could carry and take it back to the dorm for a gargantuan midnight feast. All went well until they reached the quad, when one boy spied the senior master turning the corner by the tuck-shop and making for the library: a route which would directly cross their path.

'Duck', hissed Murgatroyd Minor. 'If he sees us we'll all be expelled.'

Expelled? The very word drove a stab of fear into Clive's heart. Not expelled, surely, for wandering around the school at night? As the other boys hid behind the wall of the quad and waited till the coast was clear, Clive slipped back to the dormitory by himself, feeling fearful and ashamed. He had so much wanted to be part of the adventure. He had even enjoyed being frightened but he wasn't brave enough to take the consequences. The other boys returned shortly afterwards laden with tuck. No one offered Clive anything.

As expected, Clive won a full scholarship to Winchester and, five years later, an open county award to St. Catherine's College Cambridge. Predictably he gained a first in law, was called to the Bar, and rose to fame and fortune at a meteoric rate. It was shortly after he had been called to the Bar that he met Antonia Cavendish. Clive was just twenty-four. Antonia was twenty-two.

Antonia Cavendish was a prude. There was no doubt about it. Even her best friend used the word, though only once. Antonia had been extremely upset.

'You know you're a prude, Toni', Sarah had insisted.
'I hate that word. And don't call me Toni.'

Antonia was thirteen at the time and shared a dormitory with Sarah and two others of the same age. Almost
all their conversation centered on sex and their individual rates of physical development. While the other three
compared menstrual cycles and breast sizes Antonia
either stood aloof or hurriedly left the room. In the
shower-room after games most of the girls walked
around completely naked. As the showers were communal this practice seemed natural to everyone except
Antonia - who always showered in her underwear. At
first the girls laughed at her but as they quickly became
accustomed to her priggish habits, they took no notice.
At bedtime in the dormitory Antonia undressed quickly
with her head down, leaving her skirt on until her
nightie was in place. She always slept in her vest, feign-
ing the cold, even in the heat of summer.

Antonia was afraid of her sexuality. She was fearful
of approaching womanhood and the carnal desires of
men. But she was quite clear about sexual intercourse.
The class had already studied reproduction in biology.
The miracle of conception amazed and intrigued her
and she had no fears of the pain of childbirth. It was the
idea of penetration that appalled her. Surely no man
would ever do that to her?

Antonia had great difficulty in eradicating from her
mind a particularly unpleasant incident that had taken
place some years ago. In fact, from the onset of puberty
this incident had become increasingly to dominate her
thoughts. She was ten years old and still attended the
local day school. On Wednesdays she stayed late at
school for a dancing class. None of her friends went to

that particular class, so she always left the school alone. There was a short cut to the bus stop across a small piece of wasteland at the side of the school used by everyone. No one thought anything of it, as the alternative route was at least ten minutes longer.

The day in question was in mid-November. It was already after five o'clock and quite dark. Antonia set off with jaunty confidence across the narrow belt of wasteland to the bus stop. The ground was rough scrubland but the trample of many feet had worn a clear path so the going was easy, even in winter weather. The evening was cloudy but occasionally a full moon broke through, lighting up the common for a few seconds. About halfway across there was a small thicket of thorny bushes and shrubs; not large enough to be called a wood or a coppice but sizeable enough to be classed as a noticeable landmark. As Antonia passed this shrubbery the clouds parted and a full moon came into view for several minutes, its pale translucent light shining on the figure of a man, completely naked, penis erect, standing facing her on the path.

'What a bit of luck! And just the right age too!'

He reached out and grabbed her arm. She could feel his warm breath on her cheek and sense the urgency of his carnal desire. He put his hand on her thigh underneath her skirt and with absolute horror she saw his penis quiver and enlarge. Revulsion and fear welled up in her; her knees shook, her stomach churned. Like a cornered animal she struck out, using the only primitive weapon she knew. With a sudden violent movement she bent and bit his penis extremely hard. As he howled with pain she kicked him ferociously in the groin and he fell back into the scrub grass moaning in agony. In a frenzy of fear and anger she thumped him several times on the head with her satchel and fled across the common.

Before they met Clive and Antonia had each dated several members of the opposite sex, but rather as a matter of social necessity than with any idea of forming a permanent relationship. It was more important to Clive to establish his legal career before he burdened himself with a wife and family. As for Antonia, although she realised in her heart of hearts that she was destined for marriage rather than spinsterhood, her now long-established fear of sexual intercourse meant keeping a safe physical distance from men. She enjoyed their company on social occasions but was in absolutely no hurry to rush into anything permanent.

However, she felt safe with Clive. He was well-bred, perfectly mannered and extremely considerate. Having such high aspirations as a barrister created an immense workload so his social life was strictly limited. He preferred to reserve his few leisure hours for the more important events of the sporting and cultural calendar and so he became a regular patron of such events as Ascot, Henley, Glyndebourne and the Chelsea Flower Show. Clive hoped these visits would produce the right contacts and Antonia, when invited to accompany him, realised that a day out at the Chelsea Flower Show would be less likely to end up in bed than a weekend in the country.

Their friendship continued in this vein for almost two years. They saw each other regularly but not too frequently and became more relaxed in each other's company. Neither broached, nor even thought very much about the subject of marriage. They each assumed that they would one day marry someone, possibly even each other, but at present that day seemed a long way off.

It was parental pressure that brought matters to a head more speedily than either of them had anticipated. One glorious June day at the Henley Regatta Mr and Mrs Montague were introduced to Mr and Mrs Cavendish. Their joint ambitions for their offspring subsequently led to Antonia's and Clive's engagement. These ambitions differed only in the fact that Mr and Mrs Montague were ambitious for their brilliant son's illustrious career, whereas Mr and Mrs Cavendish were merely seeking an outstanding husband for their pretty, though far less able daughter. The Montagues supplied the talent and the Cavendishes supplied the money. It seemed a perfect match and as near an arranged marriage as could be found in England at that time. Clive was twenty-five, Antonia was twenty-two. They were both virgins.

The first two years of marriage were a revelation to them both. Introduced to the practical joys of sex for the first time Clive's carnal urges knew no bounds. The more he experienced sex the more he craved it. The physical release of his libido gushed forth in a torrent, demanding daily satisfaction. During his climax he felt liberated, satiated. His spirits soared like a bird and he felt physically omnipotent.

By contrast, physical intimacy increased rather than diminished Antonia's deep-seated sexual fears. At first the warmth of their naked bodies lying close together had begun to inspire some confidence in Antonia's dormant sexuality. She genuinely loved Clive and sought to please him but she was completely unprepared for his voracious sexual appetite. Though his initial approach was gentle and caring and the foreplay was always lengthy and tender; once fully aroused Clive became violently passionate and over-excited. His climaxes were mistimed to Antonia's and he became so over-wrought during ejaculation that he barely considered her at all. His forces spent, he would lie beside her, panting, elated and satisfied while she felt limp and physically bruised. After the first two years of problems they settled down into what can only be described as a sexual compromise. Antonia demanded separate beds and shortly afterwards, separate bedrooms.

It was before they moved into separate bedrooms that Clive broached the subject of starting a family. Stretching out in vain to reach his wife's hand across the great divide Clive asked:

'What about children?'

'Well, children would be nice. I've always wanted a son. Let's try for a son, shall we?'

So they tried for a son; Clive coming too soon like a storming bull, randy, panting; Antonia lying still and clinical, gritting her teeth, clenching her fists as Clive came again a second time; all in darkness, as Antonia didn't wish her husband to see her naked body.

Their first child was a daughter. As it had been a long labour and a difficult birth, Antonia's dislike of sex increased even more. It was a year before Clive felt able to broach the subject of sex again. Separate bedrooms had long been established and Antonia shared hers with their beautiful baby daughter, Sylvia. Clive was a proud and adoring father but he badly wanted more children, especially a son. By now the lack of relief for his sexual urges had become quite over-whelming. Denied the chance to stroke his wife's smooth shapely body or even to see her naked, he began to be obsessed with the sight of any presentable young woman. Very short skirts were fashionable at the time and a pair of pretty legs under a thigh-high skirt never failed to give him an erection.

He considered divorce, but apart from sex they were curiously compatible. He had a brief affair, wild and passionate, with another married woman. They considered eloping and giving up everything for each other but after a while the violent sexual attraction wore off. They realised that sex had been the only thing that had brought them together and it didn't seem worth sacrificing his career and her husband's money for something so tenuous. They parted on good terms and Clive's sexual frustration built up again.

One day Antonia allowed him back into her bedroom and Sylvia was placed in her nursery at night. They would try again for a son. This time conception took longer and Clive savoured every moment. Antonia finally became pregnant, banished him again to his own room 'for the sake of the baby' and nine months later gave birth to another daughter, lovely fair-haired blue-eyed Rosalind.

A son had still eluded them.

Now nearing thirty-five, Clive was the envy and admiration of all his friends and acquaintances. His legal career was well and truly established and he was becoming recognized as one of the leading prosecuting barristers of the day. He had specialised in criminal law and was now handling some of the most notorious murder, rape and drugs charges; many of them at the Old Bailey, others in Crown Courts throughout the country. In court he was a charismatic figure: tall, slim and debonair, with steely grey-blue eyes, which struck a chill into most of the defence witnesses and often over-whelmed the defence counsel as well. He spoke eloquently, putting the prosecution case succinctly in his closing speech, speaking directly to the jury and explaining everything clearly, never patronising or condescending. It was a rare defence counsel who could match his oratorical skill and even rarer that the defendant was not found guilty and sent down.

Clive's social life was equally successful. Having reached the pinnacle of his career at such an early age, the pressure formerly exerted by others, as well as by him, no longer existed. As his professional stature and financial security increased he found he had more time to relax. Although his caseload was still heavy, he found for the first time in his life that he had some time for leisure. His quicksilver mind and out-standing powers of retention placed him head and shoulders above his colleagues. He was able to prepare his cases in half the time taken by his peers and he took every advantage of his free time. He took up golf, not with any pretension of achieving excellence or playing competitively but just for the sheer joy of walking on a golf course and making a completely different circle of acquaintances and friends.

Now that money was no longer short, a nanny was engaged to take care of the two beautiful little girls, Sylvia and Rosalind, so Antonia also found herself with more leisure time. They went to the theatre, the opera, dined in smart restaurants and gave elegant dinner parties that were regularly returned on the same opulent scale. Clive and Antonia Montague were the envy and admiration of their social circle.

But sex remained a thorny problem. Now that Antonia had the services of a living-in nanny to hand she realised she could no longer offer permanent exhaustion as an excuse to refuse occasional sexual advances. Clive had managed to persuade her to share the same bedroom again, on a trial basis only and he tried to make his carnal urges coincide with any faint sexual desire on Antonia's part.

But it was always the same. She would undress in the bathroom and avert her eyes while he undressed beside her as she lay in bed, securely covered by the duvet, wearing her nightie and a bed-jacket. Before he gently peeled back the bed-clothes and lifted up her nightie, she would switch off the light, saying that it hurt her eyes and Clive was denied the pleasure of slowly revealing his wife's beautiful sensuous body, delicately rounded firm breasts, a small mole on her navel. He could only feel his way around a far too infrequently uncharted territory; the nipples on her shapely breasts becoming pointed and rubbery in an involuntary reaction to his search for her clitoris. Having stifled his desire for so long, often several months, Clive found it impossible to hold back his climax and the result was that he came too soon, leaving Antonia resentful and unrequited.

It was a chance conversation on the golf course that persuaded Clive to seek out a prostitute.

'It's exhilarating,' David said. 'Those tarts are real professionals. They know all the tricks and so many different positions. It's given lovemaking with my wife a real boost. Try it and see. It's an adventure. It'll enrich your sex life.'

What David didn't know was that Clive rarely had a sex life.

Clive spent the week pondering the possibilities of prostitutes and broached the subject cautiously to David during their next game of golf.

David roared with laughter. 'You mean you haven't tried it yet?'

'Well, er, no. I'm quite ready to try - I just don't know where to start.'

'I see.'

'I shall have to be ever so careful,' continued Clive earnestly. 'Soliciting is illegal, as you know. I am a prosecuting counsel and I can't afford to loose my position.'

'I know, I know. Soliciting's only illegal if you're caught. You're not going to be that careless and stupid are you? Besides, you either have to be caught making two approaches to the same woman or approaching two different women on the same occasion. You have to be pretty thick to do that.'

'Yes, I suppose so.'

'The crazy thing is, that prostitution in itself is legal. It's just soliciting that's against the law.'

'Only in England. I could always go to Holland or Germany for the weekend but that would take some explaining to Antonia.'

'No need to go that far,' said David cheerily. 'Just take a walk along Praed Street, near Paddington or a stroll around Finsbury Park. Then you have a wealth of choice south of the river such as Brixton or Streatham. But if you don't want to travel so far the first time and wish to sample the bottom end of the market there's always York Way behind Kings Cross Station. And for a touch of class you can't beat Shepherd's Market in Mayfair.'

Driving back from the golf club in Pinner, Clive felt a sense of mounting excitement. It wasn't just urgent sexual release that he sought. This was something that went deeper and was even more fundamental than pure sexual desire. He craved danger; he longed to pluck the forbidden fruit; to do something that was both reckless and illegal.

It was Sunday. Usually on Sundays Clive would have the perfect excuse that he had to go to his chambers to study a brief after dinner. Unfortunately, on that particular Sunday, they had been invited to dine with friends in Highbury, Islington. In fact, the evening turned out to be less tedious than he expected. He almost admitted to enjoying it. They were a party of eight at the elegant home of a fellow barrister and his pretty wife. The lady seated next to him at dinner was extremely attractive and very well endowed on top. The close sultry heat of the July evening meant that the ladies wore the scantiest of dresses, his neighbour's being of a dangerously low-cut design. As the evening progressed Clive felt his excitement and sexual desire mounting, watching the cleavage of his companion rise and fall with her animated conversation and feeling her warm breath on his cheek as she turned to face him, emphasising a point. Clive would happily have taken the good lady up to bed long before the dessert but there are certain things one cannot do in the house of a best friend and Clive was forced to let decorum prevail.

The route home to their house in Muswell Hill led past Finsbury Park. The ladies of doubtful virtue were already out plying their trade and Clive vowed to return as soon as he had taken his wife home. Once in the house Clive hastily gathered up some papers, muttered excuses to Antonia, who showed only a little surprise, and drove off again in the direction of Finsbury Park. The raid on the tuck shop at school all those years ago flashed through his mind. The dimly lit streets reminded him of the shadowy quad; the lonely figures of the prostitutes became as fearsome as that of the senior master, prowling around the school in search of miscreants. As fear intermingled with sexual excitement, Clive wasn't sure whether he was the hunter or the hunted. Should he give up and go home? The craving for danger and the desire to pluck the forbidden fruit overcame his fear. No, he wasn't going to chicken out this time. He scanned the whores as they stood leaning against a lamppost or walking with ambling provocative gait on their own small patch. My God, some of them were ugly! Some of them were old too, probably well past the menopause. Suddenly he felt a wave of pity towards them. What a terrible thing to have to do for a living: to sell sexual favours to a complete stranger. Surely there were other, more dignified ways, of earning money? His feelings of compassion were immediately engulfed in an even greater one of guilt. Surely these prostitutes were giving an essential service? There must be many men besides him, unattached or whose wives were frigid like Antonia, who found essential solace in their ministrations.

The first time he must choose with care.

He drove so slowly that he was no longer unnoticed. By now it was quite clear to the prostitutes why the sleek grey BMW was cruising around Finsbury Park. Several of them called or waved. Clive drove on at a snail's pace, uncertain whether to get out of the car when he had found his prize or invite her to join him. A slim brunette stood under the next lamppost; her shapely legs encased in black fishnet stockings, showing a tantalizingly amount of bare flesh under a skirt which barely covered her buttocks. As Clive came level with her she turned round, her pale oval face translucent in the lamplight. She was beautiful and looked very, very young. Guilt overcame Clive again as he stared at this lovely vulnerable creature. No, it wouldn't be possible. It would be like going to bed with his own daughter.

But before he could drive off she was sitting in the car beside him.

'Hello, luv. It's twenty quid in the car round the back or forty in bed at the brothel. Personally I'd recommend the brothel. It's more comfy like and it's got more equipment.'

Equipment? thought Clive. He'd never thought of equipment. He settled for the brothel and the girl directed him through a few small side streets, chatting as easily as if they'd just met at a party.

'Park here is best. The house is just around that corner.'

He parked the car and followed her along the street. The houses were of the Victorian cottage type; too small for a well-off middle class family and too run down for anyone with insufficient money to renovate them. Their destination turned out to be one of the most run down in the area. The front door was scarred and peeling and the entrance hall smelt of rotting garbage. The girl led the way up the creaking uncarpeted staircase flanked by a wall with peeling paper and large patches of damp. There were several mushrooms growing along the edge. The whole place smelt of decay and disease.

By now Clive's sense of excitement and sexual desire had completely worn off. He was filled with revulsion and despair tinged with fear. But it was too late to chicken out now. On the top floor, the girl unlocked a door and stood back to let him enter. His heart was thumping and his fear turned to terror as he stepped into the room, where he was taken completely by surprise. The room was of medium size and seductively lit by strategically placed table lamps. The walls were hung with luxuriant drapes and tapestries, the floor covered in a deep pile carpet. The predominant colour was of a deep rich red. A fire was laid in the Victorian grate as if prepared for cooler evenings. As the present evening was particularly warm the curtains remained drawn back and the window had been thrown wide open. There were two easy chairs on either side of the fireplace and in the far corner was an enormous four-poster bed hung with opulent rich red hangings and covered in fur rugs. The girl went to the window and closed the curtains.

'Sit down, do,' she said, indicating one of the two easy chairs. 'It's your first time, ain't it? I always know a first timer. Some of 'em lose their bottle and leave quick but they're usually back the next day.'

Clive sat down, his terror gone, a warm feeling stealing over him. The girl came and stood beside him, remaining motionless at first, then reaching out to touch his face; stroking slowly, gently. He closed his eyes as desire began to stir in his loins. Antonia had never done this. The girl continued stroking, down his neck, his arms and over his whole body. She sat down on his knee.

'What's your name? Mine's Carrie.'

Carrie continued to stroke and then began to undress him, unbuttoning and peeling off his shirt, then unzipping his flies. Clive felt excitement welling up in him, his penis swelling until it was huge and erect. Carrie stood up and undressed herself in front of him, standing right beside him, so at any time he could touch her. Clive watched with delight and increasing desire, his breath coming in short pants, as she revealed her perfectly shaped naked body, pale in the soft light.

Carrie was the most skilled and perfect lover, both on the floor and in the bed. Clive stayed the whole night.

Having tasted such delicious and exotic fruits as Carrie had to offer, Clive found he constantly craved for more. The stopper had been released on his sexual desires and they now gushed forth in a torrent, like a great geyser. Conversely he found he had nothing in common with Carrie as a person. She had very limited interests and little conversation. Once she had satisfied his sexual appetite and drained his capacity for the evening he would either sleep exhausted in her arms or dress hastily and leave furtively for his chambers, returning home later to hear Antonia snoring alone in her room.

Clive discovered that Carrie wasn't always free to minister to his needs. After all, there was no contract of any kind between them. He paid her good money for her services and she was perfectly free to offer these to anyone else she wished. On the other hand, Carrie tried to be as helpful as possible. If he rang requesting her services on a night when she was already engaged, she would suggest one of her colleagues instead. Carrie didn't ply her trade exclusively round Finsbury Park. She had many regular clients who came directly to the house to be soothed and pleasured in her opulent and erotic bedroom. Many of them were from the higher echelons of society, she confided. Some of them were Very Important People Indeed.

So if Clive rang to find that Carrie already had a booking with another client, she gave him a list of telephone numbers. So in this way he came to know Christine, Monica, Rosie, Mandy and several others as well. Clive felt no emotional involvement with any of these women. There was no intellectual contact either, which he found an enormous relief. Having spent his life being driven by ambition, it gave him a great sense of freedom to have a relationship that was purely physical. It was exhilarating to watch a woman slowly undress, knowing he could utterly possess her body, but without any emotional or intellectual obligation. Although there wasn't any emotional attachment on either side, Clive felt a great respect and even certain affection for these women who worked so hard to give him pleasure.

Clive's life had now taken on a completely new dimension. He felt young, confident and vigorous. People said how well he looked. He gave up smoking, he drank less, he slept better and he stopped feeling tired all the time.

If Antonia had noticed anything different in his attitude or behaviour she failed to mention it. Clive found he was more relaxed in his wife's company. Their mutual interests increased and their marital bond strengthened after the long awaited birth of their son. Antonia had dutifully acceded once more to his sexual advances, hoping that a boy would be conceived during what she imagined would be their final effort. Feeling her frigid and unresponsive body lying beside him in the darkness after one of these attempts, Clive thought briefly of Carrie, Mandy and Monica, their images now fused into one being: a voluptuous temptress erotically encased in silk, which he carefully unpeeled as they lay together on a fur rug.

With the birth of their son, bonny bouncy Alistair, Clive was able to leave Antonia completely unmolested.

Clive's life had now continued in this vein for over six years. After his first night with Carrie his sexual appetite increased so much that he tried to find sexual release at least four or five times a week. By dint of visiting brothels on his way home from court or seeing clients, he managed to achieve this tally for the first three years. As a last resort he would pay a visit to York Way behind Kings Cross. This was generally only in real desperation, for he didn't really enjoy sexual intercourse in disused railway sidings nor did he relish the prospect of being apprehended for soliciting.

After three or four years of sexual fulfilment almost constantly on hand, his voracious appetite became slightly appeased. He was beginning to feel he had more than made up for the lost years, the lack of sowing wild oats in his youth and his sexually barren marriage. Slowly he settled down to a routine and managed to visit one of the brothels regularly on Sundays and at least once during the week. So far he had managed to conceal his identity from these ladies of easy virtue: his serving women, as he called them. No one knew either his surname or his profession, not even Carrie. For Carrie always remained his favourite. Probably it was because she was the first: the first woman ever to give him deep sexual satisfaction. She was incredibly skilled and practised in her profession. Even after an exhausting day in court, when he felt no arousal whatsoever, Carrie would manage, with her murmurings and stroking, to whet his sexual appetite. There were new ladies too, usually recommended by one of his regulars. A new contact brought a new experience, a fresh approach and many different skills. Clive thrived on the excitement and the danger. He loved living on a knife's edge.

Until now, he had been able to avoid any lawsuit directly involving prostitution. He managed to turn down a couple of cases where houses had been brought into disrepute and unsavoury pimps were accused of living off immoral earnings. Then one day he took the prosecution brief in a particularly horrific murder trail. It had similarities with the Peter Sutcliff case in so far as three prostitutes had been brutally murdered at different times in a prominent red light district of London. In his closing speech the defence took the line that the accused was mentally unstable and called several eminent psychiatrists to testify to this effect. The defence counsel tried hard to present a case of diminished responsibility and pleaded for a lenient sentence to be passed.

Clive, as the counsel for the prosecution, demolished the psychiatric reports at a stroke. In the most powerful closing speech of his whole career Clive held the court in thrall with his account of the wonderful service that prostitutes give to mankind.

'It is not only the men who gain from the skills and sexual services of this admirable group of women,' he told a hushed court, 'but also the wives of these men with exceptionally high sexual drive and appetite, who would otherwise beleaguer their womenfolk with too many unwanted advances.'

He closed his speech by affirming that when the brutal murders were committed, the accused was mentally sound and in full control of his faculties. The defendant was found guilty and sent down for thirty years with no recommendation of parole.

The next day Clive's photo was in all the papers, as well as substantial excerpts from his closing speech. Carrie was amazed and delighted. Her room was full of newspaper cuttings of Clive's photo and extracts from his speech.

'Well I never,' she remarked. 'Us women has surely got a friend in high places.'

Clive was a little uncertain as to how to take this remark. On the one hand he felt that as a human being he had as much right to avail himself of the services of prostitutes as anyone else. On the other hand he realised that as a prosecuting barrister, he was responsible for upholding the law and bringing down some of the people who roamed the underground world of prostitution.

He was living even more dangerously than before.

It was shortly after this much highlighted case that Clive was made a High Court Judge: a judge who judges others and visits prostitutes. He would have to exercise extreme care and caution. No more soliciting.

Now that he was honoured - and burdened - with one of the highest offices in the land, Clive decided he would try to live without the extra dimension that had completed his life so fully. He would undertake a period of abstinence. For six weeks he kept away from all red light districts and refrained from visiting any prostitutes at all. He felt his deprivation acutely. It was a dark bleak period in his life.

Then one day disaster struck like a bolt from the blue. One morning at breakfast, slitting open a letter with unfamiliar handwriting, Clive was appalled to find that it contained a full-length nude photograph of him in a most compromising position with a lady whose picture was sufficiently blurred as to be unidentifiable. As he pushed it hastily back into the envelope he saw a note scrawled in untidy uneducated handwriting, different to the one on the envelope, which ran:

'I know all your dirty tricks, Judge Montague. If you don't pay hush money to the amount of £1,000 a month at the above address I will tell all to the Sun. Ruby.'

Clive felt rising panic. His heart beat faster, his hands felt clammy and a cold sweat broke out on his forehead. This was blackmail. He, Judge Montague, was being blackmailed for an indiscretion committed by thousands of otherwise upstanding and law-abiding males. He was being punished for a weakness of the flesh that was a basic and deep need of human nature. He couldn't think clearly. Decision was beyond him. If he gave in to blackmail where would it all end? If his sexual pleasures were already over, it was beginning to look as if his career and his marriage would also soon be finished.

Luckily Antonia hadn't noticed anything. She was busy with the toaster and the coffee machine. Perhaps a holiday abroad would be a good idea? But could someone as responsible as a judge take a holiday at such short notice? Especially a judge who had so recently been appointed. Thank heavens he had a few days to think about it. A few days grace in which to decide whether he should succumb to blackmail or have the seamier side of his life revealed to the world at large.

He went into court and sat in the judge's seat. He felt humbled and afraid. Who was he to sit in judgement over criminals and wrong doers when he himself was living a life of sin? Professionalism came to the rescue. He got through the day and then the next few days. The days stretched into weeks and then the calendar month was up.

The following day at breakfast he received a letter in the same handwriting as before. There were three more photographs of him naked, in even more compromising positions than the first one. Again his female partner was unidentifiable. The letter ran:

'Unless I receive £1,000 at the above address by 10.00 am tomorrow the Sun will know all. Your alternative is to resign from the judiciary. Ruby.'

Resign! He would have to resign! That was the only way out. How would Antonia take it? There would be no knighthood now.

Today was Friday. He had the weekend to explain things to Antonia.

Clive hastily stuffed the letter into his dressing-gown pocket and struggled to finish his breakfast, his appetite completely gone. Antonia was engrossed in the morning paper.

'Goodness gracious! Listen to this, darling!'

'Yes?'

'You remember the Harley Street surgeon who bought kidneys from Turkish peasants for practically nothing to use in transplant operations?'

Clive stroked his chin ruminatively.

'Yes. I seem to remember something unsavoury of that nature. A colleague of mine, whom I used to know quite well, sent him down for unethical medical practices. He got at least five years.'

'He's just come out after serving only three and a half with remission for good conduct and now he's just been caught soliciting.'

'Soliciting?' Clive's stomach gave a tremendous heave. For a moment he thought he was going to vomit.

'Yes. Soliciting.' Antonia's voice sounded thin and very far away. 'You'd think, wouldn't you, that now he'd try and keep out of trouble. It's quite amazing what risks people will take; especially those in prominent positions.'

Clive tried to sound matter of fact. 'It sounds to me as though he had nothing to lose.'

'It sounds to me as if he's playing with fire,' retorted Antonia. 'Imagine, an eminent surgeon soliciting on York Way behind Kings Cross! His poor wife! She must feel dreadfully ashamed.'

Dreadfully ashamed. Clive felt his mouth go dry and the back of his throat tighten. The palms of his hands felt clammy.

'Well, dear, this prominent person must get a move on or else Court No. 6 won't begin sitting on time.' His voice made a harsh rasping sound.

'Not getting a cold are you, dear? It would be too bad if you were to come down with one of your throats during an important case.'

'No, no. Not a cold. Just the early morning strain on the vocal chords. Must be the poor air quality. Most cities suffer from it nowadays. Maybe we should go away for a little holiday when this session is over. Would you like that, darling?'

'Oh, yes. Very much.'

'The country or abroad?'

'I don't think it matters. Any change is nice.'

'Maybe you'd like to pick up a few brochures at the travel agent during the day.'

'I certainly will.'

Antonia stood up and started to clear away the remains of breakfast. With a heavy heart Clive slowly made his way upstairs.

Antonia finished loading the dishwasher and wondered how she should spend the day. Since Alistair's departure for university last autumn she often found time hanging heavily on her hands. Antonia had enjoyed motherhood, despite the often tiring work involved. Now somewhat at a loss, she had tried her hands at various pursuits, which other women of a similar age and station had successfully filled the vacuum created by the flight of their young. She joined a swimming club but discovered that the chlorine ruined the artificial colour in her hair. She took up golf but found no exhilaration in striking a small ball that was never returned. She tried her hand at tennis but after a few lessons she tore a ligament in her shoulder. It took weeks to heal so she decided, without much regret, that tennis was not her game. And anyway, she wasn't a very sporty person.

A few months later she joined a ladies' bridge club. They played in the mornings, twice weekly, taking it in turns to visit each other's houses. But she could never take either winning or loosing seriously. And the prattle-tattle conversation was so boring that Antonia soon abandoned bridge.

As Clive was now often away, Antonia found herself watching more and more television. With a vast number of channels to choose from the choice of viewing was endless. Not that there was a great deal on that was interesting. The more she watched the soaps and sitcoms the tawdrier they became. The chat shows and panel games were of more interest and she became very up to date with current affairs; but it was the late night movies that began completely to absorb her. With no set hours to keep day or night she often watched films well into the small hours.

The content varied. Sometimes perverted, often violent, some of the scenes sickened her so much she was forced to switch off. But she always switched on again in the hope of watching another erotic scene. Lying back on the living-room sofa, with a whisky on the table beside her, she would watch scene after scene of naked couples, sometimes in small groups, copulating in various positions. The scenes drove her into such a physical frenzy that she would end up half naked, giving herself one orgasm after another as she rolled on the floor in ecstasy. From then on she longed for the nights spent alone. The movies had given her life new meaning.

It was a chance remark at the hairdresser that gave her the idea.

'Is that short enough, Mrs Montague?' The harsh North London accent of her hairdresser broke into her thoughts.

'Oh, yes. Yes that's lovely. Thank you so much.'

She stood up, shook the hairs off her skirt, and went to the desk to pay. Two of the junior hairdressers were chatting amongst themselves.

'Did you see the late night film last night, Marlene?'

'Which one? The one when the two couples did...?

'Yes. That's right. 'Love's Twisted Tail'. Derek and me didn't half have a good ding-dong on the rug after.'

'There's a better one on a DVD,' replied her friend. 'It's called 'Sex all the Way'. It really is too. You can get it from any of those sex shops...'

Antonia paid her bill and went out. 'Sex all the Way'! A DVD from a sex shop! She took the tube to Oxford Circus.

Antonia's life took on a new dimension. She not only joined three local DVD clubs but she also combed the area in search of sex shops.

Watching the soft porn DVDs on her own late at night, Antonia's vicarious sexual gratification widened and deepened. As her skill in giving herself orgasms increased, her thoughts began to turn to the real thing. In over twenty years of marriage she hadn't given Clive very much sexual encouragement. She wondered if he had approached her the wrong way and had misunderstood her needs. She gave the matter serious thought during the day as she went about the household chores. How could she make a fresh start?

Having cleared up the kitchen, she decided that she would tidy upstairs and take a trip up to town in search of some new DVDs. Perhaps she and Clive could watch one of them together? That was an interesting idea and might have a very productive outcome. A candle-lit dinner with his favourite food... A bottle of wine followed by a couple of brandies...

Antonia walked into the bedroom and picked up Clive's dressing gown, which he had thrown carelessly on the floor. Something rustled in the pocket. She put her hand in and took out a rather crumpled envelope. The fact it was addressed to her husband didn't stop her from opening it. When he was away she opened all his mail. Hardly concentrating on what she was doing she opened the envelope and drew out the contents. As her fingers fastened around some photographs, a letter, folded up quite small, fell to the floor. Antonia glanced at the top photograph. A picture of a man, completely naked, penis erect, sitting astride a woman, also naked, lying on a bed. Why should this photograph be in the pocket of her husband's dressing gown?

Antonia was now completely alert, concentrating fully. She stared hard at the face of the naked man. No! It wasn't possible! It couldn't be! Not... Clive! Surely not!

But it was.

Distraught and sobbing Antonia bent to pick up the letter, which had fallen to the floor. Sitting on the edge of one of the single beds she opened it with trembling fingers.

'I know your sort. You toffs are all the same. You think you can use and abuse us whores as much as you like. I wonder how your wife would like this pretty picture. Unless I receive £1,000 at the above address by 10.00 am to-morrow, the Sun will know all. Your alternative is to resign from the judiciary. Ruby.' The address at the top was 10, Copenhagen Street, Islington, N.I.

With a howl of despair Antonia rushed out of the house.

Clive had left home a little earlier than usual. As the court didn't sit till 10.30 am he had plenty of time to get to Islington and back. He looked up Copenhagen Street in the A to Z. It was very near York Way. How ironic. He stopped at a cash-point on the way and withdrew £1,000. There was nothing else for it. He had quite resigned himself to blackmail. There was too much at stake: his career - and Antonia. Dreadfully ashamed. Antonia would feel dreadfully ashamed. He stuffed the notes into his wallet; all in £20 denominations and glanced at his watch: 9.25. He would have to hurry.

Antonia realised she was driving dangerously and took her foot off the accelerator. After all, there was no particular hurry. It was just a question of getting to No 10 Copenhagen Street, Islington. She had looked it up on the map. Goodness gracious! What a terrible neighbourhood! It was just across from York Way. York Way. Soliciting. It all began to sink in and a sob choked her. She had no idea what she was going to do when she arrived. Would Ruby be there? If she wasn't should she leave a message?

'Just tell Ruby that Mrs Montague called. It's about the blackmail. Yes. You see, she's trying to blackmail my husband.'

It sounded ridiculous.

And if Ruby was in what could she say? Could she confront her?

'Ruby, I'm Mrs Montague. Could you tell me, please, why you are trying to blackmail my husband?'

That sounded equally ridiculous.

Should she turn back? No. She was over half way by now. Perhaps Ruby would be at home and she could try having a chat with her. Antonia drove on, taking more care.

Driving slowing along Copenhagen Street Clive picked out No 10 quite the tattiest house in the terrace. He drove on and parked round the corner. His elegant BMW looked very conspicuous in such a run down neighbourhood. With a heavy heart he got out of the car and took off his jacket and tie. It didn't do to look too smart in such shabby surroundings. He walked round the corner. His legs felt like lead and he had difficulty putting one foot in front of the other. Maybe Ruby wouldn't be there after all. Maybe it was all a hoax. He couldn't remember being with a prostitute called Ruby.

But then, over the years he had been with a great number of prostitutes.

Suddenly he heard the sharp ring of high-heeled shoes coming along Copenhagen Street from the other direction. A broad in a hurry? That was indeed an unusual sight. Quite unprecedented in fact. But there was something curiously familiar about the now rapidly approaching figure.

They met outside No 12.

'Antonia?'

'Clive!'

'How did you guess?'

'I didn't guess. I found the letter and the photos in your dressing-gown pocket.'

'You must feel dreadfully ashamed of me.'

'I'm ashamed of myself.' Antonia started to cry. 'You can't give in, Clive. You mustn't give in to blackmail. It'll ruin your life.'

'If I don't, it'll ruin my career.'

'Your life is more important than your career. I'll stick by you.' Antonia made a superlative effort to control her sobs. 'I'll come to court with you.'

Clive took a month's leave to let the whole thing blow over. It made far less impact than they had feared. The Sun printed the photo in one of the inside pages with a short piece about 'new judge found in compromising position.' As the face of his companion was completely unidentifiable no one could ever prove he was with a prostitute.

And who was to say it wasn't his wife?

They went to Spain for a holiday. The morning they left the headline in the Independent ran: 'Director of

Public Prosecutions apprehended for soliciting in York Way.' It quite eclipsed Ruby's little story.

Clive lent on the balcony rail, taking in long deep breaths of clear pure air as he gazed in awe at the beautiful bay shimmering in the moonlight. The lights of the villas and farmhouses on the opposite hillside twinkled like hundreds of stars. Courting couples strolled arm-in-arm along the quayside below.

'Clive! Clive! Do come in here, darling!'

Antonia's urgent voice from the bedroom wafted out onto the terrace. 'There's such a good film on the telly at the moment. I'm sure you'd enjoy it.'

Clive turned and walked slowly into the bedroom. His heartbeat quickened as he saw Antonia lying on the bed, completely naked, legs wide apart. On the television screen a couple were copulating in various intricate positions. As he approached Antonia stood up and began to undress him, murmuring endearments. He felt his excitement mount as his penis swelled. He lifted her onto the bed. With their eyes constantly on the television screen they fondled and pleasured each other. They emulated all the positions of the lovers in the film.

It was the beginning of a new life. Clive never had to visit York Way again.